CAPTURING A COUNTESS' HEART

CARYN EMME

CAPTURING A COUNTESS' HEART

Copyright © 2020 by Caryn Emme

Excerpt from *The Earl Who Won My Heart*

Copyright © 2020 by Caryn Emme

Cover designed by Graphic-Lane

ISBN: 978-1-9992204-1-9

❀ Created with Vellum

PROLOGUE

"Mother did try suggesting marriage years ago," Charlotte muttered as she grappled with the columns of her ledger which refused to produce a value greater than zero. She sat in her study enshrouded by the shadows of the midnight hour, her body hovering over the books in a manner which would have earned her a half-hour lecture from Mother. Furrowed brows shot up when her only source of light flickered over the page casting long shadows across the columns.

"You wouldn't dare expire. I won't find funds to keep you lit if you abandon me now."

She stared at the weak flame willing it to stay strong. After a few moments of held breath, her head fell upon her book. She had turned to an inanimate object for moral support over her financial woes.

A weak laugh of self-mockery escaped her lips. Raising her head, she threw the plait of black hair over her shoulder. Was this what Father had envisioned when he had spent every last effort making her a peeress in her own right? She was one and twenty and the Countess of Bentwick, Lady Charlotte Elizabeth Ashbury, a peeress in her own right.

Mother had engraved the words into her on the day Father, Lord Henry Ashbury, Earl of Bentwick, had died. Of course, Father had been as good as dead years before his physical passing.

Childhood memories of Father were always of a man who had kept to his study and then to his rooms. There were rarely any visitors save for a solicitor and never any trips to care for his estates. Brief visits with him had left the distinct smell of something sharp and sickly sweet embedded in her nostrils. In fact, if she closed her eyes over the ledgers, she was able to elicit the smell instantly. A quick peek at the ledgers through one eye made Father's need of inebriation clear.

It was well known that before his death the Earl of Bentwick had been a hermit, a drunk and one prone to bouts of deep moroseness. He had spent a fortune without adding much to an already crippled estate. It was not well known, however, that he had exhausted himself until his title and its entailments would be bestowed upon his only heir, his daughter, Charlotte Elizabeth Ashbury when she came of age.

From the privacy of his study, Lord Bentwick had ensured that Charlotte would become Countess of Bentwick, a peeress of the realm in her own right. Many ladies throughout British history had received the honor for life only, the Duke of Marlborough had achieved succession to his daughter and, if Barons could do it, Lord Bentwick made it possible for an Earl to accomplish the same. He used every favor, every weapon in his arsenal to keep Bentwick alive and under the protection of an Ashbury for one more generation in the hopes Charlotte would have a son. Until that time, it would be Mother, also known as Lady Catherine, Countess of Bentwick, who would act as guardian.

Charlotte sighed. Mother's tenacity had inspired her to

learn quickly and manage her Earldom. She wrapped her woolen stole tightly around slim shoulders, staving off the cold air and wrestled the ledgers with new found vigor.

An hour later, she stretched a sore back and a stiff neck with a satisfied smile. Creative budgeting in the maintenance of Bentwick Manor while they were in London, in addition to the small profit made from a conservative investment, would cover the expenses of all essential items until the summer because their circumstances were supposed to be different by then.

Tomorrow, she and Mother would depart to London. Mother had set aside enough to fund one season when Father had died and had refused Charlotte use of the money for Bentwick regardless of how many times she insisted it would be put to better use on the estate. Despite Mother's kind support, it had been a painful defeat admitting that a husband was necessary to save her estate and even worse to be grateful for the carefully guarded sum which would ensure success in London. It had been her goal to save her Earldom so she could find a husband without desperation for money.

She had run out of time and Bentwick was still struggling. It seemed desperation, not love, would lead the hunt for a husband. The ledger was closed with a firm thud, casting infinite particles of dust to float through the weak beams of light and onto her face. She sneezed three times.

Charlotte carried the lamp through her study and quietly closed the door. The dim light of the lamp did little to conceal the faded paper on the corridor's walls. Tarnished door knobs and gaps where well-appointed art pieces once hung stared at her bluntly refusing to appear anything but abandoned. The weight on her chest spread through her limbs reminding her that a wealthy husband was the only way to save her cherished home.

The midnight stroll through a darkened Bentwick Manor took her to one of her favorite rooms, a once elegant parlor dressed in ivory and peach. Even the soft glow of the little lamp could not mask the weathered furniture and faded drapery. Her fingers found the worn chintz. Looking around the room, she suddenly recalled this was the place she had last seen her best friend.

Her only friend.

Matthew Harrington had embarked on a grand adventure to India five years ago shortly after a brief visit with her. Her head fell slightly to the right, curious that such a memory would choose to come to the surface now. Their last exchange swam into view materializing before her as though she was eavesdropping on their last conversation. As the memory of that day appeared before her, so too did a pink hue spill across her porcelain cheeks, warming her face.

Matthew had carried her into the parlor after a less than graceful fall from her horse that late afternoon. He had gently placed her upon a chaise by the window, allowing the stirring butler and maid to care for their sixteen-year-old mistress. Once they had all left and the doors were left open, he had sat next to her, smiling ruefully. "Another adventure with Lady Charlotte comes to an end."

"Apparently not a very good end for me," she had muttered, pointing at her ankle.

"This is what happens when I let you win all the time, you expect it to happen and when it doesn't you become down-right reckless."

"Let me win? Our race history is quite evenly matched, and I've earned every victory without any pity from you. Recklessness notwithstanding."

Her laughter had rung through the parlor. "Will you be home for long?"

"No. I only returned for a few days at Robert's request. I

rush home when my brother, the Earl, needs to see me. It's the after-effect of losing one's father at a young age," he had said, looking at her with deep understanding. "The remaining members of your family suddenly become of paramount importance. Apparently, we're supposed to discuss my future." His typical lopsided grin had softened any danger of becoming sentimental.

She had been momentarily taken with the appearance of a small dimple on his left cheek. Looking up into sky blue eyes and brown hair wild from their horse race had done little to still the sudden and bizarre flutter of her heart. She had cleared her throat, hoping to drive away such a strange reaction to the boy she had known her entire life. "And what shall you tell the Earl of Elmvale?"

"That I will live as I like. I'll be the fun-loving second son everyone expects because he'll have an heir and a spare one day, and I'll just be Uncle Matthew. I doubt I'll ever even marry."

Charlotte had released a most unlady-like laugh, her head falling backwards. "You, Matthew Harrington have more nerve than any man deserves. Lord Elmvale is far too kind to receive such treatment, although I wish I could see his reaction. Sounds a lot more intriguing than my future. Imagine being able to marry whenever you like. Or, even not marrying at all. What a luxury."

"It is, isn't it?" He had said through a cavalier smile.

After five years, the envy she had felt that afternoon about Matthew's fortune still lived inside her. Matthew didn't have to think about marriage at all. He did not have the title which demanded an heir. He was wealthy, educated, from an influential and respected family, and he was a man. He had all the freedom in the world.

"I, on the other hand, must save Bentwick, so I have to marry."

"Marry? To whom?" He had asked preposterously. "Save Bentwick? You're not responsible for the mess your father left." She had watched with a small smile as he ran his fingers through his wavy, brown hair. The gesture had been imprinted into her since their childhood.

"Alright, you're not a child anymore," he had conceded. "Bentwick may not be profitable at the moment, but it's a desirable title with equally coveted holdings which, if properly managed, can make you enviably rich."

She had raised her brow at his reference to money.

"Oh, did I offend you?" His hand had risen to his chest with mocking sensibility. "It took the brief mention of money to embarrass you? Not the less than gracious fall earlier which nearly brought your skirts over your head?"

"You're a shameless cad for daring to mention any of it," Charlotte's voice had sliced his attempted mockery.

"You'll be a force when you're Countess dear," he had replied with a raised brow. "You know you won't last long on the Marriage Mart. I can't believe you'll let some despicable member of the *ton* lay claim to you because of what your name offers not because you're…well, you. And, you'll do it for his money?" He had locked his eyes on hers. She could not look away, nor give in.

"I don't have a choice."

"There's always a choice."

"Really, Matthew? I wonder why I haven't pondered all of those options before."

"You cannot marry someone for his money."

"Why not? Women have been doing it for centuries! I certainly can't marry someone for love! At least not yet," she had said with a twinkle in her eye. "I'm going to do everything in my power to save my Earldom on my own, so my only criteria for a husband doesn't become amount of wealth. I'm only sixteen and have five years before I become

Countess. If I save Bentwick now, perhaps I will be able to marry for love," she had looked at Matthew with wide grey eyes.

"You remind me of the child you're supposed to be when you speak and look like that."

"I'm not a child," she had scoffed in the way young people whom believe they are no longer children do. "I can't deny the fact that marriage to a vastly wealthy gentleman will speed up the process. But, I just can't accept it yet. I have to rebuild on my own." The straightness of her spine and determination in her eyes had flinched slightly when she saw herself being studied, truly studied.

"I hate that you have to do this. I hate that my dear friend has to give herself to a seedy old man for his money."

"What if it isn't a seedy old man?" Her tone had become cheeky, brushing away the growing tension.

"Someone you might actually fall in love with? That will surely be intolerable. We won't be the best of friends anymore."

"I suppose not," she had said while her hands had repeatedly pleated the skirts of her gown. "But, if I can save Bentwick first, perhaps I may actually have a chance at love."

"You know love requires baring one's soul and all that? It means being vulnerable. It means trusting another. Are you ready for those kinds of expectations?" His eyes had settled on her with an intensity which rushed through every inch of her skin. All thinking had stopped as she watched him continue to look at her in a way he had never done so before.

"I wish I could make things different for you," he had finally said.

For an instant, in the dropping rays of the late afternoon sun, she had permitted herself the fantasy that Matthew could be the one she would marry. She recalled how the fantasy disintegrated before it had fully formed.

He was her friend. How could she possibly place upon his shoulders the ruin that was Bentwick? She and Matthew could never be. He was five years her senior and had far better prospects than to be shackled to a desperate Countess. She had never permitted herself to wallow in the injustice of her future marital choice and she would not start now. Any fantasy about Matthew becoming her husband was probably because she loathed the thought of ever losing his friendship.

It was nothing more.

He wanted freedom, fun, excitement. He wanted everything she could never offer.

Then, he had leaned towards her. She remembered his form coming closer, the heat of his body entering her personal space and his scent of sandalwood, soap and his own essence diffusing into her nose. Her heartbeat had turned into a gallop as he had ever so gently brushed her lips with his own. Within a breath, she had felt the lightest of pressure on her mouth send shocks through every limb and making her stomach plummet. Velvet warmth had brushed over her lips, and then it was over.

When she had opened her eyes, dazed heather grey in the morning dew, she found herself swimming in his eyes of sky blue. She had swallowed as she watched the intensity of his gaze, his eyes refusing to leave hers. The weight of so many questions, of so many words remaining unsaid hung between them. Wordless, he had stood. With one last look, he had taken his leave, offering her a very polite and solemn goodbye. She had barely been able to respond.

The illusion disappeared under ripples of unshed tears and she was back in a cold, dark parlor. Squeezing her eyes shut, she stopped the onslaught of tears which attacked each time she felt beaten by the unfairness of her situation. It was after that particular visit when she had received news of his trip. He hadn't come to see her before he left. It was as though he had sentenced their friendship to end since upon his return the assumption was she would be married and they could no longer be the dearest of friends. She sighed aloud in the dark parlor. Her first and only kiss could only be remembered as an affectionate farewell.

Instead of spending any more time on a memory which still sent shivers through her, she focused on images of the people who had loyally remained in Bentwick, stubbornly refusing to see their Countess fail. Each reminded her she had no choice but to find the wealthiest gentleman she could, and quickly. Recalling Matthew's friendship, his compassion, his blue eyes, his kiss would not serve her in the enormous task she had set upon herself by going to London for the first time at the late age of one and twenty. She firmly closed the door to the parlor.

Ignoring any more signs of an impoverished Earldom's seat, she rushed to her bedchamber. She had to convince the *ton* she belonged in London as a peeress in her own right and find a wealthy peer to offer marriage. Despite her age, despite never having attended a season, she would keep true to her vow to save her Earldom and all of the people whom depended upon it. With that final thought, Charlotte smiled at the little lamp for steadfastly maintaining its flame, and then, doused it.

CHAPTER 1

1828 ~ LONDON, ENGLAND

Charlotte entered the grand ballroom of Somersby House like she was falling into the loveliest of dreams. Wafts of delicious smelling food invaded her nose and the heat of too many bodies enjoying the Duke of Somersby's ball enveloped her. Impeccably dressed footmen carrying trays of refreshments seamlessly flowed through the throng. Perfectly spaced white columns adorned with sconces provided a lovely romantic glow. And, through the large garden windows the starlit night proved dazzling romance had been on order for the freshly titled Duke of Somersby. Two weeks of morning calls and studying Burke's Peerage were insufficient preparation for the opulence of a London ballroom.

Charlotte fidgeted with the rose gown which complimented the natural blush across her porcelain ivory skin perfectly. The cap sleeves barely touched her shoulders and her silk gloves rode up past her elbows. Her black, silky hair was arranged in a pile of curls atop her head bringing emphasis to almond-shaped grey eyes. Simple pearls adorned her ears and neck, one of the few sets of jewelry Mother had managed to keep.

"It's incredible," she whispered, feeling the pull of the spell.

"Don't tell me you're falling for all of this?" Lady Evangeline Fitzroy, youngest daughter of the Marquis of Hexbrook, murmured beside her. Her dark brown hair was neatly in place and the candlelight revealed red strands running through it. The contrast to her yellow dress and the flash of her amber eyes gave her the appearance of being a living flame. She raised a brow with a look of such irony the dormant buds of hope for a wealthy husband whom was also romantic and dashing unfurling deep within Charlotte shriveled instantly.

A long exhale and sharp shake to her head reminded her the time for such a prospect had long passed. "I suppose not."

Evangeline beamed and Charlotte's arm was immediately taken by Miss Isabella Wynthorpe, daughter of Viscount Wynthorpe. "Ignore her. Just because she has vowed to never marry doesn't mean the rest of us must succumb to her disdain for all things lovely and romantic."

"I didn't say it isn't lovely. I just meant Charlotte can't be sidetracked by romance. She said herself yesterday at tea, she must find a husband to marry and the wealthier the peer, the better. Her only loyalty is to her Earldom. And, us of course," Evangeline finished smugly.

"I declared my loyalty to you?"

"Yes, right after I told you I would never marry and Isabella swore to only marry for love, and Julia admitted many things about her newly-wedded state. We divulged our deepest secrets to each other over too much tea and too many biscuits. Now, we're bound for life," Evangeline smiled gleefully.

"I've sold my soul," Charlotte said.

"You've no idea!" whispered Lady Julia Bexley, Countess of Westcott, joining their conversation. "My goodness it's warm in here," she said taking a deep breath. Her honey blond hair was pinned back in abundant curls and her green eyes sparkled. "They've packed every member of the *ton* in here it seems. I witnessed all three of the Miss Burnhopes nearly falling over themselves for Viscount Laurel. Normally, the shy peers don't receive any attention until the end of the season. Perhaps, it's their new strategy, seeing as this is the older one's fourth season."

"It's my second season, are you saying I still have time before I have to start chasing timid peers?" Isabella asked cheekily.

"You won't have to chase anyone with your beautiful face," Julia responded loyally. "And every one is enamored with your blue eyes. In addition to your other attributes," Julia's eyes widened in a not-so-innocent fashion.

"Everyone? And, what attributes?"

"Oh, please Isabella, Julia's referring to your plentiful bosom and luscious curves," Evangeline said enthusiastically. "You make us all rather envious."

Charlotte's eyes widened too, but more in pity for her new friend who looked extremely uncomfortable and whose deep blush was beginning to compete with the gleaming ginger curls atop her head.

"I'm positive they didn't fail to mention the freckles adorning my face which happens to turn the color of my hair whenever a gentleman approaches me. That is bound to be more fun to discuss than my eyes or figure. I may as well start my hunt for someone quiet and dull now. If I don't, I might just end up with one of the old, decrepit ones," she said with a resigned sigh.

"Not to worry Isabella! I'd never abandon my best friend," Evangeline said with an air of conspiracy, "you may live with me in the independent household I aim to maintain."

Charlotte laughed louder than she should have when Isabella rolled her eyes, whispering, "Heaven, help me."

She took a moment to look at the three ladies, whom were vastly different from her, both in appearance and personality. She had met them at the Marchioness of Hexbrook's private dinner six days ago. Mother's dearest friend had welcomed them to town with a heartwarming dinner attended by all of Mother's old friends, and she had met their daughters. After a less than stellar introduction to a Viscount, Charlotte had been drawn to them by a strange magnetic force. The four of them had congregated, ruminating over the expectations of gender and marriage. They had somehow forged an unwavering foursome which each instinctively knew would help them survive the idiosyncrasies of a season in town.

"Evangeline's right and don't get used to hearing that," Charlotte raised her brow at the triumphant look on Evangeline's delicate face. "Thinking of any trait other than boundless wealth as criteria for my future husband is a grave mistake. Unfortunately, money is what Bentwick needs and, therefore, it's all I require. But, let's try not to make my desperation for it too obvious."

"Your unfailing sense of duty makes me appear downright evil," Evangeline said.

"That's probably because you are dear," Charlotte smiled broadly.

"Good evening Lady Bentwick," the deep voice of the Duke of Ellis cut through their conversation. His frosty glare chilled her as she returned the cordial salutation, and then he disappeared.

"That was odd," Charlotte noted.

"He is odd," Isabella said, "He's been a widow for twenty years. He has twin sons at Cambridge and isn't the kind of man one would trifle with."

"Is there any kind of man one would trifle with?" Evangeline asked pointedly.

Isabella rolled her eyes. "I suppose you wouldn't believe so, but for those of us who wish to marry, yes, I suppose there is," then, she turned to Charlotte. "It was a rather strange interaction."

"I've been managing merchants, farmers and bankers for years…I've learned to trust my instincts and every single one is screaming about the Duke of Ellis."

"And they should be. He truly isn't a man to trifle with. Father warns me about him before each ball and Oliver becomes a pontificating nightmare," Evangeline added.

"It's not often I agree with Evangeline," Julia said, "But a few ladies have had to take extended holidays to Italy and France after being in his attention for some time."

Charlotte pursed her lips. "I may have no other choice but to accept his attentions."

"It's still early in the season. You have plenty of time to find your perfect match," Isabella said encouragingly. "We all do actually." Her bright smile faded when her eyes landed on Evangeline.

Charlotte almost joined the friendly banter on the perils and benefits of marriage but her attention was suddenly caught by a jolt of awareness running through her.

She tilted her head to the right, as though someone had just called her name. All thoughts of Ellis, money and ruin were swiftly swept aside by a curious tingle shooting through every limb. The voices of her friends died away as she searched for the source of her exhilaration. Overpowered by a loud buzz from head to toe, she turned her head various times to scan the room. Why was there a sudden flutter in her stomach and current in her veins?

Charlotte nodded at the comments being made by her friends for her ability to produce coherent language was gone. Every sensation running through her body told her she was being closely studied, but she could not tell by whom or even guess as to why. Her fingers lightly grasped and released her gown as she tried to locate the source of her fire. Many a lady she had met in the past week had raptured on about the magical spark which would determine their acceptance of a proposal. But who was making her world spin? She scanned the room one more time and stopped at a pair of blue eyes set in a rather tanned face across the room. She knew those eyes. She knew that face, the smile, the dimple on the left cheek.

Matthew was home!

He was home and no one had told her!

Her face broke into a smile and her eyes suddenly watered with joy. The room stopped. Her heart nearly stopped. Everything came to a screeching halt and she was no longer in Somersby's ball room. She was at home, by her favorite pond and Matthew had come upon her, interrupting her sketching, as usual. All noise ceased and no one existed except for Matthew weaving his way through the crowd towards her.

His six-foot three frame was handsomely poured into his evening dress. Jacket and cravat crisply fitting over broad shoulders and strong neck. The starched white shirt accented his alarming tan far too well and the strength of his arms, the power in his legs were barely contained in the formal attire. But, what Charlotte remembered most of all, was the wild brown hair which refused to adhere to decorum. His blue eyes were trained on her with a seriousness she had never associated with him.

Her entire body brimmed with happiness at the sight of him. The boy who had been like her older brother had returned safe and whole.

It was the only reason her heart was racing, she told herself.

It was the only reason butterflies had overtaken her body.

It was the only reason she was consumed by sheer joy at the sight of him.

CHAPTER 2

Charlotte heard Evangeline's voice far in the recesses of her mind, and then Isabella and Julia's intonations floated in. Their voices became louder and pulled her back to the present moment. Images of Somerset faded and Charlotte recalled where she was. She set her face to its neutral look of contentedness. Gone was the smile, but her eyes remained fixed on Matthew as he approached her.

"Who is that?" Charlotte heard Isabella ask through her hypnotic state.

Evangeline and Julia glanced up as well and all four ladies watched Matthew approach. Evangeline, oblivious to Charlotte's trance, piped up. "Oh, I remember him! The Earl of Elmvale's brother…what was his name?"

"Matthew," Charlotte said, her eyes fixed on his approaching figure.

"Right! The Honorable Mr. Matthew Harrington!" Evangeline giggled. "He visited Hexbrook several times. He was at Eton and Cambridge with Oliver – they were very good friends. I remember he used to make me call him that, and once he and Oliver left a frog in my bed."

"Yes, he would have," Charlotte replied mechanically, her eyes focused on the figure walking towards her.

"He's so tan!" Julia remarked.

"He was in India," Charlotte supplied without a glance.

"…positively gorgeous!" Isabella murmured which made Evangeline snort in laughter. "So tall," Isabella continued to comment.

"…tan makes eyes bluer…" Julia mumbled.

"Why are we speaking in partial sentences?" Evangeline wandered aloud to no one in particular.

"…and, face is perfect – it isn't fair for a man to have such perfect lips," Julia continued almost to herself.

"You're married!" Evangeline pointed out.

"But not blind!" Julia blushed deeply.

"And the hair, he looks…." Isabella trailed off.

"Wild. Daring. Dangerous." Evangeline said with a huff of annoyance at the sudden stupefaction of three highly intelligent ladies over a handsome – well, extremely handsome - she admitted begrudgingly, gentleman.

"Actually, from what I hear he is exactly that. I once commented on his appearance and Oliver nearly bit my head off. He said not to be fooled by his friendly nature – he's a rake and I should stay far away from him. Which of course I wouldn't have done had he not gone to India," Evangeline informed them.

"Of course, Carters would say so. All brothers warn their sisters off of men who are exactly as they are," Isabella said pointedly.

"That is the first coherent thing you've said since we saw Mr. Harrington," Evangeline noted. She turned to urge the gentleman in question to hurry his step and cease all of this nonsense immediately, but she stopped herself when she saw the lopsided grin and then, Charlotte was positive she knew what had finally frozen her outspoken friend, the dimple.

They formed quite the tableaux once Matthew finally arrived at their quartet.

"You're back," Charlotte broke etiquette. She stood completely still, arms at her sides, her face remained placid. Only the rise and fall of her chest, and her words escaping in a breathless whisper, betrayed her state.

"Lady Bentwick," Matthew flashed his most charming smile and bowed slightly. "Lady Westcott, Lady Evangeline, Miss Wynthorpe."

Charlotte permitted a small smile to break through her Countess countenance when she noted the effect Matthew was having on her friends.

"Pardon me. After so many years abroad, I seem to have forgotten my manners," he turned to Julia and Charlotte saw her beaming, "Lady Westcott, I knew Westcott at Cambridge and believe the best decision he ever made was to marry you."

Then, he turned to Evangeline and Isabella. "We haven't been formally introduced, though I also attended school and remain friends with your brothers."

Charlotte watched Evangeline respond knowing they would be rooted to the spot for the evening if she didn't. Isabella was crimson and would not speak a word to a strange man, while Julia had lost all sense of proper conduct and simply smiled.

"Pay no mind, Mr. Harrington. We are sophisticated ladies who can forgive these tiny lapses in propriety. Besides, I recall your visits to my brother, and the frog you left under my pillow can be said to be our formal introduction. I'm also sure that if you're a friend of Lady Bentwick's you will soon know Miss Wynthorpe."

Charlotte cleared her throat knowing the rules well enough to avoid scandal, "Mr. Harrington, may I introduce you to Lady Westcott, Lady Evangeline and Miss Wynthorpe." The accepted nods and pleasantries were exchanged as they remained on the right side of decorum.

Charlotte bit her lip to sustain the bubbling urge to laugh when she saw Evangeline cleverly push Julia towards the elderly Lady Westmount. The Marchioness was torturing some poor lady with the rules of proper conduct and behavior. Next, she took Isabella's hand on the pretext of desperately needing to see her new satin gloves, pulling her away from Charlotte and Matthew – far away enough to give them some semblance of privacy and close enough to satisfy the rules of propriety.

She turned from her friends to face Matthew and her breath caught. His eyes had not moved from her. She stared into a sea of blue before noticing his lips twitch as though he were instructing them to stop from laughing too. She swallowed, remembering the warmth of those lips.

"Good evening Lady Bentwick."

Five years of separation melted away as his voice and twinkling blue eyes instantly transported her home. They could have easily been riding through the meadow discussing their horse's attributes. But they weren't. They were in a London ballroom. He stood before her looking positively god-like and his voice was velvet.

She bit her lower lip slightly and her fingers gently folded and unfolded the delicate material of her gown. Being with Matthew had always been a source of comfort for her, and while she did feel the familiar ease of their friendship arise from a deep slumber, she also felt something else. There was something strange passing between them. Perhaps it was five years of separation, or perhaps it was sheer happiness that he had returned unharmed. She could not begin to describe the emotions flirting with her in the presence of her beloved friend. S he wished for time to ponder the strange feelings, but there would be none in the midst of a party. "Matth- Mr. Harrington! What are you doing here?"

She saw the familiar lopsided grin. "I'm enjoying Somersby's ball."

"And you just happened to receive an invitation for it while abroad?" She countered, her grey eyes determined to obtain an answer. She regained some composure in the face of his familiar smile and easy manner, compelling the strange emotions his sudden appearance caused into the deepest part of her. She breathed deeply and continued questioning him as she would have in Somerset on one of their adventures through the woods. "When did you arrive? Why did you come home? What are you going to do now that you're here?"

"Yesterday. I felt it was time. Whatever a second son and still heir is expected to do I suppose," he shrugged one shoulder with such charm, Charlotte pursed her lips.

She turned to look at the dance floor appearing far more interested in the dancing couples than she was. The intensity of his gaze which refused to leave her face forced her to turn back to him.

He was studying her, remembering her. Her lips parted, but no words escaped. Her tongue ran over her lips and she saw the flicker of his eyes watch the tender skin moisten. Recalling where they were, she set her face to neutral even though she knew her eyes betrayed the vibrancy and passion she had always felt when she was with him. She lowered her voice, so only he could hear her. Though, her tone was insistent and commanding, also a familiarity between them. "What prompted your return, Matthew? Truly?"

She heard his breathing slightly catch when she dared to use his name. He cleared his throat as he dropped the beguiling attitude. "I had seen enough damage. Actually, it was the moment I started to think of where I was as home.

My place is here, as Robert's heir – but don't let him know I admitted as much," he said, his eyes sparkling with some of his former mischief.

"I'll make sure to tell him you've been flirting incessantly with all of my friends," her eyes narrowed, conspiring to the crime.

"Oh, he'll love that," Matthew chuckled. "Just don't name them should he get any ideas to marry me off."

Charlotte permitted a small smile feeling positively thrilled about their moment of camaraderie. For an instant, they were at home discussing the million injustices committed against them by their families. In that bubble of comfort and ease, which only Matthew was ever able to provide, she permitted herself the freedom to be intimate.

"They really missed you," she said softly. And, after a beat, the words deep in her heart could no longer be contained, "we all did."

Her voice was barely a whisper, but she knew it reached his ears and meandered its way deep inside him because he offered a small smile in return. Charlotte knew it was his most honest of smiles without the intention of charming or eluding. It was a smile she had only ever seen when in private, and somehow knew, he reserved for her.

"Me too," his blue eyes deepened, locking onto hers, making her throat shrivel. Her lips parted, but for the second time in one night, she lost the ability to form words.

"In any case," he cleared his throat, "it's nice to see you aren't in need of my help at the present moment." The cavalier attitude returned, brushing the fragile moment aside.

Charlotte squared her shoulders realizing he was clearly evading becoming too sentimental. She hid her disappointment and played his game. "You're the only one who ever thought I was in need of your help. I'll have you know Mr. Harrington that I'm most capable."

"And beautiful and graceful too," he drawled provocatively.

Her stomach dropped to her feet. Why would he say such things in the middle of a ballroom? She suddenly realized that he felt different. Aside from the strange feelings surrounding her, there was something markedly different about him.

"Dance with me," he raised a brow, laying the dare for her to accept or face endless mockery for cowardice.

"No," she stopped the game because he never flirted with her like she had seen him do with others. He had always patronized her like an older brother. She realized he wasn't the same Matthew she had known growing up, and therefore she couldn't trust him as she once had. At least not until she figured out what sort of game he was playing and decide whether or not the stakes for her were too high.

"No?"

"Not used to hearing that word, are you? You know why I'm here and you could ruin my chances with your attention. You're also a renowned rake and charm oozes so easily from you many a lady has convinced herself of being desperately in-love with you. I'm happy you've returned unharmed, but I can't disrupt my chances of an honorable proposal."

"Honorable or lucrative?" His tone became slightly sardonic, but his eyes questioned her. He was unsure if she was looking for love or money, and she wouldn't give him the satisfaction of accurately assessing her situation.

"How easy it is to judge from where you stand," Charlotte levelled him with her finest Countess countenance. "I will marry honorably. Clearly, your compliment was nothing more than a wish to thoroughly annoy me."

"Since my compliment meant nothing," his brow raised for emphasis and his voice lowered dangerously, "then you shouldn't fear dancing with me."

She glared at him remembering all too well that besides offering comfort, camaraderie and competition, Matthew also knew interminable ways to irk her. And, it appeared, it was something he recalled far too well.

She clenched her jaw when she recalled a space in her dance card and saw the beginnings of a victorious smile lift the corners of his mouth. Within moments she was in his strong, yet gentle grip. She felt him hold her just a little bit closer than was proper, and his arms contracted as he tightened his grip ever so slightly. Her heartbeat a little faster and warmth spread through her cheeks. Her head spun with delight and annoyance as she realized it was the first time she was actually enjoying a waltz.

She felt Matthew's strength emanating through his precisely tailored evening dress. She winced realizing her gloved hand fit perfectly into his and their bodies moved harmoniously, effortlessly. His warmth enveloped her and his masculine scent invaded her senses. She whirled in his arms, feeling safe, protected as she always had. She also felt the flutter of a warning because her best friend could disrupt her plans to marry a rich peer.

The entire dance was maddening. Instructing herself to revel in every last second, because it would be their last, she forced herself to remember that Matthew had no interest in marriage. His sole intention was to live a carefree life. He had run away to the other side of the world after one brief kiss! Any ridiculous feeling about the perfection of their waltz had to be stamped out because he would never trade in his freedom for the chance to rebuild an ailing Earldom.

"That wasn't so bad, was it?" He taunted as he bowed at the conclusion of their waltz.

"Remember it well because that was our one and only this season," she countered, and then added for good measure, "Probably even, ever."

"Coward," he said with a lopsided grin.

"I won't let you ruin my chances of marrying well," she said with an arrogant tilt to her head as she was led back to Mother.

"You don't understand, do you?" Despite his easy manner, his voice was iron. "I have the fortune of finding you unmarried. Now, it's my duty to make sure you marry someone worthy of you and I will stand in anyone's way who dares to ask for the wrong reason."

"What you don't understand is that I'm a grown woman and I will marry who I think is best for Bentwick. You have no say whatsoever."

He shrugged his shoulder casually and offered one last infuriatingly smug smile as they parted ways. "We shall see, Lady Bentwick."

CHAPTER 3

An hour later, Matthew sat in a shadowed corner of the club. His survival no longer depended upon a sinless lifestyle and so a night of drink, game and women was exactly what he needed. Self-imposed celibacy and monk-like living had saved him abroad, but it wasn't how one thrived in the *ton*, he thought ruefully, finishing his drink and signaling for another. He needed to reclaim his former self if he was to survive being back in England. There was no use for the celibate man who had fought in battle and seen death and carnage. The man who had witnessed intense cruelties due to a very strict social system and who had risked everything in investments had learned humility, self-control and the value of dedication and discipline. But, this wasn't the man whom the *ton* expected.

He accepted the greetings of old acquaintances and friends at the club with his usual charm, many of whom made comments about his heroic return home. Each time he flashed a grin or raised his glass in response, a very uncomfortable truth began to settle around him, hugging him and slowly making itself known. Every man in the room expected jovial, arrogant, smug Matthew Harrington. Every man admired him for the nerve of his lofty goals: have an adventure, bed many women and return a hero with enviable wealth. While he had accomplished all of those things, it wasn't something he cared to share with any of the gossip-hungry faces before him. The Matthew Harrington sitting alone at the table, gently swirling the contents of his glass, and studying the faces of once familiar men, was fundamentally a different man. But, the truth was he wasn't in India anymore. Survival now meant a return to his old way of life which included nights of sinful debauchery with the very men before him.

He groaned, downing his whisky in one gulp and signaled for another. And, then requested another as it swiftly disappeared down his throat.

"Not sure if they watered down the stuff abroad, but here it's a touch too strong to drink that quickly. Unless, of course, the goal is to lose everything you have at those tables," Lord Oliver Fitzroy, the Earl of Carters, motioned with a quick nod behind him where many a young Lord overlooked cards on the tables with quiet desperation.

"If only I could lose everything I have," Matthew said wryly, pointing to his head.

"Beheading went out with guillotine Harrington," Oliver said. He sat across from Matthew in one smooth motion, casually signaling for his own beverage. Oliver Fitzroy was the most blasted confident man Matthew had ever known. He was an Earl, heir to a Marquisate and truly believed the world revolved around him. He was as tall as Matthew, a gifted athlete and more handsome than any man should be. Perfectly combed black hair and clear green eyes had made many a lady melt in his arms.

"Why aren't you at Somersby's?" Matthew asked. He finished his drink and another appeared at the table.

Oliver lifted his crystal green eyes heavenward in the ironic fashion Matthew had come to associate with him. "Because the heavens decided I had had enough martyrdom for one evening and struck my sister with a fine headache. I escorted her home and now I'm here to be repaid for my brotherly devotion. I don't take joy in my sister's ailments, well, not entirely, but I'm telling you Harrington, Evangeline will be the death of me," he sighed deeply.

"You sound like a victim of the most vicious wrongdoing," Matthew said in between swallows of fine amber liquid.

"She is the most outspoken woman in the world. I can't wait until she's married. But until then, mother won't let me breathe unless I'm watching over my youngest sister. Thank God my other two sisters married quickly and well, otherwise mother would strangle the life out of me. One has to take one's victories when one can because watching over Evangeline truly makes me the most ill-used man in the realm."

Matthew smirked at his friend's dramatics careful to avoid Oliver's steady gaze. He had known Oliver since he was a boy. They had attended Eton and then Cambridge together. The day he had mixed mud into his professor's inkpots, Oliver had been there. The first time he visited a local pub and drank more ale than he should have, Oliver had been there. The first time he stood his ground in a bare-knuckle fight against local boys, Oliver had been there and had probably instigated the whole thing. The first time he had visited a house full of beautiful women, Oliver had been there and had paid for those beautiful women to entertain him. And, when he had informed Oliver of his trip to India, instead of trying to dissuade him, he nodded with silent understanding of his need to prove he was more than Elmvale's charming heir. If there was one man who would see the difference in him, it would be Oliver.

"Avoiding me isn't going to work," Oliver said flatly.

"I'm sitting right across from you." Matthew raised a brow.

"Why are you home?

"Pardon?"

"Did you return too soon? Did you get a chance to prove to yourself you are more than your brother's heir?"

"Carters -" Matthew warned.

"Harrington," Oliver replied unruffled. "The *ton* has not changed. You must find a way to accept that and adapt your new outlook to your old world. Otherwise, you'll never be truly home."

"I suppose then that I must dance and smile and answer idiotic questions about how wonderful it must have felt to watch the enemy be defeated at my hands," Matthew said darkly before swallowing another drink in its entirety.

"You tell them it felt victorious but it's even better to be back in London. Tell them it was hot and you're happy to finally have a decent cup of tea. Then move the conversation to horses and it's all over," Oliver shrugged a shoulder, looking completely at ease.

If only he could focus and there weren't two Olivers melting into and out of each other in his line vision, Matthew was certain he'd be happy to wipe the smug smile off his face.

"I haven't your powers of political prowess," he said. His words slurred slightly but it didn't stop him from finishing his drink and requesting another.

"Pity," Oliver swirled his drink thoughtfully. Then, his clear gazed landed on Matthew. "So, how did it feel?"

The remnants of his drink caught in Matthew's throat and his words sputtered out in a loud cough. "You can't be serious."

"Completely. Speak of it now, tell me everything. Then never speak of it again. It belongs in the past. There is no use for any of it now. Honor what you did and then put it to rest so you can live with us once again."

"Since when did you become a sage?" Matthew attempted sarcasm, but the two Olivers suddenly became three and not one was going to let the question go.

Matthew's jaw tightened. "It felt like playing God with men's lives. I saw too many die, too many willing to die for a lost cause," his eyes remained fixed upon the glass in his hand though his mind easily conjured the haze of heat rising above bodies littering the ground. "I will never forget Burma and I will pray for peace for the rest of my days."

"Wonderful," Oliver interrupted a little too jovially to feel anything but contrived. "Now we talk about the two Arabs I recently acquired."

Matthew shook his head in disbelief at his friend's tactics.

"You can live here again."

"Oliver-"

"You danced with Lady Bentwick." Matthew's head spun with the sudden change in subject, though Oliver's refusal to allow him a second bout of self-pity didn't go unnoticed.

"I did. There is nothing wrong with dancing with my neighbor and dear friend."

"Clearly, the south east Asian heat made you delirious about the *ton*," Oliver said drily. "The Matthew I knew swore to never marry. Does that still hold true?"

"Marry? Carters, what the devil are you getting at?" Matthew asked looking more and more confused as the alcohol he had quickly consumed dulled his senses.

"It's no secret that Lady Bentwick is here to marry. From

all outward appearance, her Earldom is healthy. She has her choice of husband and you danced with her...I merely assumed..."

"You assumed wrong," Matthew said flatly.

"You could do it you know," Oliver lowered his voice. "Rumor has it you're much wealthier now than when you left...you could marry the Countess."

Charlotte slipped into Matthew's mind. The lady he had seen across the ball room was every inch a Countess. She had stood regally with her face set in the perfect balance of polite condescension. The cold and aloof lady had bared no resemblance to the vibrant girl he had known. In her place, he had found a stunningly beautiful woman, as warm and real as a marble statue.

Matthew brought his glass to his lips to hide his smile when he recalled the way the ice surrounding her had thawed when she felt herself being watched. He had seen that look on her face countless times, as though she would take flight any second to satisfy her inquisitiveness.

"Or, maybe I'll marry her," Oliver distastefully interrupted. "Perhaps she'll inspire Evangeline to find a husband since they've become great friends rather quickly," his hard stare belied his casual tone. "She's quite beautiful."

"If you value your life, you'll remain far away from Lady Bentwick. As shall I. I can't marry her."

Charlotte was the girl with whom he had grown up. Or, being five years her senior, was the girl he had cared for while she grew up. She was like his sister, which made the palpable current between them all the more confusing. He had missed her. It was the only possible explanation he would allow for the veritable force which had inexplicably drawn him towards her when he had seen her in Somersby's ballroom.

Even though the short kiss they had shared before his departure had haunted him for five years, he refused to think of it in any other terms than feelings of pity which had overcome him for the circumstances of his friend. His fingers nearly crushed the glass in his hand. He could never think of her in any other way because he would never dare do anything to hurt her. Even though he was no longer acting on his every whim, he knew his reputation, he knew his views on marriage, he had seen too much during his years abroad and the sum of all of his experiences made him frightfully aware of how deeply he could wound her. It was a risk he was not willing to take.

"I won't survive losing her friendship to marriage," the words quietly left his lips and his eyes kept trying to focus on the glass in his hand.

"There's no guarantee you'll remain friends if you marry her. But, you'll most definitely lose her when she marries someone else." Carters' tone cut to an unsavory truth Matthew wished to avoid for as long as he could.

"Well, then I must ensure she marries someone suitable."

"For whom?"

Matthew's eyes narrowed. He finished his drink and loudly placed the glass on the table. "From what I recall, this was normally the time we would be off in search of even less noble pursuits."

Oliver nodded, accepting the end of the conversation and looking relieved to hear a hint of the old Matthew.

Thirty minutes later Matthew found himself at a private party in the home of Oliver's mistress. Oliver disappeared and Matthew was left in the capable hands of her three friends. He studied each through the fog of alcohol. One was too insipid, the other too round and the third too blonde. None of these women inspired any excitement in him and so none were worthy of helping him to break his self-imposed celibacy.

He hated to admit it, but he was hoping for a dark-haired beauty with grey eyes and ivory skin. Fortunately, he was far too drunk to think upon it further and fell into a rather ungracious heap upon the chaise.

CHAPTER 4

Matthew breathed in the fragrant spring air to cleanse the exhaustion dominating his body after a long and rather embarrassing night. He had bathed the shameful night away and drank copious amounts of strong tea before venturing out to enjoy the weather. It was the perfect spring day as only London could produce to create amnesia for winter's dreary perpetual grey. In his case, he thought mournfully, he needed to forget more than a weary winter.

He had made the long trip home with trepidation. The charms of India had seduced him during his first year. Spicy food, encompassing heat, women with hair of ebony and skin woven by the sun had charmed him completely, and he had seriously doubted his return. Marching into battle for His Majesty's army in Burma had shown him the many ways people of a lower station suffered. It was one thing to hear about the plight of the impoverished and quite another to witness it. He returned to his post with the desire to work for those who needed a voice. He worked tirelessly, but after five years far from home and those he held dear, he knew India would entice him away forever if he did not return.

He walked slowly through the park, remaining in the shadows, feeling far too ill to strike up a superficial, polite conversation should the need arise. A few nurses walked about with children in tow. Gentlemen took purposeful strides towards appointments and ladies hid from the sun behind parasols. Flashes of those in need, of the many injured in war couldn't help but make him think of how completely coddled all those before him now seemed. He left the park and turned down one of the quieter streets in Mayfair.

He smirked, remembering his own less than challenging life as heir to the Earldom of Elmvale. He had blazed quite the trail, reveling in his position as second son, certain he would never inherit the title. He remained without said title because his brother, Lord Robert Harrington, was alive and well. But, Matthew knew he could not simply pick up the thread of his former life. Five years had changed everything. Unfortunately, even though his world had changed, the *ton* and those dear to him continued on as though nothing had happened, as though he had never witnessed carnage, nor had fought desperately to improve the lives of others. He had returned to an unchanged world as a very changed man.

His pace slowed until his body came to a full stop. Matthew looked around and his eyes stopped at a quietly elegant structure. His feet had brought him to Bentwick House – he had been there as a young man once. Strange how his body had simply known the way. His eyes followed the lines of the home and landed on a solitary figure. His limbs froze.

He would recognize her form anywhere. Slender yet strong, and far more confidence than any lady should be emboldened with, the lady in rose was Charlotte. The angle of her hat and her insistence on remaining still, something he never thought possible, only permitted the lower half of her face to be seen. His brows furrowed once more as he studied his friend. Gone was the girl of sixteen full of bravado. She was every inch a Countess. He remembered her stormy looks and the laying of her challenge the night before with a grin in full admiration of how capably she wielded her authority. Then, he noticed her maid was standing in the doorway. Was she planning on going somewhere alone? "Hell," he muttered as he marched directly towards her.

"I'll return in time to dress for dinner, Riley," Charlotte said to her maid. "Hexbrook House is not very far. You don't need to trouble yourself."

"My Lady! It's no trouble at all," the plain, brown haired young woman said nervously.

Charlotte smiled. "Thank you, Riley, but you needn't bother. Honestly, you can watch me walk there. I'll be perfectly fine."

"It seems, Lady Bentwick, that your maid has more sense than you do," Matthew said smoothly, signaling to the maid who blushed upon recognizing him that he would care for her mistress. He offered a patronizing smile when she jumped, turning to see him standing slightly behind her. "Your maid just closed the door and now you're alone on the street. I could've been someone with less than honorable intentions."

She narrowed her eyes and glared at him. "You did that purposely. Where did you come from anyway?"

"Of course, I did. You need to learn that you aren't safe here like you are at home. You can't go walking about without a chaperone."

"Thank you for the life lesson," she replied her voice dripping in sarcasm. "Now, if you'll excuse me, I'm heading to Hexbrook House."

"Perfect. I'll walk you there."

"There's no need. I'm completely safe. I've been there

several times already, so you see, your services aren't necessary."

"Services?" He arched a brow at her audacity. Ire crept up his limbs when she smiled triumphantly.

"Precisely," she beamed, beginning to walk past him. She stopped suddenly and turned to him, her nose crinkled. "You smell positively awful. How dare you approach me smelling like that?"

"My lady, you are artful in your treatment of a gentleman."

She raised her brow in response. "A gentleman in your state wouldn't go near a lady."

"I'm in no state. I bathed and shaved before stepping out. Not that I should be discussing my morning ablutions with you."

"Fine. But in future Matthew I would appreciate more self-control around alcohol."

"I'm sorry, are you Adelaide?" he exaggerated looking around for his mother, "I thought not. You may be my friend, but do remember I'm five years older-"

"Older being the key word," she interrupted. "A gentleman of your age should take better care of his health," she pursed her lips as though deciding on her next statement. To Matthew's chagrin, she continued speaking her mind, "You're back for a day and have already taken up the thread of your former life?"

The disappointment in her tone stung deeply, but he casually shrugged it away, refusing to admit it mirrored his own feelings about how he had handled his first night back. "The thread of my former life seems to be the only available option."

"Really?" The heavy sarcasm in her voice made him smirk. This was familiar territory and not the disappointing pity for his less than honorable actions of the night before.

"What else is there for me in London?" He fell into large pools of sparkling grey and his heart stopped when he saw her eyes shimmer with the threat of tears.

"Much more than you think, but you fell into drink without even considering another option. I'm sure gambling and women were involved too. I thought five years away would have changed all that," the ache in her voice nearly strangled his heart.

She took a deep breath before looking at him squarely. "You, of all people, know exactly how I feel about spirits of any kind," her voice cracked and even though they were separated by mere inches, he felt as removed from her as he had been when he was abroad.

"Charlotte?" He froze when she stepped away from him realizing it wasn't his scent she was recoiling from, for he had thoroughly bathed away the humiliation of the previous evening. He recalled every conversation in the woods about her father's lack of sobriety and he flinched when she spoke again even though her voice was full of sadness.

"Complete freedom to enjoy your life as you wish, wasn't that your goal? Well, I shan't keep you with the weight of my ailments. Good day, Mr. Harrington."

"Ailments?" he asked sharply. "Is it you or your Earldom who is ill?" He ran his hands through his hair. He had promised to interfere in her search for a husband last night to protect her, and maybe even to annoy her, but the thought of his friend giving herself to an undeserving man because of her financial needs turned his blood molten.

"I'm looking for a husband, my reasons are my own," she doused his anger with cool collectedness.

"Enlighten me, Charlotte because if you're simply hoping to find love, I'll do my duty as your closest friend and watch over you. But, if it's money you still require, I'll protect you so fiercely anyone with a remote smudge to his honor will abandon any notion of courting the Countess of Bentwick."

"I've been taking care of myself and an entire Earldom for years. I don't need you swooping in to save me or protect me."

His chest seized when she turned to walk away. And, just as he moved to take her arm, to bring her back and...and...he wasn't even sure what he would say or do but he nearly screamed bloody murder when they both heard her name being called.

"Lady Bentwick!"

A quick turn right revealed Lady Julia Bexley, Countess of Westcott, a few paces behind them on the arm of a gentlemen Matthew recognized immediately.

"Lady Westcott! You're on your way to Hexbrook House?" Charlotte's eyes brightened as though her prayers had been answered and Matthew clenched his jaw. He saw her change her demeanor instantly. Tears, painful memories all buried as she turned to greet her friend and became a little too friendly eyeing the gentleman by her side.

Lady Julia Bexley was lively and slightly nervous. Her mint visiting gown accentuated her green eyes and a few honey tresses stubbornly refused to remain under the protection of her cap and bonnet. She was Charlotte's height and also her exact opposite, exuding warmth and sunshine in contrast to his friend's cool reserve. He realized instantly he preferred Charlotte's serene beauty. Lady Westcott couldn't possibly compete with the porcelain beauty of his friend.

"Is everything alright?" asked the insufferably polite gentleman with Lady Westcott.

"Oh, heavens! I nearly forgot," Lady Westcott exclaimed with an eager look. "Lady Bentwick, may I present to you Lord Simon Huntsbridge, Viscount Hunstbridge. My cousin."

"Thrice removed," Huntsbridge added.

"No need for specifics. I'm your favorite cousin after all," Lady Westcott raised her brows.

"Highly questionable under the circumstances. You forgot I was standing next to you the instant you saw Lady Bentwick," Lord Huntsbridge's tone carried a whiff of sarcasm mingled with what appeared as a tried manner between them. "Not that I blame you," Huntsbridge added in a soft whisper in spite of the pink hue sprouting from the base of his collar.

Matthew nearly snorted at the arranged introduction. He was also starving, had a fine headache coming on and was still suffering from the embarrassment of being unable to give into the obvious desires of three willing ladies. In addition to his fury at Charlotte's refusal to confide in him, there was fury for her judgmental, though accurate, assessment of his behavior. He was in no mood to stand by while she made a connection with a bloody Viscount. "Lady Bentwick is absolutely fine," he said brusquely. "In fact, we were on our way to Hexbrook House."

"I was on my way to Hexbrook House," Charlotte corrected him sweetly. Then, she turned her attention to Huntsbridge. Matthew felt his body burn.

"Lord Huntsbridge."

The blond peer bowed on cue with a small smirk on his face and Matthew instructed his hands not to create fists at his side.

Lady Westcott, on the other hand, was beaming. "How lovely that you may join us on our short walk Mr. Harrington!" She immediately took hold of Matthew's arm, pushing Charlotte aside and in Huntsbridge's direction. She marched quickly ahead nearly dragging Matthew with her in order to give Charlotte and Huntsbridge privacy.

With Charlotte and Huntsbridge walking slowly behind

him, Matthew ordered every muscle in his neck to keep from turning back. His ear caught bits of what seemed to be a one-sided conversation for only Charlotte's intonations reached his ears. He did manage to turn once on the pretext of showing Julia a robin perched in its nest and was happy to see they were walking alongside each other with enough space between them for at least two others. He shot a teasing grin at Charlotte who scowled in return.

"Don't you think so, Mr. Harrington?"

Matthew turned to see Lady Westcott's wide green eyes expecting an answer to an important question which he hadn't heard. He put on his most charming smile and stopped at a blossoming lilac, in front of the gates to Hexbrook House's courtyard. He carefully pulled a delicate bloom, offering it to her.

"I think you've the right assessment of matters Lady Westcott," he said smoothly. "And, I also think this bloom has its fair share of competition in your presence."

Lady Westcott's lips pressed together as she received the flower. "You, Mr. Harrington, have more nerve than any man of my acquaintance. I know you didn't hear me because you were far too preoccupied with listening to my cousin's conversation with Lady Bentwick."

Matthew laughed. "Have all women changed so much in the five years I've been gone?"

"I don't think we've changed at all. You probably have just begun to take real notice," Lady Westcott raised an eyebrow.

"Please tell the Earl of Westcott he has made a fine choice in his wife. Though I doubt he needs my assessment to verify what he already knows," Matthew winked, making Lady Westcott blush deeply.

"You're obviously incorrigible," she giggled, "except I doubt Westcott notices much beyond the management of his Earldom." She sighed.

"If you march into his office looking as you do now, and sighing as you just did, I would wager any amount that you would have his attention," Matthew continued in his beguiling attitude and his laugh deepened when Lady Westcott's face nearly matched the color of the lilac she kept bringing up to her nose.

They were suddenly startled out of their banter by a deep clearing of the throat. Matthew looked up and found himself facing the furrowed brows of Charlotte. His smile widened, if only to irritate her further.

"How was your walk Lady Bentwick?" He asked grandly. And, he should have been ashamed of himself, but he took absolute joy at the pursed lips of the Viscount. From what Matthew recalled, Huntsbridge possessed a healthy and respectable estate, and also happened to be quietly handsome. Blond hair and green eyes did nothing to belittle his masculinity, he admitted begrudgingly. But, he was also exceedingly quiet, bordering on shy. While other peers had had their fun tormenting Huntsbridge when they were at Eton, Matthew had always held him in high regard. Though, at the moment, he couldn't have been happier for Huntbridge's lack of elocution.

"Lovely," she answered icily. "Yours?"

"Divine," he said smugly.

"Come, Huntsbridge," Lady Westcott said, "escort me in."

Huntsbridge bowed at Charlotte, almost apologetically, and said a stiff goodbye to Matthew.

"He's not for you," Matthew said as the blond pair slipped through the gate towards Hexbrook House's grand entrance.

"He's perfect for me," Charlotte snapped. "He's handsome, exceedingly polite, gentle, and doesn't possess a shred of arrogance. Unlike other gentlemen I know who are clearly so enamored with themselves they believe they can charm anyone into doing their bidding."

"You'd be bored within a week and Huntsbridge wouldn't know what to do with you."

"Oh, I believe Lord Huntsbridge would know exactly what to do with me," Charlotte threw back with a confident tilt of her head.

Matthew froze. What on earth had happened to fine bred ladies since he had left? Outspoken, daring, willful, he groaned realizing Charlotte had always been that way. The same qualities which had brought them close in childhood were infuriating as adults.

"Really?" He took a step forward, happy to see a fissure in her cool confidence. He kept stepping towards her until her back was up against the lilac tree. Within the cover of the fragrant blooms, his face hovered just over hers. Her eyes were wide, grey saucers and her breath deepened. His gaze fell to her lips and their feather light softness which had been seared into his memory came racing back. He was suddenly consumed with need to claim those lips once again.

"I doubt very much anything the genteel Viscount of Huntsbridge would do with you would come close to this," the low-toned whisper was instantly followed by a kiss far less innocent than the one he had given five years ago.

The instant his lips met her velvet warmth, his body sizzled and it took every ounce of control not to take more. His arms remained at his sides fighting the instinctual need to wrap themselves around her. But, he knew he was playing a dangerous game. They were in broad daylight and the blossomed branches offered duplicitous protection from the watchful windows.

Unless he was prepared to offer marriage on the spot, he had to stop. But first, his greedy tongue took more. In one luscious stroke he parted her lips. Roses and strawberries assaulted him as he entered the eternal warm softness of her mouth. He immediately wanted more and the instant he heard her sigh deep him her throat, he released her. Hard breaths ran through him and he was gratified to see the kiss had produced a similar effect on her.

Her breasts rose with each ragged breath and her eyes shone with desire.

And, anger.

She stepped away carefully, her hand on a branch showing the ever-seeing windows they had been discussing the blooms. Her voice was ice and sliced away at every feeling of lust the kiss had awakened within him.

"I'd always excused your selfishness with the fortune of your life. As a wealthy second son, you don't require an heir. You can live as you like. But, I can't believe that you would rather ruin me than see me married to a respectable man whom, for reasons only you seem to possess, you find unworthy."

She gave him one last mournful look before walking directly toward Hexbrook House.

Her words were a shot in the stomach. She was right. He stood on the empty street, under the fragrant lilac tree staring at the hard door beyond the courtyard which now lay between them. He had been lying to himself when he had assumed his vested interest was to ensure she was well wed. In truth, his only interest was to ensure she didn't wed anyone at all.

CHAPTER 5

Charlotte followed the butler alongside Lady Westcott towards Lady Hexbrook's parlor. Her body had exuded coolness and control as she had said a pleasant farewell to Lord Sheffield, even though her mind had been whirling with Matthew's ill-timed and, much to her chagrin, enticing kiss. Her jaw clenched as she made the silent vow to ensure Matthew Harrington received a slow, painful death.

Sitting next to Evangeline, she nodded politely and exchanged pleasantries with Evangeline's mother, the Marchioness of Hexbrook and her two elder sisters, Viscountess Vale and the Baroness Redding. Her insides were ready to explode and the deluge came forth the instant Evangeline's mother and sisters left them alone in the elegant rose parlor.

"I did everything I could to save Bentwick so I might marry for love," she said, her throat tight. "It didn't work. Now, I need the richest husband I can get. So, falling in love isn't an option. And, even if it was, it appears I won't have the opportunity to find out because the person whom I believed to be my best friend has vowed to ensure I don't find it."

Evangeline's eyebrows shot up. "What?"

"This has something to do with Mr. Harrington, doesn't it? The way he was looking at you and Hunstbridge…" Julia's voice trailed off.

"What happened behind the tree?" Isabella asked. She was in a light blue visiting gown. Her red curls were swept back, revealing the most perfect cream complexion brought to life by vivid blue eyes.

Charlotte met those eyes and knew they had seen something. "Nothing happened behind the tree, why?"

"It looked like two people who could have been carrying on an innocent conversation or two people trying to conceal themselves," Isabella responded, moving to sit beside her.

"Let's go with the former," Charlotte said pertly.

"You're blushing. And, you were hiding behind a tree with a man whose appearance mesmerized you," Isabella noted, "Perhaps you have found your love match?"

Charlotte's eyes widened. "Absolutely not! Matthew was my only friend until I met the three of you. And, now instead of behaving like my friend, he's behaving like an overprotective mother hen trying to guard me from men that are…men that are exactly like him. It's ridiculous."

"Tell him I've convinced you to be a spinster. After all, what else could be expected when you've become friends with an outspoken bluestocking?" Evangeline's eyes sparkled. "Throw him off to give you time to catch the husband you need."

"I doubt he'd believe me," Charlotte pursed her lips. "I can't let him ruin my chances with any of the peers I've met."

"Do you have to marry a peer?" Isabella asked slyly.

"What are you getting at?" Charlotte's eyes narrowed.

"She means," Julia said with a knowing gleam, "would an extremely wealthy second son be suitable? After all, wealth is the goal."

"No."

Charlotte stared at the three smiling faces. "He vowed to live a bachelor. He flaunted his life-style every chance he could get. Freedom. Fun. Frivolity. It was practically his own personal coat of arms. Matthew has no intention whatsoever to settle down, to marry, to tie himself to one woman. And, even though it might make me an awful person, he doesn't have the wealth Bentwick needs. Besides, it'll ruin our friendship."

"And, his interference or your marrying someone else won't ruin it, dear?" Isabella asked quietly.

"I can't start creating fantasies about marrying my childhood friend," Charlotte said resolutely. "I can't deter from my only goal, to marry for my Earldom."

Silence descended upon them. Charlotte held her breath as she saw the others wrestle with her statement. It was honorable. There was nothing to criticize, and yet it was so very hollow.

"Duty, then?" Julia broke the silence, blond curls bouncing with the turn of her head.

"Yes," Charlotte said, lips pursed in a sad line across her face.

"Well then, I suppose it's settled," Evangeline said pragmatically. "You'll continue to meet worthy peers and we'll make sure Mr. Harrington doesn't get in your way."

"How are we going to do that?" Isabella looked startled.

"Oh!" Julia said with a conspiratorial air, "I'll maneuver him towards Westcott who will have him talking politics for hours!"

"And, we'll make sure Oliver is kept busy chaperoning us with his friend, the well-known rake," Evangeline added devilishly.

"If this didn't affect the future of my Earldom so dearly, I might actually enjoy watching Matthew's plans be thwarted,"

Charlotte laughed. "It might actually give me a chance to find more than wealth."

"No one has left a lasting impression?" Julia asked with a look of expectation.

"No, dear. Not Hunstbridge either," Charlotte answered softly.

"Don't worry, the season has just started, there's plenty of time for the spark," Isabella's voice became a romantic whisper and her hands mimicked an explosion of fireworks.

"I don't believe in the spark."

"Of course, you don't," Isabella turned to Evangeline with a raise of the brow.

"As much fun as the spark sounds, at this point I'm hoping my future husband will respect my duty to Bentwick. I feel like I'm racing the clock. It's only a matter time before the *ton* catches wind of my financial situation. Mother and I have done all we can to conceal it, but our ruse won't last long." She sighed, then as though remembering something, she turned her attention to Isabella. "Shouldn't we be helping you find a husband too? I can't monopolize all of our resources."

"True," she admitted, "However, I'm not willing to give up on love. I don't have an ambitious father who wants to marry me off. Sorry dear," she said to Julia, "I don't have an estate depending on me and, I haven't seen anyone I remotely feel is worthy of any effort to overcome my shyness. I won't marry for any reason other than love. Even if it takes years. Well, maybe not years, but I'd rather share in Evangeline's household than marry without love."

"Why do you make that sound like a death sentence?" The brunette feigned being affronted. "It's settled then. We distract Mr. Harrington and find a wealthy peer for Charlotte. Once you're married, we'll help you," Evangeline said to Isabella.

"Can we find a peer who is rakishly handsome, terribly romantic and fun? There's nothing worse than marrying solely for duty," Julia said.

"I cannot afford such a dream," Charlotte's flat tone instantly deflated Julia's romantic musings.

"Dreams can come true," Julia whispered so softly, only Charlotte could hear her wish.

"Immense wealth is the only criteria I require and the sooner I find a gentleman to fulfill the qualification, the sooner I'll breathe with ease. Love, regardless of how terrifying, will have to be put aside," Charlotte said.

"Terrifying?" Isabella looked puzzled. "I thought you were a romantic like me. How can love possibly be terrifying? It's the most wondrous emotion to look forward to, I'm sure."

"Because it leads to heartache. Mother was so broken for so long. I've only recently seen her smile again. She suffered a long time because of Father's neglect and death. I wished so hard as a child that his love for her would be strong enough to pull him out of his sadness. It never was. After he died, I wished for my married life to be completely different. I really believed if I could save Bentwick, I would find love. But, if I really think about it, I don't know what I'd do if someone did love me. I might be too scared to let him because look at what happened to Mother. I have been a fool. In any case, my wish did not come true. I need to marry for money. End of story," Charlotte smiled ruefully.

"Dreams can come true," Julia repeated, louder for all to hear. " You might fear love, or believe it isn't meant for you after all the years of hardship. But, I truly believe you'll find it. And, when you do, I hope you're strong enough to embrace it, not to back away in fear. I believe Isabella will marry for love, as it's been her greatest wish. I even believe, that at some point, in my cold, distant marriage, love will come. It has to. I can't live the rest of my life without any faith in love. I even believe Evangeline will find her true match."

Evangeline harrumphed loudly. "I certainly won't go looking of it. You're right about the three of you. But as far as I'm concerned, love will have to literally fall on my head."

She theatrically imitated being bludgeoned over the head and they all enjoyed a thorough, and necessary, bout of laughter.

Charlotte breathed deeply, ignoring the tug in her heart, reminding herself money was the only way to save Bentwick. Matthew's completely inappropriate kiss had to be forgotten. His vows to protect her had to be ignored. He would never be able to give her what she had wished for, a faithful marriage of love. And, considering her deep-rooted fear about the havoc love could wreak, there was no point in hoping for the emotion, despite Julia's promising predictions.

There was also no point in pining for Matthew's kisses or enticing stares. He couldn't save Bentwick and he most definitely wasn't the marrying kind. The time had come to put his friendship and all which he had meant where it belonged. It was the only way to move forward and forge a future which was completely different from everything she had endured and overcome. The past had to be laid to rest, even though Matthew Harrington had been her only source of light within that stormy past.

CHAPTER 6

Matthew stared out the window, watching the evening sky fall from a symphony of orange and pink to somber purple. Only when the newly darkened sky exposed its first twinkling light did he notice his brother standing behind him. It was like looking in a mirror, fifteen years in the future. Matthew saw Robert's six-foot two frame, blue eyes lined at the creases and brown hair gleaming with strands of silver at the temples. Surrounded by peaceful solitude in the dowager's library, he smiled at the brother who had been more like a father. Both men were impeccable in evening dress awaiting the announcement of their first guests. Or, rather, Lady Adelaide, their mother's first guests.

Despite Matthew's protests, she had insisted on hosting a party at her home welcoming him back. He had managed to talk her down to a private dinner party, but after having faced a formidable Burmese force, seemingly insurmountable challenges in India, and investing in extremely risky financial ventures to be rewarded tenfold, he realized his mother was a far more striking contender.

"The dinner party will be absolutely lovely," she had said with the same sparkling blue eyes her sons had inherited.

"You know none of it is necessary. Being in your company again is celebration enough."

"You're far too charming for your own good, Matthew Edward Harrington," a scolding mock as she had gazed lovingly into the face of her youngest.

"In any case, thank you for conceding. I know you would have preferred a more elaborate affair. A small dinner party will help ease the transition home far better than a large party where I'll sound like an old curmudgeon forgetting everyone's name," he had given her a warm embrace.

Then, a soft, melodic laugh had escaped her lips as she had withdrawn from the room. "If that's what you choose to believe, then yes. I acquiesced to a dinner party."

"Mother has outdone herself," Robert interrupted his thoughts.

"She definitely threw it together quite well considering she decided to do this a week ago," Matthew replied, realizing it had also been a week since he had seen Charlotte, since the kiss amidst the lilacs.

"She had plenty of help from Clara," Robert referred to his wife. He poured golden liquid into two glasses from a tray which had quietly been delivered.

"Lady Elmvale was eager to welcome me home?" Matthew received the glass and raised a brow.

Robert laughed. "Give her some credit Matthew. She may not be the most forthcoming with her emotions, but Clara is a woman of deep sentiments. And, passion," he added for good measure.

Matthew nodded his head uncomfortably, taking in his brother's intended meaning. "I'm glad you're happy, you deserve it. But, please, no more details."

"And, I'm relieved you're home," Robert said with more

seriousness. "Especially since we're still without child, and it isn't for lack of trying," he said after clearing his throat to dispel some of his own discomfort.

"I'm sorry Robert," Matthew's face remained neutral.

"Thank you. Though we have not lost hope." Matthew noticed the flat quality to Robert's voice.

"It'll work out. You'll see, these things always do."

Matthew knew he was offering a platitude but he could not think of anything else to say about such an intimate subject even though it directly affected him.

"If it doesn't work out, as you put it, before I die - "

"But it will."

"If it doesn't, Matthew, you will be the next Earl of Elmvale."

"That's not possible." His words were succinct with sheer contrariness. He refused to believe that his hero was vulnerable for the fates which had conspired to take away his father when he had been but six years of age would surely allow him the company of his brother, whom had essentially become his father, for years to come.

"Matthew," Robert said with a sigh, "Did being away for five years teach you nothing?"

Matthew remained silent, his jaw clenched.

"You went on this wild venture to prove something to yourself, to me, to the world that you are more than a charming, frivolous second son. Yet you arrive home without notice and still cannot accept the fact that you are my heir."

Matthew stared at his brother, then spoke through a tight throat. "My wild adventure, as you put it, was littered with dead bodies, the stench of disease, weeks of downpours and incessant work to help living conditions in a country very much unlike our own." Robert remained silent and Matthew breathed deeply before continuing.

"I'm returned for but a week and you immediately assume

I'm ready to take up the thread of my former life. May I spend a few days at home to gather my thoughts, to adjust and to enjoy my family before we start speaking of your death? May we assume for a little while longer that you and Clara will have a son and I'll simply be Uncle Matthew?"

He tried to hide his desperation from Robert's piercing blue eyes, swallowing his whiskey in the heavy silence and allowing the amber fluid to slowly burn its way down. After a few more moments of silence, Robert's voice cracked before it filled the air.

"I almost went into that jungle myself to get you out."

"That would have been a sight," Matthew smiled ruefully at the vision of his ever-proper brother marching self-righteously through the mud in search of him. "I wasn't always in the jungle," Matthew sighed at how little was known in London about where he had been and what he had done. "In any case, I'm glad you didn't."

"I think I can understand that, but I can't help to ask, why?"

"I simply prefer the man I am now." He could not truly put into words the horrors he had witnessed and the challenges he had faced. He definitely could not describe the changes which had occurred within him as a consequence of it all.

"I'll sell my commission – my military career is over," the words quietly spilled out as he contemplated the empty tumbler in his hand.

"Naturally," Robert nodded, refilling both glasses. "As my heir, it's expected. But, are you certain? Are you ready?"

Matthew confidently met his brother's gaze. "I'm honored to have served, but one war is enough to last my entire life," he said and admitted that he had amassed a substantial amount of wealth, his holding was not only thriving but he had added significantly to it. He had also become rather skilled in the world of investments – though his immense fortune was something he hoped to keep secret.

"I need to stave off as many of the husband-hunting mamas for as long as I can." A mischievous grin showed a glimpse of his former self.

"Many mothers are a little cautious to have their precious darlings too close to an incorrigible rake. You should be safe for some time," Robert reminded him with a smile.

"Let's hope the reputation I had before I left will hold. I'm afraid I'm more monk than rake of late." He walked back toward the window and pondered the starlit night.

"You're doomed once the *ton* gets wind of that! Every mother with a daughter of marriageable age will be at your heels," Robert laughed softly as he stood alongside his beloved brother. He turned towards Matthew, squarely, encouragingly. " You're back physically and soon you'll be mentally returned to us too. In time, you'll bring into your present life the lessons of the past five years. If there is one man I know who can navigate this transition with some sort of charm, it's you."

Matthew looked at his brother with gratitude and the two men shared a look of deep understanding which defied language.

"By the way," Robert's voice became light again, "Don't expect tonight's dinner party to be too small. I have a feeling Mama invited a fair share of eligible ladies to encourage you to peruse your prospects."

Matthew groaned. "I won't be chased after for my money or family connections, nor will I simply settle into marriage with some eligible Lady or Miss because Mama seems to think it's time."

Robert's eyes widened. "You'll marry for love, then?"

"I didn't say love. And, I didn't say I'd marry either." Matthew saw Robert's raised brow and released a loud sigh.

"I'll take your response as an improvement. Before you left, any talk of marriage would have you racing for the nearest door. Now, you won't settle, which means you have expectations of another kind. You're maturing, Matthew." Robert's smile eased his condescending tone.

Matthew emptied the contents of his glass and placed it on a table. Then, quietly turned to face his brother. " If I ever marry, and that's a big if, I will do so with someone who chooses me for me. Not my money, not because I'm a Harrington, and not because I'm currently your heir. Robert," he ran his hand through his hair, his voice suddenly shook with rare vulnerability. "Everything I've lived through, the reasons for my celibacy, war...life is precious. It's to be lived with passion – that part of me hasn't changed. But, it's also to be lived with gratitude because at any moment, it can all be snatched away. I want someone who believes in the beauty of life, not just what my money and name can offer her."

"I had no idea you were such a romantic," Robert said with a touch of irony, his eyes shrewdly watchful. "I hope you find the right woman. Marriage is hard enough when you're married to someone you love. I wish for you what Mama and Papa had, what I have with Clara. You're lucky to have the luxury of time in your selection of a wife. Use it well."

Matthew winced remembering someone else with heather grey eyes who had said something similar to him. "I thought Mama was supposed to be the one shoving marriage down my throat."

"She'll begin doing so tonight," Robert answered pointedly.

"Perhaps I'll begin management of the Earldom sooner than I thought. I could start with a trip to our estates in the north. We have homes in Scotland, don't we? The High-lands?" Matthew retorted.

Robert enjoyed a deep chuckle as he left to find Clara. After a few more minutes of solitude, Matthew left the library for his command performance at his mother's private dinner. He strolled through the brightly lit corridor stopping when he noticed an attractively framed drawing hanging on the wall. Upon closer inspection, his heart leapt. Only one person drew flowers to look so splendid and real.

Charlotte.

The instant her name entered his awareness, he realized she was standing regally in the empty hallway. He turned towards her and saw the slight catch of her breath. She had been contemplating him as intently as he had been eyeing her drawing. She was within arm's reach, and she took his breath away.

CHAPTER 7

Charlotte walked through the dowager Countess of Elmvale's home in search of the library. Lady Adelaide had sent her to find Matthew. Her guests were starting to arrive and her son, the guest of honor, was not present.

She smoothed the blush pink gown and pulled up satin gloves ensuring her ensemble was all in place. Her raven hair was smoothed back into an elegant braided chignon highlighting her luminous porcelain complexion. Her grey eyes were vividly accentuated by well-shaped brows and thick, long lashes. A velvet ribbon holding a pretty, ivory cameo was tied around her neck in the same midnight blue as the sash which encircled her upper waist.

She didn't know why her appearance had mattered so much. She wanted to look perfect, without looking like she had tried too hard to look perfect. Being their closest neighbor in Somerset, she and Mother had dined with the Harringtons more times than she could possibly remember. The bristling in her stomach and slight shake in her fingers made no sense. Except, she didn't recall ever having to sit through a dinner after having been kissed by Matthew.

She saw him standing in the hallway, absorbed by a frame on the wall. Her shoes were soundless as she walked up to him, taking in his tall, strong form. He looked positively dashing, perhaps even dangerous, she told herself when her heart fluttered at the sight of her gorgeous friend. He turned when he sensed her near, his eyes of infinite blue now trained upon her. Her breasts lifted as her breath caught.

He smiled, his dimple deepening slowly. "Good evening, Lady Bentwick."

The low tone of his voice shot through Charlotte's body right down to her toes. She swallowed in an effort to compose herself. "Lady Adelaide requests your presence. She'd like her guest of honor to be present as her other guests arrive."

"And I thought you were searching for me because you'd missed me this past week," he tilted his head, looking adorably cheeky. Infuriatingly cheeky, she corrected herself.

She began to squirm under his playful stare. She smiled hoping he'd say something, but he just looked on as absorbed in her as he had been with the frame. She felt warmth begin to spread across her cheeks, then cleared her throat. "What was it that held your attention with such rapture?"

He grinned as he glanced briefly at the frame on the wall before returning his attention back to her. "They aren't quite as striking in your presence. In fact, their beauty has diminished since I laid eyes on you. I was looking at lilacs."

"Pardon me?" Her cheeks grew warmer from both his blatant compliment and reference to the flowers whose fragrance had haunted her all week.

"You're breathtaking this evening," his voice dipped to a whisper. "Even the lilacs drawn by your very skilled fingers cannot compete."

Charlotte swallowed hard trying to still the sudden thump in her chest. "Thank you," she smoothed her gown nervously, "I - I drew those for your mother the year you left."

"She clearly appreciates your artistry very much for she had them beautifully framed and in a spot where they can be vastly appreciated," the intensity of his gaze made her feel as though he wasn't speaking about appreciating her artistic abilities. "Speaking of lilacs…" he said almost lazily.

"Let's not," she said a little too quickly. She attempted to purse her lips, to cease Matthew's intended avenue of conversation, but her mouth gave way to a small grin as her body succumbed to a wonderful, tingling sensation all caused by his overt admiration of her. She didn't know why his flirtation didn't offend her as it had in Somersby's ballroom. Perhaps, it seemed more honest in the empty corridor where they could be themselves without the prying, expectant eyes of the *ton*.

"Why not? I'll be happy to meet you by the lilac tree tomorrow, since I'm positive you'll leave your maid at home when you join your friends to dissect all of the gossip you'll gather here tonight."

"No, I don't think another meeting under the lilac tree will be necessary," she fell into the moment of flirtation, fully grinning, her eyes sparkling with mischief. "And what makes you think we won't be discussing politics, the latest botanical lectures or watercolors?"

Matthew's look became downright sardonic and Charlotte felt laughter bubbling out of her. Nervous laughter, fun laughter, exciting laughter relieving the tension of being in his presence again and realizing the kiss under the lilac tree hadn't changed them as much as she had feared. His charm no longer seemed so dangerous because it was weaved into the comfort of their friendship.

"Come, let's go before Lady Adelaide sends someone to gather the both of us," she casually took hold of his hand, noting instantly the surge of energy between them. Charlotte felt the warmth of his hand creep into every crevice of her body. Holding his hand had never produced such a reaction and she couldn't help but wonder how and why.

"It'll be like all those years ago when your governess would angrily take you home for behaving like a wild creature and not the future Countess you were supposed to be," his hand tightened around hers.

She smiled wistfully. "Strangely enough, those now seem like easier times," she looked up at his face. A nostalgic look flitted across his eyes as he looked at her. They stood rooted, unable to move, enjoying the simplicity of a moment of closeness, of friendship.

She breathed deeply, glancing down, somewhat breaking the spell, releasing his hand. Her eyes swept upwards again and locking with his, unfiltered words spilled out before she could think about how they would fall, "Just so you know Matthew, I'll never forget being amidst those lilacs with you. You've probably had countless moments like those, but for me it was a memory to be treasured."

She wished she had the courage to see his reaction, but she turned on her heel and moved swiftly to join the others.

"For me as well," the velvet soft murmur reached her ears half-way down the corridor and judging from the heat surging through her back, she would have sworn his eyes followed her to the drawing room every step of the way.

"The plan is to distract Mr. Harrington as soon as the gentlemen return to join us after their drinks and whatever else it is that keeps them busy after dinner. Then, Julia can introduce you to the other eligible gentlemen present. I believe there's several Viscounts, two Barons and a few Earls. There's also an offensively wealthy French Count who's lived in London for years, but I don't think he'd quite do for you," Evangeline said conspiratorially. Most of the female dinner guests gathered around tables set up for cards and settees arranged for after-dinner conversations. The four friends opted to stand on the far side of the room, by the opened windows to enjoy the warm air of a spring night and have some privacy.

"Are you sure you don't want to marry Carters and we can avoid this whole thing?" Isabella asked nervously. Her face was flawless cream and the curls atop her head glinted coppery gold in the candlelight. The soft blue gown gave her an ethereal look and Charlotte wondered how someone so beautiful remained unmarried.

"As wonderful as that may sound for you my reserved friend," Julia intervened, "I can't possibly advise Charlotte to employ those tactics," she motioned to the way the elder Miss Burnhopes sprung from their seats the moment the gentlemen entered accosting Viscount Laurel once more. The poor thin man looked both gracious and terrified at their eagerness to continue their conversation on the latest architectural designs sweeping through the continent.

Charlotte looked at Isabella almost apologetically. "Carters hasn't shown any interest whatsoever, therefore I must search elsewhere."

"Alright, let's get on with the plan then," Isabella mumbled, causing the other three to unsuccessfully stifle a bout of laughter.

Charlotte's merriment was interrupted by a tingle along the nape of her neck. With a small smile, she turned slightly towards the door. Her eyes were immediately locked with Matthew's. He entered the room, politely stopping to acknowledge the ladies vying for his attention, but his focus remained with her. His overt observation of her caused ripples to run through her body. She forced her eyes away before the gossip started.

She hid a smile as Evangeline cunningly intercepted him. Charlotte suddenly realized Evangeline's beauty was fire-bred. Dormant while she was sedate, but the instant she rose to a challenge she was transformed with enviable attraction stemming from her ceaseless confidence. Rich brown hair pulled into soft curls and her primrose gown moved lithely over her tall, thin frame. She offered a stunning smile and her amber eyes sparkled with mischief.

"Mr. Harrington, you must absolutely satisfy our curiosity and settle a lively disagreement we've been having while the gentlemen have been away. In fact, our discussion was precisely about the need for gentlemen to have private time at these affairs. Aren't they meant for social interaction?"

"Normally, I'd be happy to oblige," Matthew replied with a lopsided grin, "but, in the short time of our re-acquaintance, Lady Evangeline, I must admit, I'm a little unnerved by any matter involving the four of you. I suppose therein lies the answer to your question. We need time to prepare for such social interaction."

"Don't tell me we frighten you," Isabella said quietly, her lovely creamy complexion slowly turning pink.

"You're right to be more than a little apprehensive. Any matter involving my sister is terrifying," the deep voice of Lord Oliver Fitzroy interceded.

"That's probably because you expect to control her as you do everyone else," Isabella replied with far more confidence than Charlotte had seen her display outside of their foursome.

"And, I thought I could trust you to temper her, but it seems I've been mistaken Miss Wynthorpe," Carters replied pointedly.

"It wouldn't be the first time, my Lord," Isabella quipped. "Besides, Evangeline is beyond tempering," her reddened face was subdued to a gentle blush.

"Thank you, Bella, I take that as a compliment. Now that you've been settled," Evangeline arched a brow at her brother, "we can ask Mr. Harrington what gentlemen possibly need to prepare for. After all, there aren't many fruitful or life-altering conversations in here. Perhaps we could encourage ladies to become more political."

"Yes, because that's what the world needs, political ladies," Carters rolled his eyes. "Lady Westcott, what would Westcott have to say about such a suggestion?"

"I'm afraid Westcott is at the opposite end of Lady Evangeline's political spectrum, Lord Carters," Julia's smile dazzled, but she leaned in conspiratorially when Carters was about to agree with her. "However, I feel he could use a healthy dose of feminine opinions when deciding on matters which affect us all."

"I've a feeling there are numerous governesses and teachers at lady's schools whom need extreme reprimanding," Carters replied with a mutter full of healthy disapproval for the four pairs of mischief-filled eyes which landed on him. "In any case, Harrington doesn't need to offer you opinions on any matter," he said pointedly to his sister, then turned to Matthew. "I expected to see you at the card tables."

Charlotte was forced to admit Evangeline's brother was an exceedingly handsome man. His dark hair and obvious strength exuded a touch of arrogance while green eyes hinted at the possibility of danger. She pursed her lips, wondering if perhaps it would be easier to simply find a way to get his attention.

A quick look at Matthew's knowing gleam and she realized with her friend close by she would have no chance with any eligible gentleman. He was obviously reading her looks for his smile broadened when her jaw clenched.

She cleared her throat and turned her attention to the Earl with a playful shrug. "I thought you knew Mr. Harrington well, Lord Carters. A group of young ladies is always more palatable than a table with cards. After all, a deck of cards can't giggle and swoon at his supposed charm. Although, I have to admit, he didn't choose his group of ladies quite so wisely this time."

Carters turned to Charlotte with renewed appreciation. "How right you are," he flashed her quite the smile, "perhaps I should leave Harrington to their whimsy. He'll be running for cover in no time."

"Between Lady Evangeline's modern world-view and Miss Wynthorpe's well-read mind, he won't stand a chance. And, I'm sure Lady Westcott's feminine opinions will finish him off."

As Charlotte and Lord Carters exchanged knowing smiles about Matthew, the man in question shrugged, his dimple appearing with a lopsided grin. "I'd be more than happy to be schooled in suffrage or the applicability of Greek philosophy to modern times. Besides, I'm positive I'd have something to add to feminine opinions, so an evening spent in the company of these three ladies, will be time well spent indeed."

Carters scowled. Evangeline's face lit up with glee and Isabella's face competed fiercely with the crimson dress worn by one of the Burnhope sisters.

"Lady Bentwick, Westcott is speaking with Viscount Fairchild, come with me," Julia said lightly, then turned her attention to Matthew with a knowing look. "My lord, I'm afraid you'll be without our company for now, but I'm sure Lady Evangeline and Miss Wynthorpe will be vastly entertaining."

Julia whisked her away before she could say another word. A brief glance back showed Carters with a stern brow much to the delight of Evangeline and Matthew who continued in banter while Isabella stood by with a worried look on her face. Except, as she turned her attention back to Julia, she was positive Matthew had dared to wink at her from across the room. Charlotte bit her lip to keep from smiling but couldn't help the wave of relief washing over her. Matthew knew what they were up to and he played along. Perhaps he wasn't going to stand in her way as she searched for her husband after all. However, when she met the Viscount and discussed inane subjects with the less than dazzling Lord Fairchild, she realized Matthew's lack of interference was perhaps more disconcerting than his promise to impede the possibility of a proposal.

"Not quite what one expects from a Viscount who looks as he does," Julia said echoing Charlotte's disappointment.

"Perhaps because he is so handsome, he's never had to practice conversational skills," Charlotte answered with a sigh. "Did you see that?"

"What dear?" Julia asked placing a hand on her forearm.

"I thought I saw Matthew's hands shaking," Charlotte frowned. She watched him a little bit closer and saw him pull at his collar.

"I doubt it," Julia interrupted her observations, "seems Carters was able to firmly interrupt his conversation with Evangeline and Isabella. He's moved on to charming the Burnhopes. He's most likely comparing them to the vase of daffodils nearby," she finished with an ironic tone.

Charlotte watched as their circle was joined by the French Count. Her eyes narrowed with sharp focus. Matthew exchanged pleasantries on cue, he smiled on cue, but his humor did not reach his eyes. Then, she saw him run his hand through his hair and she knew he was in distress.

"Julia, I must go," Charlotte abruptly left her friend's side. She reached the small group and squeezed in between the Burnhope sisters whom had Matthew sandwiched between them. The elder Burnhope was about to protest, but the moment she realized it was Charlotte, moved aside.

"Pardon me, Countess," she murmured with cool politeness.

"Lovely dress Miss Burnhope," Charlotte said with warmth hoping to show the young lady her intention wasn't to diminish her presence. Her words took immediate effect and Miss Burnhope's face softened.

"Mr. Harrington," Charlotte turned to Matthew, "I need an escort to Lady Adelaide's library. There's a book in there which I absolutely must see, apparently it's a first edition."

"And which book might that be?" he asked. His voice was light, his tone mischievous, but his hands still shook slightly at his side.

"You know the one," she said through wide eyes, commanding him to listen to her.

"But, you've arrived at just zee moment in which Mr. 'Arrington was about to tell us about his 'eroic acts in battle," the French Count said with the hint of a challenge.

"Heroic acts remain so when they aren't repeated by the person whom enacted them," Charlotte replied smoothly. "Now, if you'll excuse us," she nodded politely and turned on her heel knowing Matthew had no choice but to follow her. She led him straight into Lady Adelaide's library and didn't stop to look at him until she heard the soft thud of the closing door.

His brow arched over one eye and his lips began to move into a lopsided grin. "A first edition which my mother owns? You could've come up with something better to get me all to yourself."

Charlotte faced him fully, her hands at her sides, her tone

gentle. "Don't," she said softly, "you can stop pretending with me. I don't believe for one moment that you spent as long as you did far from home and marched into battle only to return the absolute same. You aren't the same, are you?"

His smile faded. Arms crossing his chest as his head fell to the side, "And, what would you know about battle, Lady Bentwick?"

It was odd to hear such irony in Matthew's tone. She knew better than to be dissuaded because it too was nothing more than a pretense. She tilted her defiantly. "Nothing," she said, "However, I know what it's like to fight for everything one holds dear because one's survival, and everyone else's, depends on it. I would imagine battle is the same, with weapons and more blood. And, therefore, more gruesome memories."

She watched him closely as her words settled. Matthew was clearly struggling with her directness. There was nowhere to hide, and she knew he realized this when his hand moved through his hair. The gesture had been seared into her on the day he had told her he had no father. She was five and he was ten. They had been playing hide and seek in her home. It was the first time she had ever seen Matthew not smile, not laugh, not tell a joke, not try to make her feel better.

The slight shake of his hands returned. Without a thought, she stepped closer and took them in her own. The warmth of their joined hands once again emanated through every region of her body, and while it elicited the same excitement there was also deep comfort in their touch. They were inches from each other and her eyes locked with his.

"You're home now."

"I don't believe I shall ever be truly home," he squeezed her hands as though fighting to hold on to the brief moment of peace.

"As long as I'm around, you can always feel that you are home with me."

"That's the problem, dearest," his voice penetrated her heart. "You won't always be around," he lifted his brow ruefully and the meaning of his words sunk into the deepest part of her.

In true Matthew fashion, before anything became too sentimental, he changed course. "Besides, I can't fathom letting you into the gifts of surviving a war: darkness and hopelessness."

Charlotte watched him struggle with the images in his mind, with the darkness in his heart. She squeezed his hands harder as though by sheer will she could bring him back to the present.

"You're the reason I have any good memories at all. Any darkness or hopelessness won't scare me, you must remember I'm far braver than that."

"I always forget how much you've had to live through," he said full of thought. "It doesn't mean I can burden you further. I'll find a way even though the *ton* certainly won't let me forget what I lived through. Everyone seems fascinated by war stories which will never arrive at their front door."

"They can't be blamed," she said, "war is so romanticized as is the war hero. Perhaps you can find a way to deflect their questions until the next interesting gentlemen appears and they forget all about you," she said cheekily, trying, *trying* to bring him back. "Besides, I don't think I can hunt after every first edition housed in every library of the *ton*." She dared a small smile.

It seemed to work. Matthew's lips moved into a grin and the hint of a sparkle returned to his blue eyes. His hands remained firmly wrapped around hers and gone was any trace of a shake. She didn't dare move, staying like that, hand in hand, staring into the deepest parts of each other in utter silence for many moments, waiting for Matthew to return fully.

"Thank you for the brief escape," he said softly, "I believe I'm ready to return to impertinent questions now. And, since when has Mother been friends with a French Count? Seems like our roles have reversed tonight, Charlotte. You have saved me."

"I've always saved you, it just didn't seem that way because you were always the one carrying me," she said flippantly, her smile widening. "But, without me, your life would have been a complete bore."

Radiant joy ran through her when Matthew's head fell back and he laughed. A deep throaty laugh filled him and she couldn't believe how much happiness the sound of his laughter brought her. He suddenly released her hands and she was surprised to feel cold without them.

He looked at her with curiosity. "The last time we saw each other you accused me of easily falling into my former life and tonight you tell me I'm not the same. Which is it, Charlotte?"

"Both."

"Both?"

"Yes. You're trapped somewhere in between and while falling into your former life is most definitely easier, it isn't who you truly are."

His face fell slowly closer. She was able to detail each dark lash lushly framing eyes the color of a summer sky. The warmth of his breath caressed her lips when he spoke. "How can you be so sure?"

She swallowed. Hard. "I see you truly are feeling yourself. Flirting with me isn't going to prove anything other than what I've already stated. You see, I know you better than you do, clearly. You are charming, handsome, stubborn and incorrigible."

"I don't know if I like everything on that list," Matthew started to say, but Charlotte continued her assessment.

"And, you are also thoughtful, perceptive, kind and deeply caring. So while you may think that putting me at unease with your charm and promises to stop me from marrying make a good mask for the man you truly are…well, you're wrong." She swallowed again and bravely, squarely met his gaze, hoping he couldn't detect the tension in her body created by his mere glance. She was so unnerved, she almost, almost wished he was back under the spell of darkness and hopelessness. Almost.

He chuckled. "I think you're being far kinder than I deserve. Except, there's something I can't quite understand."

His words landed so close to her lips, if she flinched she would be able to feel their infinite softness one more time. She refused to flinch. So, she merely raised her brow as though asking, "What's that?"

"Why do you care so much about who I am or who I am not? Why is Lady Bentwick so intent on understanding who I am now, or who I could be?"

"You're my dearest friend."

"Is that the only reason?"

"What other reason could there be?"

Her question lingered unanswered. Matthew brought her hands to his lips, slowly kissing each one. He paused before releasing her and wordlessly accompanied her out of Lady Adelaide's library. She did not breathe until they returned to the drawing room. She was happy to see Matthew slide back into the social scene seamlessly, but couldn't quite explain the little tug at her heart when he spent with rest of the evening away from her.

CHAPTER 8

The next morning, Charlotte was on her horse the instant she sensed the black night dissolve to dark grey. The expectations of ladies out for a ride with a groom within prescribed areas and at a prescribed speed frustrated her. She wished she could gallop her horse as she did at home. While in London, she would have to settle for a docile ride in the lush greenery of the park to find calm.

Fortunately, her groom respected her skill with a horse, so when she demanded space and privacy he offered more than was allowed. Protected by the blanket of the early hours of the morn, she rode faster than polite society allowed and her horse stirred the rising mist of dawn through the deserted park.

Memories of every moment spent with Matthew since his arrival swirled through her. Despite their numerous disagreements, she was forced to admit, each moment had been heavenly. She groaned and nearly kicked her horse to a gallop. Since when did any descriptor of Matthew Harrington include heavenly? He had always been bothersome, arrogant and unbearable. Dancing in his firm grip, being the focus of those eyes and feeling his lips upon hers searching, insisting, warming her all the way to her toes had changed everything.

Hence, her need to think.

Yet no amount of thinking could rationalize the deep happiness she felt for Matthew's return. She knew she had missed him, but it wasn't until he appeared before her and weaved his way towards her that she had realized how much. Matthew was the only person with whom she could truly be herself and after five years of hardship, Charlotte realized she needed more than anything to race wildly through the flats, laugh loudly after falling into the stream and climb a tree to pick apples because they were both starved.

She sighed knowing those days had long passed.

Her teeth tightened. If she was being truly honest on this early morning in the empty park, she feared that her happiness extended beyond reconnecting with her dear friend. She feared her elation was for reasons beyond the rekindling of a lost friendship.

A loud groan escaped her lips.

She had to marry someone like Viscount Sheffield or Fairchild or the Duke of Ellis. She simply could not go back on her word to protect Bentwick because Matthew had caused a stir deep in her stomach.

Beautiful, he had called her.

And, don't forget graceful, her traitorous memory recalled.

She allowed herself a grin at the memory. Not one gentleman since her arrival had dared such intimacy, such a trespass in propriety. Her mother had always told her she was a beauty – but in all of her years working to save an Earldom, she never gave her appearance a second thought.

While in London it had become of primordial importance, but even with all of the special attention to detail, she didn't think herself beautiful. Nor, graceful. She was strong, rode well, and knew more about farming, animals and business than a refined lady should. She was able to stand straight, keep still and use the look of boredom as a mask for the *ton*. But, she knew she was far from graceful. Nonetheless, his words warmed her heart and touched a part of her she did not know existed.

She sighed as her grin dissolved into a frown. He was a gentleman and complimented her with more intimacy due to their deep friendship. It was nothing more. Falling in love Matthew would never do.

Charlotte's eyes widened.

Falling in love with Matthew?

The thought stormed upon her so ferociously she scurried away and hid from it before it pounced on her again. Falling in love with anybody, much less her childhood friend, was not an option anymore. Her wish for love had been made the day her father had shut himself up in his rooms with moroseness and drink. Loving a man who was a charmer of women and who had vowed to live unmarried and free would bring her the same amount of pain she had felt as a child. Falling in love with a man who would cast her aside for something more fun and interesting would reignite the scars of having loved a father who preferred solitude and drink over his own daughter. She had to carefully guard her heart. Even though Matthew seemed different, was it enough to allow charm and flirtation break down the meticulous wall protecting her vulnerable heart?

No.

She groaned. All silly notions and any fanciful feelings about flirtations with Matthew had to be eradicated. Falling in love indeed! She scoffed. She could not risk losing her heart because of an inappropriate kiss and a promise to interfere in her plans to land a husband. She may have yearned for love, but it was too late for her. Searching for love at this late stage could destroy her Earldom and undo her.

She rode farther into the park than was deemed appropriate. The solitude offered by the lush trees and peaceful pond was too enticing, reminding her of home. She found a beautiful tree in front of the pond, slid out of the saddle, and readied her sketchbook. She looked down at a lovely patch of grass but chose to climb a low hanging branch.

Drawing. Drawing while sitting in a beautiful tree always obliterated stray thoughts. She opened her book, readied her pencil and her wish for distraction was soon granted when she heard a distinct buzz far above her. It was the sound of a wasp's nest.

Charlotte slowly looked up and stared at the horror of a multitude of wasps which could readily descend upon her in an instant. She tried to quietly climb down but part of her gown had somehow caught itself along the uneven surface of the bark and into a slim, deep gash. Her bottom was essentially attached to the branch. With her open book and pencil on her lap, she gently leaned onto her right hip and tugged at the dress under her left thigh in an attempt to loosen it. She sat back down. Only by tearing the dress would she be free. She was trapped. Even if her groom had been closer to help, she certainly could not ask him to help her release the underside of her dress from a branch. How on earth would she get down?

The little beasts hovered over her head. She would be humiliated. She would be mortified by the stares and the gossip which would surely follow her everywhere. She would have to leave in shame without a husband and be completely ruined. Bentwick would be sold off, everyone left destitute.

The dreary images swarmed her and her head fell into her hands. She was stunned when she felt moisture along her fingertips. She had not cried since long before her father died and here she was, in a London park, stuck on a tree branch, ready to succumb to tears. She released a little nervous laugh of helplessness and wiped her eyes dry because crying had never offered a solution to any of her problems. A deep inhalation to bring everything to right was interrupted by the sound of horse's hooves coming upon her. She opened her eyes expecting to see her groom. Instead, the man who had invaded her every thought appeared before her.

"I was almost convinced of your change from precocious young girl to an elegant Countess in her own right. My instincts were right; you haven't changed at all. My Charlotte is very much the same and still resides within the grand Lady Bentwick."

"Your Charlotte?"

"Always, my Charlotte."

She swallowed at the smooth tone of his voice. Though his dashing smile turned her stomach to water, she would have to pretend all was well or he would tease her mercilessly about being trapped on a tree under the wretched wasps at the age of one and twenty. She set her face to clearly show Matthew he was intruding. Hopefully, he would leave and she could find a way to hop out of the tree with her pride and dress unscathed. One look at his wide smile with the dimple on his left cheek told her he wasn't going anywhere.

She decided to return her focus to her sketch and thought it best not to smile. "The only thing which hasn't changed is you interrupting my sketching."

Out of the corner of her eye, she saw Matthew's dimple deepen. "Naturally. Interrupting your sketching always leads to the best adventures."

Raising her eyes from her sketch book, her body stilled. Her ever-confident friend caught his breath the moment her gaze met his. She didn't dare move, absorbing the blue of the purest summer's sky.

Why did she keep comparing Matthew's eyes to the sky?

Whatever was passing between them was incomprehensible. And, terrifying. She closed her eyes needing to break the moment because she had to stop all of this foolishness. Matthew was a very handsome man, but he was also her best friend and the most bothersome, arrogant person she had ever known.

She opened her eyes feeling more confident. The sudden surge of bravery was dashed when she saw a look of disappointment cross his face. He was questioning her with his gaze, as though assessing whether to proceed on his originally intended path.

"Perhaps those memories are best if kept in the past," he finally said bowing slightly, ready to leave.

She should have let him go. It was the perfect moment to break the spell cast in Somersby's ballroom, which had been haunting them ever since. Her heart raced and her senses were overwhelmed by his tall, strong presence. To her chagrin, or anticipation, or desperate need for help, she could not really tell which of the emotions was dominant, she couldn't let him leave.

"Matthew?"

The familiar tones of strength, friendship, and ultimately, comfort rang through her voice. She saw his shoulders soften and hoped the one thing they could rely upon was their history and deep friendship. In the single intonation of his name, Charlotte brought them back to Somerset, to the flats, to an afternoon spent riding. She brought them home.

"It's rather early to be trapped on a tree, even for you," he smirked and crossed his arms looking far too paternal for Charlotte's taste, though she was happy to see the momentary tension disappear. They were back on familiar grounds – he was chastising her for what he perceived as her lack of judgment and naturally, her response would have to be total defense of her actions.

She tilted her chin in what she hoped would be a regal look of condescension. "Trapped? What on earth would make you think I'm trapped?"

"Then I gather you are willing to sit still while those wasps prepare for a delicious feast!" He raised a brow and pointed at the large nest just above Charlotte.

"What wasps?" She asked bravely, refusing to admit defeat.

Matthew chuckled. "Right then! I'll leave you to your sketching!" He turned with a grin to walk away.

"Wait!" Charlotte yelled with a touch more desperation than she had intended.

"Yes?" His blue eyes were wide with innocence.

Her nostrils flared knowing she was without another option. Releasing a groan when he looked nearly giddy at her discomfort, she narrowed her eyes. "Don't just stand there – get me down!"

"I don't appreciate your tone. How about more pleading?"

"Get. Me. Down."

"Very well then," he sighed and reached for her hands, but she yanked them away.

"I thought you needed me to get you down?" She saw the baffled look on his face at her skittish response. "Give me your hand."

"It's not as simple as giving me a steadying hand," she mumbled feeling the return of the burn on her cheeks.

"It's not?"

"No. It's not," she ground out.

"Of course, it is! Give me your hand," Matthew said with infinite patience. "Don't be ashamed. Even the most skilled tree climber encounters problems from time to time."

She stared at him indignantly. "This has nothing to do with my skill. I'm perfectly capable of climbing and descending from a branch which hangs five feet off the ground."

He inclined his head and arched his brow. "Really? All evidence points to the contrary."

"Insufferable man!"

"That might be so, but I'm the only one around who can help. Unless you wish for me to call your groom," he suddenly looked around. "Where is your groom?"

"Around," she waved in the general vicinity of the park. When Matthew looked less than satisfied with her response she explained further, "I needed space to think."

"We need to have a serious discussion about this infernal habit of yours. You cannot be permitted to leave your maid at home or your groom on the other side of the park," Matthew said through gritted teeth.

She crossed her arms and scowled. "Permitted?"

"Yes. Permitted," he repeated emphatically and tried to pull her down again, but she refused.

"Very well," Matthew sighed in the way Charlotte recognized as his need for increased patience, "what is the problem?"

She felt her cheeks flare and knew crimson wouldn't come close to describing their shade. She gently leaned onto her right hip and pointed to the mess caught in the tree.

He raised his brows. "Ah. I see." He said no more for it

was clear that Charlotte was precariously perched upon a precipice of fury. And, humiliation.

He leaned in to try to loosen the dress but she skirted away. "Don't!"

Matthew groaned. "How exactly am I supposed to help you off this branch if you don't let me near the spot which has you so securely fastened to it?"

She glowered, speaking through gritted teeth. "Keep your fingers on the dress and only the dress."

"You dishonor me with your warning."

"Dishonor you? Your reputation leaves much to be desired. It was a miracle no one saw us under the lilac tree, but if anyone catches us now, I'll be ruined. I have to let you near my...and let you touch...and.... Oh, this is awful!"

"I assure you my lady, despite what you may believe about my reputation, I've never had to wait for a woman to be trapped on a tree in order to be permitted near her back side. And when I have, she has certainly never claimed it to be awful. Now, let me help you down." His face was smug with satisfaction when her eyes widened indignantly.

She pursed her lips and continued to glare at him. After another intolerable shrug of his shoulder, she reluctantly leaned to the right and closed her eyes tightly wishing for a large hole into which she could crawl and hide forever. She felt his fingers moving directly under her and was certain her cheeks would remain shocking pink for the rest of her life. She winced and flinched every time she felt the faint pressure of his fingertips or his knuckles brushing by her. When she could barely stand any more, she opened her eyes and saw the hovering wasps inspecting her. She moved in an attempt to deflect them but they seemed quite undeterred. She bobbed her head hoping to gently usher them away.

"Will you stop moving?" He ordered as he yanked at the dress which would not budge.

"You're going to tear the gown!" She shrieked skirting another buzzing beast.

"If you would remain still I could do this faster," he ground out and as several wasps congregated around his fingers.

Charlotte slowly raised her hand above her head. Ignoring Matthew's eyes wide with incredulity, she crashed her sketchbook on his forearm.

"What was that for?" He cried out. Her only response was to crash the book upon his forearm again. "Stop! You're going to make them angry and -"

Whack! She hit him again.

"Will you stop?" He demanded, violently yanking the book out of her hand. In a single moment, Charlotte saw Matthew's eyes blaze with both anger and terror. "The wasps will get angry and – AAAHHH! Sting!" A wasp retaliated against her attack.

Matthew tried to swat the rest away, but there were too many. The sharp pain of the stinger shot through his hand and as he swung her book at the buzzing vipers he lost his grip on the branch. He quickly lost his footing, stumbled backward and fell directly into the pond.

He shot her a murdering glance. Her hand flew to cover her gaping mouth and she used every ounce of willpower not to laugh. The sight of Matthew sopping wet chased all terror of the wasps away. She covered her face with her hands and fought for the self-control to remain completely motionless. Once the wasps perceived no threat from her, they retreated to their nest. She viewed Matthew from a small space between her fingers.

"Now you decide to remain still?" He said through gritted teeth, rising from the pond.

"If you hadn't taken away my book I could have swatted

them away for you," her lips quivered as she fought to maintain them in a straight line.

Matthew marched directly to her, "A few weeks in London and you've suddenly developed amnesia about the proper way to deal with the little beasts," he muttered. Without another word or look, he deftly dismantled the dress without a single tear. However, the same could not be said for the many brushes of his fingers along her bottom. She winced each time but knew to keep quiet as he worked it free. Then, he unceremoniously threw her over his shoulder, and ignoring her yelp, took her to the other side of the pond, as far from the wasp nest as possible.

"That was rather ungentlemanly of you." Charlotte scolded him with her best angry governess face when he plopped her down on the ground.

Matthew arched his brow and pointed to his wet backside.

It was all Charlotte needed to finally allow the bubble to explode. Her laughter pierced the still woods reverberating through the leaves and she was positive it reached the outer edges of London.

He assessed his sodden riding clothes and soon matched her loud laughter. "So much for saving a damsel in distress."

"I wasn't in distress."

"According to you, you never are. If it hadn't been for me, you would have been in utter danger for most of your life. You must remember the time you were leaping over the rocks in the stream, fell and scraped both of your knees so badly you could barely walk. I carried you home. Of course, you were much smaller then. Remember the day you managed to tangle your dress in the shrub moments before the Marquis arrived at Bentwick Manor? You don't have much luck with your dresses in the woods, do you? My favorite memory is of the day my life was in most peril. The day I had to chase a fox away from the tree you had decided you had to climb because you absolutely had to pick apples. He had you trapped up there for hours, encircling the trunk awaiting your delicious fall. You would have been there all night had I not, what were your words again? Oh, yes, had I not 'interrupted your sketching.'"

She heard his voice mimic her intonations and she couldn't remember the last time she had laughed so hard. She held onto her side and howled the most unladylike and the most delicious howl.

It was all true.

And the worse part was, Matthew had heaps of stories about helping her out of the most precarious situations. It was awful to give him the upper hand, but she was smart enough to admit when he had bested her, even though he was dripping wet. She wiped the tears from her eyes, sighing contentedly.

"How's your hand?" She asked and gently picked it up in her own. She had forgotten neither were wearing gloves, and though she had held his hand before, she had never noted its weight, warmth and strength. Her breath caught in her throat.

"I've sustained worse injuries. I'll survive." He slowly gripped her hand to prove he was well and held her gaze steadily. She watched as his eyes lost their mirth and he suddenly became somber as though a weight was being placed on him.

"Charlotte, I'm sorry," his eyes fell.

She furrowed her brow, deeply confused, when she saw a deep sense of shame revealing itself across his face. All trace of laughter and fun gone. "Whatever for?"

"Last night, I told you I'm a danger to you and I think you very briefly witnessed it a moment ago. The sound of the book slamming down, the chaos of the moment was too much for me and in an instant, I was overcome with both rage and fear. Rage that I couldn't help you and fear that you would be hurt. These episodes happen when I least expect and all I see is the extent of damage from the war," he nodded his head as though trying to shake away the pain.

"But, how could that possibly be a danger to me? All you wanted to do was protect me, which is what I've been battling you about for as long as I can remember," she dared a soft smile, "Matthew, I'm fine and you are too. We shall keep being friends because I can't imagine us not being a part of each other's lives. And, none of your dire warnings will change that. Your feelings about the war will subside, I promise."

"Promise me if I ever sound like that or look like that again, you will get as far away from me as possible."

"I've always tried to get as far away from you as possible, you just always find me and interrupt my sketching."

"Charlotte," he groaned, "I'm serious. Please, I would die before I hurt you. You have to promise."

"Fine," she said looking up into his eyes realizing it was odd to see him frown for so long. One of the things she was so fond of was his constant smiles and laughter. But here he was standing before her, so utterly serious. The same Matthew and yet not the same. How odd to know him so well and yet not know him at all. "I promise."

She reluctantly released his hand because it was the proper thing to do. After a moment she smiled, hoping to lighten the moment, to bring him back but she didn't receive one in response.

"I suppose we should return home. Perhaps we can take our time riding back?"

When he ran his hand through his hair, she knew he was in deliberation. "I spy your groom. And, I have appointments I must keep. Lady Bentwick, I believe today's adventure ends here. It seems we've added the final memory to our catalogue of memorable moments before you become another man's wife. Good day."

Charlotte watched him leave once he ascertained she would be safely escorted home. Entirely alone, with her groom behind her, she watched as Matthew left her at a near gallop without a single glance back. A shiver ran through her as she realized watching him leave her was the most unpleasant feeling in the world.

CHAPTER 9

The next morning, Charlotte opted for a short walk in the park and brought along her sketchbook should inspiration arise. Wearing a cool morning dress of light blue and a straw bonnet dressed with flowers in similar shades, she breathed in the refreshing spring air hoping to spend the morning drawing. She nodded politely to other ladies out for early morning walks, appreciating that not all were still in bed sleeping as ladies of her station normally did. Her eyes scanned the park, looking for the best spot for a good morning sketch. They landed on a solitary figure sitting with his back to the walking paths, facing the most perfect peony bushes which begged to be captured on paper.

She frowned. Why did the gentleman have to sit there, precisely? He had his pick of any other bench in the park, and he chose the one which most suited her sketching needs at the moment. As she drew closer to the gentleman in question, she recognized the shape of him, the wild brown locks escaping from under his hat. What she didn't recognize was the darkness surrounding him. His shoulders were actually a little hunched and his head bowed. He was positively defeated.

Charlotte swallowed away the ache spreading through her chest at the sight of her dear friend in such moroseness. Panic at remembering her father in such a state told her to walk away. He clearly desired to be alone and he had left her as fast as polite society allowed only yesterday. Intruding on someone who wants desperately to be alone only leaves one feeling empty, she reasoned.

She sighed.

It was impossible to leave the only friend she had as a child in such painful contemplation. This was Matthew, not her father. Regardless of what had transpired yesterday it was her duty as his friend to help him. She took a sharp breath in and squared her shoulders. Placing a smile on her face, she walked purposely toward him.

"Well, you've outdone yourself this morning, Matthew," she called, her voice far more cheerful than she intended, "you've managed to interrupt my sketching before I've actually begun. These are the most beautiful peonies I've seen and must sketch them. But, now I can't," she said. She released a breath of relief when he stood and turned to offer a half-smile.

"Then come sit by me and sketch them regardless. I'm sure your maid won't mind," he immediately stood upon hearing her voice. Taking a long look around, he shook his head disapprovingly. "You're incorrigible. No maid again?"

"I don't need one for an early morning walk to the park. It's the only time ladies with any sense can take advantage to have some time for themselves. Unless we're walking to church," she replied pertly, though her heart sang to hear him challenging her.

She was thrilled to see his eyes roll upwards and hear a

hearty chuckle escape his lips. "Charlotte, I don't envy your future husband."

She dared a wide smile since there was no one around for what seemed like miles. "Does that mean you've renounced your promise to interfere in my search for a husband?"

"I won't need to," he replied sardonically, "Being seen speaking to a man of my ilk will do plenty for keeping undesirable proposals at bay." He looked at her pointedly with an arch brow.

"I didn't think my humble opinion would sting you so," she teased.

"There's never anything humble about your opinion, dear. And, it did," he replied in what seemed to be only a half-mocking tone.

She sighed loudly before responding. "Yesterday's incident was vastly different from this one. I'm at a respectable distance and anyone looking at us would think I'm barely looking in your direction. Also, you're a dear family friend, so either way, I'm safe," she gave a satisfied, self-righteous nod.

"Safe is not a word I would use for being around me," his tone suddenly dropped and so did Charlotte's stomach. He stared at her with such open admiration she felt the immediate need to hide.

She swallowed and smiled nervously, refusing to let him flirt his way out. "That may work with other ladies, but not with your oldest friend," she lied smoothly. After clearing her throat for emphasis and to still the flutter in her heart, she added, "I thought you rather enjoyed being known as the merry younger brother to the Earl of Elmvale."

"Being known as merry and being accused of being an epic rake is vastly different."

"Is it?" Her eyes were wide with feigned innocence. Her

lips pursed with secret satisfaction when she saw him rise to her challenge.

"Are you sure it's wise to have such a conversation with me, dear friend? You're after all, a refined, delicate Countess and I'm quite the opposite," his eyes narrowed and his lips moved into a devilish grin.

With each word he uttered, the broken man she had found on the bench slowly disappeared. She was not about to stop now. "Why? Are you afraid of continuing?" She challenged, knowing it was the bait he needed to fully come out of the sad, self-pitying trance.

It worked.

"I'm acutely aware that I made a veritable profession out of wooing women and cleverly escaping marriage all while remaining delightfully beloved. But, my rules were strict," he said with utmost seriousness. Except, Charlotte saw the return of a sparkle to his eye.

"There are rules for such behavior?" She mocked him with an equally serious tone.

She rolled her eyes when he offered a patronizing tilt of his head. "My dear, I was never involved with ladies whom did not have any previous experiences, any married ladies whom had not borne at least two sons, nor the sisters of my friends." He stared at her as though daring her to swoon or to accuse him of being a cad or behaving like a beast.

Instead, her tone matched his own level of sarcasm. "Yet you remained charming and witty enough that most mothers, though weary, would gladly receive your proposal for their daughters. Amazing."

They looked at each other for a moment. The game was ending and his face revealed the friend she had always known.

"Thank you," he said softly. "It's distasteful to hear you use the very epitaph I happily worked so hard to obtain, especially since it's no longer true. I know what you just managed to accomplish, even though you did promise to stay away from me if you ever saw me in this state again."

"I'm not very good at following rules and all that," she laughed when he snorted. "It was the least I could do after the wasp sting and the pond," she gave a small shrug of her shoulder. Then, after a moment, she thought about what he revealed. "What do you mean it's no longer true? Just a few days ago I came across you and you smelled positively –"

"Still charming as ever with your honesty," Matthew interrupted her. "It's the Matthew Harrington London expects – wild, carefree, fun. And, so, I deliver until I figure out my place here."

"Perhaps you have it backwards. No, of course you have it backwards," she said with an exasperated sigh. With one hand on her hip and accentuating head nods, she made her point, "Matthew, you must let them see who you are now and then your place in London, in the *ton*, in your own family will make sense. You can't expect to be who you were and then by magic a new role will suddenly make itself known to you. Why are you smiling like that?"

"This is the Charlotte I know. Not the cool, collected lady of the ballroom. I don't know why I'm so pleased, but I am," he smiled boyishly as though discovering the best of secrets.

She exhaled loudly. "That's completely irrelevant. How do you expect to marry well if every lady worth knowing is skittish about being near you because your very presence may ruin her reputation?

"You're not afraid to be near me."

"I don't count."

"Really? If you don't count then why am I haunted by the scent of your fragrance? Roses. My body can easily conjure the perfect synchronicity of our waltzes, of the way we moved together. And, the memory of your petal soft lips which taste like an overripe berry teases me at every turn since each time I take measures to avoid you, I find myself in your presence. So, please explain how it is you don't count."

She felt her face warm with his bold appreciation. His eyes took in the blush spreading over her fair skin contrasting with her raven tresses and he seemed stunned by her. She was positive she heard a murmured "ethereal" escape his lips as he continued to take in every inch of her.

"Of course, I don't count," she repeated succinctly, putting an end to his overt flirtation. She refused to fall. It was too dangerous to fall. "Stop playing games Matthew. We aren't children anymore. Your teasing and mocking aren't going to help either of us. I'm going to marry and you need to start behaving like the gentleman I know you are. We're neighbors and it's well known that our families have always been close. Everyone knows I'm committed to Bentwick. I don't even know why I'm explaining myself."

"The Countess never explains herself," Matthew muttered. "Your careful abiding by the rules and your commitment to your duty makes my own promises to never hurt you and to ensure you're well married easier to fulfill."

She saw him breathe deeply. When he looked up, he did so with a small, teasing grin, "Some ladies are not quite so skittish to be around me. After all, I didn't earn my reputation all by myself."

"I suppose you're right," she said softly, refusing to allow his inappropriate insinuation to distract her. "Nonetheless, you have to live with it all by yourself."

"I'd rather be alone and completely happy than married and miserable."

The honest, yet grave pronouncement, pierced her heart. Despite his attempted charming tone, it was clear Matthew was not interested in the kind of marriage the *ton* offered or the kind of marriage to which she would be sacrificed. It seemed he wasn't interested in marriage at all.

"Some people have no choice," her small whisper unraveled the lie, revealing the truth about the Earldom of Bentwick; but, somehow, it no longer mattered that he should find out.

"Please tell me you're not speaking of a rich husband."

She looked at him defiantly. "You know very well that I don't have a choice."

Matthew pulled his hat off, ran his fingers through his hair, and plopped it back on. "So, the wealthy Countess isn't so wealthy after all."

He furrowed his brow, as though forcing himself to think. She took a step back when he came closer. He stood completely still, arms at his side, but his eyes told her he would move mountains for her if necessary. "Listen, I can help. I found solutions to the most unsolvable of problems abroad. I was an honored officer and was relentless in my pursuit of improving sanitation, hygiene, infrastructure and business. I always mediated between two opposing sides and found middle ground fruitful to each. Surely, I can find a solution for you. Charlotte – there's always a -"

"Choice? No, Matthew, not for me. I must submit to marriage regardless of how miserable it will make me because it will save so many others."

"Marry me!" He blurted and Charlotte was positive the thought had not fully formed in his head before it came out of his mouth.

"No. I can't." Her throat dried and her chest ached when she saw the crestfallen look on her dear friend's face.

Except, he didn't give up. His eyes lit up in a way she hadn't seen since he weaved his way to her in Somersby's ballroom. "I don't have the sum to save Bentwick, but we're friends, we can make a marriage work. I can help you and our friendship will be safe."

"Will it? It would mean marrying for every argument you've ever used against marriage."

How was this happening? Her dearest friend was proposing to save her and she was rejecting him. It didn't make any sense. This was the moment which could save her Earldom and she was rejecting it because...because...no answer came. The only certainty she knew was that every inch of her shook with fear.

"God help me, Charlotte," his hands clenched at his sides and he nearly growled, "I'm willing to sacrifice all of that nonsense to save the girl with whom I grew up."

She felt the beginning of tears sting her eyes. She would not cry. Using every ounce of will power, she stilled her heaving stomach and spoke as evenly as she could. "I have to sacrifice myself to marriage Matthew, I would hate to ask the same of you. I'll accept a marriage of convenience from anyone else, but you," she smiled softly. "As your dear friend, I wish to honor your desire. You don't want to marry and be miserable. Well, I would hate to be the one to make you miserable. I appreciate your gesture, but it's not the answer to my predicament," her tone indicated complete finality to their discussion and her demeanor transformed.

Gone was the girl with the great laugh and perceptive gaze. She stood once again as the well-bred, cold-faced Lady Bentwick, and they said farewell with severe politeness.

CHAPTER 10

Charlotte stood in the Burnhope's concert room feeling less like the Countess of Bentwick and more like the girl with the braids who would rather be out riding and sketching than at home next to Mother receiving a morning call. The low tones of the cello as the musician warmed his hands and instrument for the evening's performance mirrored the dread in her stomach.

Another night in search of a wealthy husband, yet at some point in the very recent past, she had lost all desire to fulfill her goal. She needed a rich husband and soon, but she did not care to find him. Her entire world had been brought asunder by Matthew Harrington.

Despite his infuriating interference, heavenly kiss and constant flirting, she was reminded of how deep their friendship ran. Upon marrying another man, it would be impossible to maintain such a close connection with him without causing gossip or scandal. B ut, now that he was returned from abroad and wandered back into her life, the thought of giving him up again seemed unthinkable.

Yet, she had refused his proposal of marriage. Marriage to

Matthew was the only way to keep him in her life and she had said no. Perhaps, she had refused because it hadn't seemed like a true proposal. What if he had been less rash and impulsive? Matthew was always led by his instincts and when he heard her true reason for being in London he had acted out of honor. She nearly stamped her foot in frustration. Did it really matter how a gentleman proposed or what she felt as long as she reached her goal? For some reason, because it was Matthew's proposal, it did matter, which infuriated her even more.

The cellist intoned a most grave night of love just as the invitation had heralded and Charlotte was certain the musicians had conspired to put her most intimate feelings on display. Everything within her was chaos. Matthew's unexpected proposal proved the depth of his loyalty and friendship. She gritted her teeth, knowing she could marry any man for honor and duty except for Matthew. Ruining their friendship with a marriage of convenience would break her heart.

She wished to shut every note out and censure every ridiculous lady moaning about the epic romance the evening would certainly produce. Everyone present would be under the spell of beautiful notes and beautiful poetry. It was enough to make her cast up her accounts. But, her friends had insisted. So here she was, ready for a miserable night showcasing love, romance and all which would certainly remain out of her reach forever.

"Charlotte, this way!" Evangeline came upon her, steering her towards the opposite side of the concert hall. "We must keep away from my mother. She's been providing me with maternal advice on how to attract a good husband which includes keeping quiet and smiling demurely."

"Sounds like the sum of all maternal advice on marriage is not to be yourself for as long as possible. Perhaps that's how it was in their day, but haven't times changed? Don't gentlemen prefer a woman with some kind of wit?"

Evangeline's eyes widened. "I suppose that's always been part of my argument. But I didn't realize you felt the same way."

"I didn't either. I didn't allow myself to think of marriage as anything more than a duty to my Earldom. But, what if there's more to it and I'll be denying myself the chance of discovering what it is?" Her tone was pure misery. She begrudged Evangeline's indulged life. Imagine being so wealthy and sure of her future, she could choose not to marry. Pure pain shot through Charlotte's chest.

"Are you completely sincere about your vow to never marry?"

Evangeline carefully considered the question with her amber eyes ablaze. "I'm completely sincere about never giving myself to someone who is undeserving. And, since I've yet to meet a deserving gentleman, then my answer is I'll never marry."

"What if a deserving gentleman walks into your life? Would you change your mind?" Charlotte persisted.

"I doubt it very much," she said, giving a shrewd look. "I have a feeling these questions are not about me."

The penetrating stare almost made Charlotte retreat but she couldn't. Her worry overcame her good sense and the words tumbled out with wicked speed. "I came to London to fulfill my duty to my title. But, what if there's more to life than mere duty? What if I can find more than duty in marriage? My parents had a miserable marriage – oh, Mother claims it was a love match, but everything I witnessed said otherwise. Even though I'm hoping for love, how can I even trust that what appears to be a love match will be one? Oh, I wish I could make the right decision for both Bentwick and me, but it seems impossible!"

Evangeline slowed her down by gently holding her shoulders. She waited for Charlotte's breathing to return. "If you cannot marry for love, at least marry someone you respect and who respects you. And, perhaps someone you believe you can grow to love," then she smiled, "Although, sometimes we really must follow our heart and forget everything else."

"It is precisely that form of thinking which has me so confused," she admitted woefully. She had been willing to accept a marriage proposal from any of the forgettable peers she had met. But, she had instantly rejected Matthew's proposal. Bentwick's need for money ran so deep, she should have accepted and been finished with this whole business of marriage and husband-hunting.

She couldn't.

She told herself she couldn't shackle him to a lifetime of rebuilding an Earldom. It was impossible to contemplate any other reason for her rejection, like fear of not being loved by Matthew, or worse, falling in love with him. It was far easier to tell herself she couldn't be the one to make him miserable in marriage than to admit she was terrified of rejection, of unrequited love.

She wished she had the liberty to apply Evangeline's sound advice. She would have to follow her original plan and completely ignore the confusion in her heart. Matthew could only ever be the friend who had helped her to survive a lonely childhood. His gallantry and charm would have to be cherished only in the form of friendship. His kisses dismissed as inappropriate moments of weakness. So too would admiration for those blue eyes, mischievous grin and adorable dimple. Blasted dimple! Her foot could not contain itself any longer and finally stomped in frustration.

Evangeline smirked. "I positively love the break in the cool exterior of Lady Bentwick. Sometimes I forget how positively blazing you can be when we are at a social event."

"And I'm thoroughly annoyed that you're enjoying my discomfort so much," Charlotte snapped which only made Evangeline laugh.

"Whose discomfort?" They were interrupted by Isabella who came upon them breathlessly.

"Evangeline's once I find a wonderful, new suitor for her," Charlotte replied coolly while giving Evangeline a look which promised revenge.

"I'd like to help with that, but it'll have to wait," Isabella said, her ginger curls bouncing as she spoke. "I'm having a delightful time watching our brothers and Mr. Harrington squirm while the mothers practically climb over each other to introduce their lovely daughters. I can't wait to tease George!" Isabella giggled and Evangeline eagerly turned to watch the spectacle.

Charlotte froze. It appeared Matthew's reputation would not be a hinderance to ladies searching for husbands. His courage and success overseas had overshadowed his past and so it seemed he would have to be gracious and entertain ladies looking for husbands, along with their zealous mamas. With a tug deep in her belly, she realized she was far less eager to watch Matthew charm unmarried ladies. Her stomach clenched as she mechanically turned around.

The three men were quite a sight. Dark haired Oliver Fitzroy, light haired George Wynthorpe and Matthew with his wild brown locks, were tall and strong and very unmarried. The mothers gathered like skilled hunters upon their prey. Lady St. Clair almost tripped as she ran up to Matthew with her daughter in tow. Miss St. Clair was a buxom and lovely petite lady who had the adorable skill of looking up through her lashes.

Charlotte groaned.

He was all ease and charm. She knew he was probably making some witty observation and both ladies were riveted.

He skillfully maneuvered them towards the Earl of Carters and Charlotte heard Evangeline snort. George Wynthorpe then turned to Matthew and included him in the conversation with the nasal Mrs. Danbury and her equally nasal though attractive eldest daughter. While Isabella and Evangeline were in near hysterics when Carters handed off the St. Clair ladies to Viscount Huntsbridge, Charlotte actually thought she felt her heart break.

She always assumed she would lose her friendship with Matthew because of her own marriage and although they had spoken recently about marriage in his future, she had not truly entertained the idea of losing him first to a wife. He seemed much more at ease this evening without any of the nerves she had recently witnessed. Perhaps, he was taking her advice and simply being his new self.

A small ironic smile came to her lips. She was helping him fully return home, only to reject him and then watch him be appreciated by other ladies. And, unlike her, he could wait to make a love connection in order to marry. Only a few hours ago she had chastised him for not finding someone suitable to marry and here she stood, in a fit of jealousy, as he did just that. She stopped watching any more of the ridiculous interactions hoping her friends would distract her, and instead found herself facing the Duke of Ellis.

CHAPTER 11

Matthew entered the Burnhope's concert room using his military training to still his insides. He had led men into battle, he could certainly handle a social event which would require artfully evading questions and hearing sounds which could make him quake. All shaking ceased the moment his eyes found Charlotte.

When his brother had informed him Lady Bentwick was attending, he had inexplicably changed his mind and agreed to attend the recital. She looked regal standing amidst her friends across the room in a gown of sapphire, but something was different. The frigid air in which she enshrouded herself to face the *ton* was thawed. The Countess of Bentwick looked far more like his friend, Charlotte. He stopped his heart from swelling with joy when the memory of her rejection bit. He clenched his jaw, turning away from her to find Carters and Wynthorpe.

The entire episode had been ludicrous. How could he expect her to accept a marriage proposal grasped at from thin air? He could not decide which was worse. His less-than-romantic and laughable proposal or that she had so readily rejected it, without even a second thought. He had barely finished posing the question before the word *no* escaped her lips with such conviction, Matthew was certain he should be feeling some kind of insult.

"Harrington! You look far too brooding to be at a 'Night of Romance by Poetry & Music'," Carters mimicked the tone of the Burnhopes' invitation.

"I'm part of the tone. Aren't all men brooding until moved to be otherwise by romance?" he countered. "Which begs the question, why are you here?"

"I'm here for the poetry," Carters replied. Then he shook his head, not a wisp of his pristinely combed black hair moved out of place. "No. I can't even feign that. Mother ordered me to attend and ensure Evangeline doesn't find herself in trouble. I 'm telling you Harrington, my sister is going to be the death of me. I wish she would just marry and become some other poor devil's problem. You know what that's like," he said a little too pointedly, "you used to complain avidly about the Countess being a pain in your backside for years." Matthew recognized Carters' grin, daring him to take the bait.

"She remains a pain in my backside," he muttered and saw his friend's smile widen.

"I don't believe she'll be a problem anymore," George Wynthorpe piped in, "Everyone is infatuated with her. It won't be long before she's married." He motioned with his head toward the three ladies standing across the room in lively conversation.

"Thought you would be happy to hear that," Carters added jovially, "No need to scowl, Harrington. Women nowadays are more trouble than they're worth." The subtle knowing undertone to Carters' voice made Matthew wince.

"Really?" He responded tightly. "Is that how you intend to

court the next Marchioness? Or, perhaps you'll regale her with the details of all your exploits."

Carters flashed a grin. Matthew knew his friend was so taken with his reputation as a rake that he didn't comprehend the insinuated insult.

"With any luck, I'll find someone less willful than my sister," he looked thoughtful for a moment and then added for good measure, "She'll talk less than Evangeline too."

"Gentleman, don't look now but we're about to be regaled with tales of the talents of these ladies by their lovely Mamas," George warned and the men were immediately swallowed by mothers shoving their unwilling daughters in front of them.

Matthew clenched and released his fingers hoping to find the calm to endure the small talk, questions, and being the man the *ton* expected, not the one he had become. He graciously accepted the introductions. After a few pleasantries, he offered a few tidbits about the music they could anticipate. Tension eased as he breathed deeply, then he added during which poems the ladies could expect the most romance. He didn't make attempts to cajole or flirt. He was charming without being overt. He handled the mothers' impertinent questions about his time abroad with ease moving all comments toward more docile conversation. After a few deep breaths, he realized polite social interaction proved to be far easier than he had anticipated. Perhaps, he would be able to live at home and leave the past behind him.

She had been right.

Enthralled by this new-found confidence, he casually looked over the auburn head of Miss Danbury and his eyes were caught by Charlotte's. He saw her grey eyes storm. She was angry and though he was taken aback, the boy inside of him loved the idea of thoroughly irking her. He tilted his head in an ever so slight acknowledgement of her. His lips pressed tightly together to keep from laughing loudly when her brows furrowed furiously. He almost began to enjoy the moment of her discomfort but the thrill was cut short when he saw the Duke of Ellis approach her.

"You may not wish to marry yet, Harrington, but do attempt to stop glaring," Carters murmured. He followed Matthew's line of vision and saw the cause of his fury.

"The Duke of Ellis is a dangerous man, but I believe the Countess will handle him well," Carters reassured.

"Precisely what worries me," Matthew said, excusing himself and walking directly towards her. With his jaw clenched, he reminded himself this wasn't battle.

"Good evening Lady Bentwick, Lady Evangeline, Miss Wynthorpe," the Duke of Ellis's voice chilled the air surrounding them.

"Good evening, your grace," all three responded.

Charlotte met his black eyes without a flinch. They emanated the warmth of an iceberg and his black hair was threaded with silver. She noticed her limbs beginning to cool in his presence.

"It is a pleasure seeing you again this evening," Ellis spoke solely to her.

"Likewise, your grace," Charlotte lied. She wasn't sure what the Duke's game was. He danced with her at each ball, greeted her at every social function, but had yet to send flowers, write a poem or pay a call. He made the obvious effort to single her out but was always cold enough to appear standoffish. He was a mystery, and one that induced anxiety, not intrigue. He suddenly became odious to her and she wished he would leave her be if his intentions didn't involve a proposal.

She realized she was doing a poor job of disguising her discomfort. Ellis was a discerning man and she was barely the same lady whom graciously danced with him this week.

His lack of amusement was evident when he spoke, practically commanding her to answer his question. "Tell me Lady Bentwick, is it the music or the poetry that you enjoy?"

"The music most definitely," Charlotte replied on cue forcing herself to see the conversation through.

"I am partial to the poetry," he finally said with the authority to expect the evening's program to suddenly become all poetic recital, "I believe it speaks more to the soul than music."

Charlotte nearly snorted imagining a soul behind those cold black eyes. She saw his brow begin to arch and his eyes achieved the impossible by darkening even more.

She matched his cold stare with her own steely one, despite the sudden wobble in her legs. "I don't mean to be contrary your grace, but musical notes sometimes communicate better than words."

"I would love to discuss this further with you," his tone sent a chill down Charlotte's back. His words opened the door toward something beyond polite conversation. The opportunity to determine if Ellis was Bentwick's savior arrived; unfortunately, she was deprived the chance to discover the Duke's intentions.

"Good evening, your grace," Matthew interrupted them smoothly. Charlotte watched as he positioned himself between her and the Duke. It was the height of rudeness and she was not surprised by the Duke's reaction.

Ellis snarled and flicked a look of utter disdain at the intruder. Then, he turned his attention toward her as though Matthew did not exist. In that moment, the call for commencement was made and all guests were ushered to their seats.

"Lady Bentwick, I trust you and I will continue our most intriguing discussion without intrusion at the conclusion of tonight's recital." His eyes were black holes which promised to consume her.

She nearly took a step back when she locked eyes with Ellis, but he was demanding to see her and she could not let the opportunity to save her Earldom pass. She was lucky to receive such an opportunity in light of her treatment of him. She opened her mouth to accept but was cut short by Matthew.

"I'm afraid Lady Bentwick is engaged for the remainder of the evening. She is far too polite to contradict your grace." The slight edge in his tone sliced through any chance of creating another encounter that evening.

"Another time then. I shan't forget our discussion." Ellis gallantly wished her a good evening. She was impressed by his sudden demonstration of charm and self-control and chose to focus on that than on his disappearance into the shadows of the crowd.

"Seems like I'm still saving you," she heard Matthew say under breath as he gently led her by the elbow to her seat.

"I don't recall requesting your help." Charlotte yanked her arm away stalking ahead to meet Evangeline. She spent the rest of the night with her eyes focused on the stage and ushered her mother out the door with the pretext of a headache at the end of the performance.

She left without a glance at Matthew and wished to be as far from him as she could. His kiss and proposal had wreaked havoc on her perfectly controlled world. His very presence warmed her body, fluttered her stomach and endangered her heart. They had rekindled their friendship in the past few days. He had entrusted her with his fears and anxieties and she had helped him through. However, he was also obstructing her marriage goals while brazenly charming ladies and their mothers as though his intention was to marry. She was wholly disconcerted by his role in her life and what she was going to do about it.

She was in chaos.

Her entire life had been a meticulous plan to save Bentwick, and Matthew's arrival did not fit into it.

She was so consumed by her deliberations about Matthew, his behavior and his role in her life, she was completely unaware of the Duke of Ellis's chilling black eyes drilling into her when she left.

CHAPTER 12

"Oh!" Charlotte cried out in surprise.

"Pardon me, my Lady," the butler said, unperturbed by her outburst, "the Dowager requests your presence in her parlor. The Dowager Countess of Elmvale, Lady Adelaide, has arrived with Mr. Harrington."

Charlotte waited for the butler to leave before throwing down her brush. Painting in the garden was supposed to have calmed the torrent she had been spiralling in since Matthew's return. Now, he was paying her a morning call and she was completely unprepared to greet him. The situation was beyond intolerable. She had to put an end to his interference. She had to bring misplaced feelings for her best friend back into her control. She slipped into her home with every intention of offering Matthew a cold greeting and dismissal. It was the least he deserved for turning her world to chaos. She practically stomped through the hall fully intending to bring order back to her world.

All stomping ceased and all determination withered the moment she came to the open doors of the parlor. Matthew stood by the fireplace inspecting one of her drawings. He studied her work with the same appreciation and seriousness which he had shown in the corridor of his mother's home when he had been contemplating her lilacs. His concentration on her art incensed the fire she was desperately trying to douse. All of the hiding, denying, and running from everything he had made her feel brought her to this unmistakable moment.

God, he was handsome; it was truly remarkable that one man was so finely chiseled. His tan was slightly less sharp and his brown locks fell just longer than acceptable tempting her fingers to run through the dark mane. Her eyes fell to the strong muscular body perfectly outlined by precisely tailored clothes. He was tall and powerful yet he looked so comfortable in his skin. Matthew's body always moved in such a relaxed fashion one could almost forget just how strong he was. So absorbed by the sight of him, she didn't realize he had turned to face her.

Her throat went dry and her lips parted slightly when her eyes met his. The infinite depths of blue absorbed her. He knew her. He held almost every memory worth remembering. He was a part of her in ways she never dared to recognize. The knowledge of their close connection had never felt so intimate, nor so terrifying.

She saw his familiar lopsided grin and suddenly wished she had stopped at her room to re-pin her hair. The black mane was barely atop her head. She hurriedly pushed back dark tendrils falling onto her collarbone. She noticed he clenched his fingers into tight fists at his side as though attempting to control them.

Charlotte strode into the room, clearing her throat. She offered what she hoped was a warm greeting but feared she came across like a screeching bird. She bit her lip wishing Matthew would stop staring at her so boldly.

"Take Matthew to the garden dear, show him the roses

you're painting for the Duke of Ellis," Mother dismissed them with a wave.

The lopsided grin disappeared. After nodding at their mothers, they walked outside in silence and Charlotte could feel Matthew's cold stare penetrating her back as she led the way.

"Since when does Lord Richard Thurston commission paintings from the Countess of Bentwick?" He asked once they were at a safe distance from the house. "Ellis paid you a morning call. You received him with no one here to protect you. And, why does neither mother deem it necessary to escort us? You're painting roses for him and I'm perceived as no threat to you at all?"

She stopped and turned around, taking a moment to study him. Why was he so angry by their lack of chaperone? They had never required one, although as the depth of her attraction for her best friend revealed itself, perhaps it would not be such a bad idea. She sat on a low wall under the shade of an elm. Looking straight ahead, she spoke softly.

"I spent ten years roaming the rolling hills and valleys of Somerset imagining a season in London. On cold winter nights huddled in my mother's room by the only fire lit in Bentwick Manor we would dream about all of the things we would do in London to give us the fortitude to go on. I've bravely faced the *ton* and squashed all feelings of homesickness in order to find Bentwick's savior. And, in just over a week, you've made every meticulous plan go awry. Your possessiveness and protectiveness have to stop."

"If there's anyone who's fully aware of your strength and determination, it's me. While they're admirable traits, at the moment, they're becoming increasingly frustrating. I'll interfere for as long as I think you're in danger. He's not to be trusted."

Charlotte stood, hands on hips, facing him directly.

"You've been abroad for five years without a single word. During that time, I ran my estate and handled my affairs without anyone to protect me."

Her nostrils flared and she gave a loud harrumph when Matthew refused to accept she could take care of herself. He stepped closer, standing directly over her. His voice was heavy with warning, "You're not going to marry anyone of whom I don't approve. Ellis? I swear I'll stop you from making a monumental mistake. The man cannot be trusted."

Why was he insisting on making this difficult for her? Her eyes were fire as she tilted her chin defiantly. "I'm not an imbecile. I know what he is, but I have no choice."

"Yes, you do," he insisted, refusing to hear her.

She nearly burst with frustration that the man whom she had very recently rejected was playing knight in shining armor and trying to save her from an alliance with another man whom could save her Earldom. She clenched her jaw as he kept up his argument.

"You can't be near him. You can't accept his attention. I don't care that he could very well own half of England!"

"He doesn't own half of England."

"You know my meaning. Ellis isn't trustworthy. No one has ever actually caught him in a despicable act, but there are enough rumors surrounding him to make any person of honor weary of being too closely associated with him, even though he's a Duke. Marrying him for his money would be disastrous!"

"I don't have the luxury for a love match! What is it that you find so reprehensible about my actions? Women have made this kind of choice since the beginning of time. I don't want his money, Bentwick needs his money. Are my actions any less honorable than those of a man who charms ladies all night and then leaves them feeling powerless about the direction of their relationship? Perhaps reflect on your own actions while in London and stop preoccupying yourself with mine!"

She felt her face flush with color and the warmth spread to the rest of her body. Anger, anxiety, excitement, frustration all came to fruition in one swift moment as she made the tiny revelation that she had been just as watchful of him. A sudden moisture draped her body, concentrating in her underarms and down the middle of her back. Her heart fluttered like a hummingbird as she watched her words sink into him, and he began to understand the depth of their meaning.

His irritation was suddenly moved aside by a predatory look. He eliminated the space between them smoothly, until he stood over her.

"Jealous?" His voice was suddenly velvet.

"Don't be ridiculous," Charlotte snapped, grasping at her anger to help her through a terrifying and rare moment of vulnerability. Fury brimmed through her because he was right. She was jealous. It burned that he knew her so well. And, in her heart, she knew jealousy meant she harbored feelings of desire for her handsome friend. Feelings which refused to be shut away and betrayed her at every turn. Her throat seized when he looked at her far longer than was appropriate.

"I would bet you would prefer all of my attention and charm." Each word was drawn out slowly, quietly, its meaning driven into the very heart of her by his piercing blue eyes.

His voice was a caress travelling down to her toes. He moved his face closer to hers and Charlotte could feel his breath brush her skin. The heat of his own raised emotions brought his scent of sandalwood to her nose and her fingers itched to run through his brown locks. Yet, she refused to give into her attraction.

She stilled her racing heart and stood her ground. The

temptation was far too dangerous and she could not give in to feelings which would cause Bentwick's ruin. I nstead, she dug up courage from deep within and showed him just how well she could take care of herself. She threw her head back and levelled him with a glare.

"If your charm were money, Bentwick would be saved. But it isn't, is it?" Each word spilled superciliously from her mouth.

Matthew's expression remained as though they had been discussing the weather, but Charlotte was positive she saw a momentary look of disappointment flash across his face.

"No, I guess it isn't," he replied far too casually. "But, I'm not the one selling myself to the highest bidder."

Her eyes narrowed. "How dare you? You've no idea what I've lived through. While you were off having adventures abroad, my mother and I were sacrificing everything to save our estate and all of the people whom depend on it. If the Duke of Ellis will help me save Bentwick, I'll happily accept him."

"Let me assure you madam, war is not an adventure," Matthew's voice lost all smoothness and became hollow.

"It's not what I meant –"

"And neither is Ellis," he continued without a beat. "He's been a widow for twenty years, why would he marry you?"

The weight of his words made Charlotte cave. After a few moments of stillness, she spoke, all of her fire extinguished leaving a trail of pitiful smoke. "Am I that undesirable?"

His eyes met hers. Reading her failure, he offered a rueful sigh. "You're every poem ever written about desire. But, Ellis preys on innocents."

Her eyes filled with tears which she fought hard to contain. In a breath, he had dashed the only hope she had. Ellis was her only card and Matthew plucked it right out of her hands with his warnings. In a few short weeks, without marriage, she and her mother would be left with nothing but an empty title. It was too much to bear and too much to allow Matthew to witness her ruin.

"I believe your morning call is over," her voice grew thick and rough with emotion.

"Charlotte -"

"Good day, Mr. Harrington." She walked purposely towards her home hoping she could hang on to her composure until reaching her room.

Within seconds she felt Matthew take hold of her elbow. Her body was quickly whipped around and he kissed her.

His hand came to her waist, gently pulling her towards him. As each inch of her body came into contact with his, her pretenses dropped. When her entire length was aligned with his, she knew his were the only lips she wanted. His was the only body she wanted this close to her. Even though her brain told her it was impossible because she had rejected his proposal and even though her heart was terrified of letting him in, she melted and finally accepted there was no other person she would rather kiss. She felt his other hand gently cup the side of her face, holding her closer, coaxing her to trust him.

Bright rays of sunlight filtering through the leaves warmed her eyelids and Matthew's lips tenderly loving her own warmed every part of her. When he finally lifted his head, she opened her eyes and was positive their kiss had created all of the little bright sparks surrounding them.

She offered a small smile and was positive he could hear the loud drum of her heart, for he looked far too contemplative after such a kiss. His lips laid gentle kisses on her cheeks, her eyes and the tip of her nose, then his forehead rested against hers. His voice was a desperate and hoarse whisper.

"Charlotte, for the love God, stay away from him."

She memorized the infinite blues of his eyes with a

mixture of desire, sadness and regret. Heavy breath suppressed her tears. Despite the haze of attraction, she had to remember, she could not marry Matthew. He didn't want to marry and she could not be the one to ruin his life. Besides, being with him meant full exposure. And, despite her yearnings for a marriage of love, she was deeply afraid she was far too wounded to ever know how to truly love.

"I have no choice," she finally said, touching his cheek and untangling herself from his grasp. She turned, quietly walking away.

And this time, Matthew let her go.

CHAPTER 13

Lady Adelaide Harrington walked home with her son. She cast a sidelong glance at him, indulging a surge of maternal pride about the incredible man her bouncing boy had become. If only Matthew would find love, Adelaide thought. No, that wasn't the problem. Her son had found love years ago. The problem was he had just discovered it and was too afraid to admit it.

"Unusually quiet," she murmured.

"Enjoying the weather and my lovely companion." Matthew smiled.

She smiled, knowing he was hoping to distract any further comments. "How was your time with Charlotte?" Apparently, directness was the only option.

"Fine." His tone indicated all was not fine and he was not prepared to discuss it, least of all with his mother. Naturally, his tone didn't deter his mother.

"She has matured into such an admirable young lady," Adelaide said with a playful smile. "I'm surprised there haven't been any proposals yet. It seems the *ton* is smitten with her." She cast her lure and waited.

Matthew scowled. "The *ton* is smitten with any regular Miss who has half a brain. If no one has proposed yet, they're proving to be the imbeciles I've always taken them for."

"Funny," Adelaide replied as they entered Elmvale House. "I've never taken you for an imbecile. Thank you for accompanying me, I did miss you terribly while you were gone." Adelaide kissed Matthew's cheek leaving him in full admiration of her subtle attack and triumphant retreat.

He spent the rest of the day in his rooms. Charlotte's face intruded everywhere. Each time he bent his head to study a document the memory of her standing in the doorway of the parlor, watching him and looking achingly beautiful popped into his mind. His fixation on her art had been interrupted by an intense tingle on his neck and the moment he had turned to face her, she had stirred every single desire he had painfully kept in check for years with one single look. It had taken all of his self-control to keep from marching towards her to sweep her dark hair off of her creamy collarbone. His hands tightened at the memory.

A deep breath and a return to reading his correspondence didn't prevent her eyes, her lips, the feel of her body compressed to his from assaulting him. He could still feel her in his arms. The tip of his tongue tasted her along his lips. He closed his eyes with letters still in hand trying to still the wave of desire coming over him as he unwittingly remembered claiming the petal soft lips. His body hardened as it recalled how her entire length had fit so perfectly against him. He conjured her oval face with the delicate blush across ivory skin, her heather grey eyes and midnight tresses, her full lips begging to be consumed. Years of celibacy gave way to need, but not need of any woman. He opened his eyes. Kissing Charlotte under the lilacs and in her garden, had methodically stripped away every layer of armor encasing his heart.

Beyond her obvious physical allure, she fit him as no other woman had. He knew her. And, she knew him. No one fit him like Charlotte did in body, mind and heart, which was why his heart had wrenched with each step she had taken away from him. There had been no thought. Only the blinding instinct to keep her with him forever when he had pulled her towards him. It was absolutely ridiculous that she was searching for a husband when the only man she needed was him because...because he could save Bentwick.

The letters slipped through his fingers, floating slowly to the floor and Matthew dropped his head into his hands.

He could save Bentwick!

Once the thought revealed itself to him, it took an immediate iron grip.

He knew he could save Bentwick. By God, he had survived and thrived in war, abroad helping others, what couldn't he do in England to save an Earldom for Charlotte? He knew the land and its people as well as she. He loved his little corner of England, well, it neighbored his corner, but that was beside the point. More importantly, it became clearer to him with every breath he took that his happiness was intricately woven into hers. He didn't know when it had happened, but Charlotte was a part of him. And, he was positive he was a part of her. It was no use denying the obvious any longer. He was hopelessly in love with his childhood friend.

Had any of the servants been walking by his rooms at the very moment during which this revelation occurred, they would have been gravely concerned about the Earl's brother for the only sound emanating from his closed door was that of his bellowing laughter.

Matthew had thought he feared love. He had run from compromise and being trapped into marriage by overly fanciful women with a tenacity many men admired. The truth was none of those women had stirred his heart because Charlotte had been nestled inside it for so long he had never truly questioned her presence. His boiling anger at her marriage plans suddenly made perfect sense. He didn't want any other man to have her because he loved her the way no other man could. She was his to love and no one else's.

He ran his fingers through is hair when the fragile admission was suddenly overcome by searing darkness, dousing every single hope about being happy. After all he had seen and done, would he ever be the man Charlotte needed?

There was no answer. He didn't know if he could offer what she deserved, but he couldn't let another man try. His only option was to marry her and hope that would be enough to bury the demons of the past five years. She had fearlessly helped him through dark episodes twice. Both in public spaces. Regardless of how changed he felt, she knew him enough to see past the pain he still felt about battle. She truly was the only woman for him. No one else would be able to see the various versions of his past and understand him so wholly in the present.

He winced when he remembered she had very recently rejected his proposal. Not that it had been the most romantic or eloquent of proposals, he reasoned. The only option was to court her, to show her how very much he loved her and leave her with no choice but to accept a proposal for love. He ignored the nagging doubts about her need for money. He might not have the wealth of a Duke, but he had had the wits to turn his own wealth into an enviable fortune. He was suddenly glad Charlotte was unaware of the extent of his financial gain. He would hate for her to turn her attention towards him merely for his money. Surely, once she agreed to marry him for love, she would be beyond thrilled to discover the extent of his wealth, it couldn't be hidden after all.

Together, they would save Bentwick and he would help her fulfill her vow. Perhaps, by being with the woman he loved and basking in her light, he might find his place and the peace he so desperately needed.

But, first, he needed her to accept him. He would convince her beyond a shadow of a doubt that they belonged together. She would want to marry him, not the incredibly wealthy brother and heir to the Earl of Elmvale.

CHAPTER 14

"You're fidgeting," Evangeline said in shock. "Isabella, have you ever seen Charlotte fidget? She's been questioning a marriage of convenience and tonight she's fidgeting."

"She's not fidgeting," Isabella defended her with a compassionate smile.

"Her dress wasn't pleated when she entered the ballroom either," Evangeline glanced at the skirts of Charlotte's gown which were currently taking the shape of an awkward looking accordion.

"Do you have a point?" Charlotte asked curtly. She smoothed the gown as best she could, knowing it was a hopeless endeavor. It looked as unkempt as her insides. She avidly searched for Matthew but she wasn't entirely sure what she would do once she found him. Part of her urged to run out of the ballroom immediately. And, another more daring, or delusional, part, she could not yet decide which, urged her to run straight into his arms.

"Now she's starting to sound like my brother, which is never a good sign. You never want to sound like my brother."

"Ignore her Charlotte," Isabella said, "Only Evangeline thinks that sounding like Carters is offensive."

Evangeline rolled her eyes. "That's because I'm the only one with any sense. All of you fall for his supposed charm."

"I haven't fallen for anything," Isabella said but Evangeline kept talking.

"Insufferable and overbearing. Those should be his middle names."

"Who's insufferable and overbearing? Are you doing your best at catching the interests of a new suitor?" The Earl in question interjected smoothly. Standing next to Lord Oliver Fitzroy was Matthew Harrington and Charlotte's dress paid for it dearly.

As her fingers pleated and smoothed and repeated their incessant movement of her gown, she could not help but recall the pressure of Matthew's lips on hers and inadvertently bit her lower lip. When she did, she noticed Matthew watching her. To the outward world, it had been nothing more than a glance. Charlotte had been privy to all of Matthew's glances and she was completely certain that he looked positively smug with her reaction.

She furrowed her brow. He was enjoying her discomfort!

She nearly groaned fearing her deep blush would never subside, and prayed fervently for Evangeline's tirade to distract everyone, especially the very arrogant man who had put her in this position in the first place, from noticing her complexion was beginning to match her rose gown.

"I wouldn't give you the satisfaction of seeing me married off quite yet darling brother!" Charlotte heard Evangeline say to her brother, though it was difficult to decipher if her words were a promise or a threat.

The Fitzroy siblings kept up their banter which seemed more like a habit of Oliver complaining about his headstrong sister wishing she would be more pliable like their other sisters who were now living in marital bliss. Meanwhile, Evangeline interjected grandly reminding him that she would never marry and that she was also very much not his responsibility while they both placed Isabella in the middle trying to force her to side against the other. If Charlotte hadn't been so consumed by embarrassment, she would have thoroughly enjoyed the clear demonstration of sibling love.

She saw Matthew chuckle at Evangeline's imitation of Oliver's fierce look and tone when attempting to order her about. She stared at his lips. They were so full, so soft and had given her the most intimate encounters she had ever experienced.

And, she could never go near those lips again.

They were friends and she needed to marry someone else – secretly kissing Matthew Harrington while searching for a husband could undo her. She had to make things right and explain that it had been wildly inappropriate of him to kiss her – for she would surely never admit to reciprocating the kiss. They had to forget the entire incident and remain the best of friends.

"Wouldn't you agree Charlotte?" Isabella looked as though she was pleading for a way out of the Fitzroy battle, but Charlotte could not offer any assistance. She had not heard a word any of them had said.

"Ah…" she saw all three waiting for her response as the victorious vote in their battle of wills. And then, the boy with the blue eyes came to her rescue.

"Lady Bentwick shall give you her answer after our dance," Matthew gallantly stated and was just about to take her gloved hand when out of nowhere another gloved hand claimed her first.

"I believe Lady Bentwick is spoken for," the Duke of Ellis's deep voice cut through the warmth of their camaraderie. He immediately led her away without waiting for a response or without a look at Matthew.

Charlotte caught herself before groaning. It wasn't supposed to be this way. S he willed herself to forget Matthew and his ill-timed kiss. She focused on Ellis which he took as an invitation to hold her tighter. Where there should have been excitement at having caught the Duke's attention, there was nothing but agonizing desire to get out of his grip. Charlotte knew she wanted nothing to do with him and the very thought of his lips on hers made her stomach churn.

Before Matthew had kissed her, she had been well aware of the expectations upon her – marry a stranger, save Bentwick, produce an heir. It had been a cold, calculated list, one she had been ready to fulfill.

His kisses had ruined everything.

She was a knot of nerves and her mind was in chaos because Matthew's interference had unleashed every single fantasy she had buried about romance and love. She needed to speak with Matthew privately and set the entire situation right. She breathed deeply and called upon her infinite patience to graciously finish the dance.

Matthew was seething.

"Chin up, Harrington," Lord Oliver Fitzroy murmured to Matthew as they both watched Charlotte dance with the Duke. "Evangeline will make sure to dissuade her from the match. As you've heard, my sister is an adamant supporter of spinsterhood, perhaps she will convince the Countess to join her." Oliver finished jovially. When there was no response from Matthew but a deadly gleam in his eyes, he said under breath, "I see. I also see the lovely Miss St. Clair on the edge of the dance floor."

Shortly thereafter, Matthew was leading Miss St. Clair in an aggressive dance to ensure his proximity to Charlotte and the Duke. He apologized to her profusely once they were done while his eyes followed Charlotte. The Duke had hold of Charlotte's elbow and was maneuvering her out onto the terrace. He saw Ellis take a sweeping glance of the ballroom before making a quick escape. He was clearly in such a hurry that he had failed to see Matthew standing behind a column.

Matthew attempted to dart out but was instantly accosted by an old school fellow and then by a few mothers with their parade of daughters. When he finally stepped through the garden doors his body numbed and his mind became frantic. There was no sign of Charlotte or Ellis.

CHAPTER 15

"Is there anything more delightful than sharing a fresh spring night with a lovely peeress?" Ellis cooed far too close to her ear.

Charlotte ordered her shoulder to remain still and not reflexively shoo away the Duke like a most unwanted fly.

"Yes, it's very warm in the ballroom," she said through a tight throat.

"I must admit, I wasn't expecting much from the new peeress. Everyone was so eager to meet you. And, for once, I was wrong. You must know, however, there was only one woman worthy of my title. My dear, late Duchess, Lady Margaret Thurston. She died right after the twins were born. Sebastian first. Then, came Charles," he spat out his youngest son's name like the most bitter venom. "I'm positive it was he who caused her untimely death, though the midwives and physicians deny it of course. Tonight, marks the twentieth year of her passing."

"I'm very sorry for your loss, your grace," Charlotte dutifully replied feeling a little hopeful the retelling of intimate family history would lead to other intimate subjects, such as marriage. It was time to go in, but she needed to see the exchange through. It could very well lead to the proposal she needed to achieve her goal. She allowed him to lead her farther down the terrace stairs and into the gardens. They stood next to a tree which obstructed their view of the balconies. It also hid them quite well. Too well. Fear began to quiver through her. Only a few more minutes and she was positive the Duke would propose amidst the distorted shadows of manicured shrubs and tall trees.

"Of course, you are," he answered flippantly, "Your sort normally is."

"My sort, your grace?"

"Yes, the kind who believes I'll give up all the fun I have with stupid girls and give away the honor of Margaret's title. Sebastian's wife will be the next Duchess. And, I will enjoy the fruits of those who are intelligent enough to ally with me."

Charlotte swallowed. This was nothing more than an indecent proposal, if it could be called such, it was more of an expectation she become his mistress. She forced an even cadence to her tone and a confident smile to mask the terror beginning to seize her. "I'm sure there are many whom wish to avoid making an enemy of you, Lord Ellis. Your wife was a lucky woman indeed to have your undying loyalty. Thank you for the cool air, your grace, we may return to the ballroom now."

"So soon?" He hissed, black eyes moving into thin slits. His body slithered, instinctively blocking her way to the terrace stairs. "We haven't even begun to enjoy ourselves Lady Bentwick. If it hadn't been for my vow on her deathbed, I would daresay you would be worthy of Lady Ellis's title. You understand that a man of my needs must find release in any way he can since I intend to keep my word to my late wife. You are every bit a peeress and far too

sophisticated for any of the young pups in that ballroom.
You need an experienced peer and protector, wouldn't you
agree?"

His salacious grin turned Charlotte's stomach. She swallowed. Evidently, rumors about her financial situation had
already begun to circulate. Ellis was using the information to
force her into his arms. As long as she complied with his
sexual demands, she and Bentwick would survive. It was not
the arrangement she was looking for.

"You certainly don't disagree, which is as good as compli-
ance," he pulled her roughly by the waist, forcing her against
his body. She struggled to be released but he only tightened
his hold digging his hips into her, making her feel his
arousal.

"Take your hands off of me your grace!" She practically
shouted. Instinctively, her knee shot up with full force. Once
Ellis doubled over and he let go of her waist, she let her right
fist fly, exactly as Matthew had shown her when they were
young. The unmistakable sound of breaking skin rang
through the darkness as the Duke fell to an unconscious heap
on the ground after receiving the perfect right hook to
his jaw.

Charlotte let out a small shriek, her hands flying to her
mouth in disbelief when she saw him fall. Her attention was
then caught by the sound of a rattling hedge. She turned in
time to see Matthew jump over the rail and race out of the
shrubs. His fists ready, his eyes wide with fear.

The instant he saw Charlotte, he screeched to a halt. The
blood pumping through him visibly slowed as he surveyed
the scene. Each breath brought him to back to London, out
of the memory of battle and fear of torture and death. When
he finally looked at her, she knew it was Matthew, not his
memories, whom addressed her.

"Did my friend just box a Duke of the realm?" His eyes

were wide with disbelief and he still managed a small grin of admiration.

Seconds ticked through the interminable silence. They stared at each other over Ellis's body. Charlotte felt her stomach revolt as the meaning of what she had done revealed itself.

"There will be a reckoning for this moment," Matthew said under breath and both began to awaken from the momentary suspension of reality. He reached her in two strides, looking her up and down to ascertain her well-being.

"Are you hurt? Charlotte, did he hurt you?" He held her by the shoulders. His voice laden with concern.

Her eyes moved from Ellis's motionless body to her best friend. Her voice shook with the tremor of unshed tears. "I – I – I'm fine. He didn't, well he didn't do anything. I didn't give him a chance. I stopped him. He grabbed me too close, he tried to – oh Matthew it was awful! But, I stopped him. You taught me how, years ago, remember? I remembered how to box," Charlotte sent her fist flying into the air again and Matthew swiftly ducked before she hit him too. "So, I stopped him."

She felt his arms slowly curl around her shaking body. His heart beating beneath her ear, his warmth enveloping her, stilled her. They remained motionless until her breathing returned to normal, until she felt safe again.

"Did he hurt you?"

"No."

"Good." Matthew frowned. "Now, tell me please, what on earth were you thinking?"

"Pardon me?" She stepped out of his arms, her brows furrowed.

He held her at arms' length and scowled. "Have you lost your mind? Or were you just thinking about all of the pounds he would bestow upon your estate?" She saw the throb in his temple as though the effort not to yell was extenuating. "You trusted the one man I explicitly said was most untrustworthy. He had complete freedom to do with you as he wished."

"But, he didn't. I stopped him," her eyes widened when he snorted in response. Pangs of betrayal inundated her chest because her best friend was blaming her for the heinous actions of the Duke. Within the span of a breath he went from being her greatest source of comfort to being her mightiest judge. "Are you angry at me because of what he did?"

"Are you so desperate for money you would put yourself in danger?" He released a long breath. "Perhaps, you aren't the Charlotte I thought I knew." Sadness threaded into his voice. His eyes blazed but his voice betrayed a hollowness, perhaps a deep sense of loss. He wasn't judging her, she realized, he looked as though he didn't know her.

She closed her eyes trying to find a way out of the mess. A Duke lying unconscious at her feet, an unholy attraction to her best friend whom she seemed to be losing at the moment. Tears stung her eyes. She refused to let them fall. "We're friends Matthew but do treat me with more respect. I needed air and he gallantly accompanied me. As you can see, I didn't give him the chance to touch me so save your sermons because everything is fine."

"Everything is not fine," he ground out. "Anyone could have seen you leave the ballroom with him, just as I did."

"The Duke made sure we weren't seen, he was most interested in protecting my reputation," she replied.

Matthew remained silent and the meaning of her words filled the air around them.

She suddenly felt sick. "I'm a fool," she groaned. "A fool of a green girl. All of my meticulous preparations...and, I fell for a trick any child would have seen through."

"I see you understand your predicament."

Since he insisted on making himself the perfect target for her anger and humiliation, Charlotte's eyes blazed when she snapped, "There is no predicament other than you standing there waiting for the moment to gloat I-told-you-so. And why were you following me? I had the situation under control!"

He suddenly smothered her mouth with his hand and pulled her into the hedge and under the shadow of the staircase. Her muffled protests were stopped by voices on the terrace.

"Are you sure you're well mother?" The voice of a concerned son floated down.

"I'm fine Reginald, don't be ridiculous!" Charlotte recognized the cantankerous voice of Lady Westmount.

"Then what are we doing out here?" Reginald's voice had the tone of one who was accustomed to showing infinite patience.

"I had a feeling someone might need my help…"

"You're the hostess mother, not every silly young Miss' chaperone."

"This isn't just any young Miss."

Reginald snorted, which turned into a cough once Lady Westmount had shot him one of her looks, Charlotte presumed.

"Well, don't just stand there! Help me back inside!" Lady Westmount's commanding bark was soon followed by retreating footsteps and the firm closing of doors.

Charlotte released a deeper groan and slowly sank to the ground. "She saw me leave the ballroom with Ellis. I've placed everything in jeopardy on the hope of Ellis's proposal. And who will marry me now? I may as well pack up my belongings and leave London tonight. I'm ruined."

Matthew crouched down next to her, scooping her hands into his.

"Marry me." A command, not a question, delivered in a hoarse whisper.

"What?" She didn't have the strength to deny him again, "I don't want another honorable proposal full of pity."

"The longer we're out here the more irreparable the damage to your reputation. Cold logic isn't exactly the kind of proposal most ladies dream about, but we don't have time for epic romance."

"I've never dreamed of epic romance, you don't need to apologize. But, this isn't what I want either. I can't do this to you."

He clenched his jaw. "I'm not going to accept a second rejection. And right now, we must move him to a less visible spot." His head motioned to the heap on the ground.

"Right. The Duke. The Duke!" Her voice surged with nervous energy. She jumped up and began to tug at Ellis's unconscious body.

They lifted the Duke onto a bench concealed by a shrub shaped into a perfect rectangular prism. Once Ellis was safely bestowed, Matthew led her by the hand through the shadows to a doorway on the other side of the garden terrace. She heard him deftly open a door and they slid into what seemed to be the library. The eerie stillness of the Westmount library was penetrated by the floating notes of a successful ball. In the safety of darkness and secrecy, he stood before her holding her hand tightly in his.

"I'm still waiting for you to say yes," he said.

After releasing a rather unladylike sob, words pushed out of her throat. "You don't have to do this!"

"Do what?"

"Sacrifice yourself. I can face the consequences of my

actions. I might yet be saved. Perhaps no one else saw...Lady Westmount isn't known as a gossip."

"Charlotte..."

"I don't give up. I'm persistent and resilient. I've carried an ailing Earldom for so long, I won't let one disgusting old man, Duke or no Duke, break me," her sobs were coming more forcefully now because even she knew when she had been beaten. While they stood in the library her reputation was likely being shredded.

Matthew's voice was infinite gentleness. "It's no sacrifice. We need to let our engagement be known. On my honor, I've always considered it my duty to care for you. I can think of worse fates than marrying my childhood friend."

His eyes seared her with the intensity of his words.

Despite the passion of his words, marrying her was his duty, his honor. Charlotte's heart sank. Despite the nobility of his actions and her previous commitment to a loveless match, his words stung her very core. She took in the blue eyes in which she could drown, the dimple which was beyond charming, the smile which lit up his entire face wishing dearly for more than his honor.

The trouble was, if he had offered his heart, she most definitely would have said, no. Despite her deep desire for love and her sadness that a love match could never be hers, she realized she feared the emotion above all others. Her father had unraveled so perfectly that her mother was left in pain for years, pain she still carried in her eyes. How could she trust anyone to keep a vow of love when love had never lasted in her home? She had been trained to abide by her duty, and so a proposal for honor seemed easier to accept than one for love. Love had been a fantasy she had harbored to fuel her strength to go on, to beat the fates which had deemed her worthy of such a heavy burden. But, could duty be felt as deeply as the wondrous emotions

Matthew had elicited? Her eyes fell to his lips and she unwittingly parted hers as the memory of their kiss overcame her.

Within a heartbeat, he kissed her deeply. She felt his hand move possessively to the small of her back gently pulling her until every inch of her body was pressed against him. He felt tense, as though fighting for self-control. His tongue parted her lips and ever so gently, moved inside her mouth, lightly stroking, igniting.

She clasped her hands around his neck. He responded by deepening his kiss and she was sure he was equally enslaved to the emotions whirling around them. They kissed through ragged breaths, surrendering to the fire. His hands moving up and down her body, squeezing her close, consuming her, leaving a throbbing heat in the wake of every touch. Tongues teased, mouths caressed, lips lovingly lingered because each kiss left a burning need for more.

The warmth of his hand travelled up her back and found the front of her bodice. Ripples of shock froze her momentarily at the intimate touch, but the light pressure and warmth of his hand melted her inhibitions. How could a few simple brushes of his thumb make her belly burn and create such a throb? She had never dreamed of such intimacy, but this was Matthew and she knew she was safe.

He gently tugged at the delicate gown until she felt the cool air of night caressing her bare skin. He leaned her back, his mouth landing on the tender skin at her throat. He left a trail of warmth as he moved downward and finally took her nipple in his mouth.

Charlotte was inundated with glorious sensations traveling to the most remote regions of her body. Sweet warmth spread through her skin. He took his time and softly, gently worshipped the pink bud, his tongue lapping and loving until she was sure she would melt. Cool air enveloped her bare breast when he moved to the other side, offering the same luscious suckling, nearly bringing her to her knees.

His mouth moved up her neck and found her mouth once more. After a deep kiss, he pulled away. His voice was thick, his body belying his words, his hands clearly unable to stop from touching her. "Charlotte, my darling, we have to stop."

"No." A forlorn protest signalling her arousal made him chuckle with pleasure.

"I can't control myself much longer. We must go or I can't guarantee the safety of your virtue."

With pursed lips, she nodded hating that he was right. They took some time to even their breathing, and he helped her to arrange her clothing and hair.

"I'd make a great lady's maid," he joked, admiring Charlotte's perfect appearance when they finished.

"I doubt very much you would find employment."

"But look at my fine work," he feigned a crestfallen look.

"No one in her right mind would trust being unclothed around you."

"Oh, but you will," his brow arched as his voice dropped and Charlotte's stomach did the same. "Or, should I prepare for a second rejection from Lady Bentwick?"

She took a deep breath and studied him. "You're willing to change your entire life's path to ensure my safety and you've put yourself in Ellis's direct line of fire to protect my reputation. Why?"

"Need I remind you of the countless times I saved you as we grew up?"

"Even as we grew up, I'm so much younger than you and I was a lonely girl. Why make me your concern?"

"I was as lonely as you," he said, his face growing serious. "Robert had the Earldom thrust upon him and unless I was at school, I had no friends. There weren't any children who lived on the estate. Then, one day I found you stuck in a tree," he smiled briefly, "You weren't a nuisance to me...well, at first you were...your tenacity, curiosity, bravery were all qualities which I admired and still do. Being friends with you wasn't a choice. It was inevitable."

"I always thought I had forced myself on you," Charlotte laughed softly.

"You did," he said with a twinkle in his eye. "I wouldn't change any of it though. I'll never hurt you. I'll protect you with my life, you must know that," he said quietly, slipping her hands into his, as though pledging himself to her that very night, in the dark, still library.

"When I came to London, I prepared to marry a stranger, but marrying my dearest friend...We know each other as no one else does..." her voice trailed off.

"And that's a bad thing?"

"Yes. No. I don't know," she shook her head. Her grave error in judgement afforded little time to analyze other options.

He stepped closer to her, taking her face in his hands. "Charlotte, we can make this work. I promise."

"Bentwick is ruined. Any fortune you've amassed will be absorbed by my Earldom," she warned.

"And?"

"Why are you not the least bit worried about marrying a penniless Countess? About the tremendous task of rebuilding Bentwick? Why aren't you unnerved about losing your beloved bachelor's lifestyle?"

"I love penniless Countesses, Bentwick is an incredible Earldom and blast my bachelor's lifestyle," his mischievous tone made Charlotte smile. Then, he shrugged a shoulder and his gaze changed as he punctuated each word with enough feeling Charlotte was positive he was baring his soul. "You said yourself, be who I am and my life will fall into place. Being with you is who I am."

She swallowed nervously, asking more questions, biding for more time. "And the dark sadness which takes over you? What of that? You advised me to keep away from you when it occurs, and it seems to me as your wife, I won't be able to do that."

His lips moved to a soft smile of understanding, aware that she was stalling. "I thought you're not very good at following advice or orders of any kind. Being married to you is what I need. You're the only one who has helped me through moments of intense memories or nerves. And, I'm the only one who can help you out of this scenario. So, you see? We're perfect for each other."

"Of course," she said, exhaling loudly. He answered every question perfectly which only increased her doubts but she was out of time. "None of this makes sense. You said you'd rather be alone than miserable in marriage and I can't see how marrying me and taking on Bentwick will bring you anything but misery. But, you seem certain marriage won't destroy us. So, my answer is yes. I'll marry you and hope to God it doesn't end in ruin."

"Let's try to impart news of our engagement to our families with a little less gloom," Matthew smiled. "You've made the right decision. Trust me."

She bit her lip, trying to hide her smile. "If I didn't know you as well as I do, I'd say that you deliberately set out to marry me."

He flashed his most charming grin. "Perhaps, you don't know me as well as you think."

She rolled her eyes, but as they walked out of the library, she couldn't help but wonder if he was right.

CHAPTER 16

Standing at the threshold of the sunny parlor where Mother preferred to break her fast, Charlotte's fingers played with the muslin of her morning gown. Lady Catherine sat in the morning sunshine methodically stirring her tea.

"Are you planning on joining me, Charlotte, or will you simply stand there like a silly goose?" She saw Mother's perceptive blue eyes lift with a wry smile.

"I'm sorry!" The apology burst out of her mouth before she had a chance to think. Her gaze fell to her hands as the distasteful tinge of failure crept upon her.

"Whatever for?" her soft tone produced a deep groan of guilt from Charlotte.

"I failed! This enormous expense for a season and I failed to marry a peer to save Bentwick. Instead, I'm marrying someone I've known for most of life. I didn't need a season to marry Matthew. Oh!" She stomped her foot. Her torment was furthered by hateful self-recriminations for measuring Matthew's worth by his wealth.

"Oh, my dear. Come sit with me," Catherine patted the cushioned chair next to her.

Charlotte moved to the chair slowly, her head down. She sat, and after a deep breath, finally looked up. "Mother, I – we sacrificed so much..."

"I must admit I was quite surprised with your news last night," Catherine said, her brow raised slightly. "But, I'm also beyond thrilled. You don't owe any apologies for choosing Matthew."

Charlotte felt a fresh wave of tears rush forward when her face was lovingly caressed by the strongest woman she knew.

"I'm truly sorry the burden of saving Bentwick became yours. You must know I'm so very proud of how you've managed it all. I regret that due to this obligation you're not happy about your engagement to Matthew."

"Without you everything would have been lost years ago and everyone left destitute! And now they're going to be and it's my fault!" Charlotte said in between heavy sobs. She was utterly miserable about feeling miserable about marrying Matthew.

She had failed to secure the wealth Bentwick needed, she had shackled her best friend to a ruined estate and she was about to marry an honorable, handsome, charming man who viewed her only as a duty which would surely lead to his misery. She dropped her face into her hands, ready to indulge another deluge of tears when Mother's gentle voice subdued the onslaught.

"Do you remember the colt you saved when you were twelve years old? Everyone said he would not last a day after you found him injured in one of the fields. Even our groom repeatedly advised 'nuh tuh waste yer time with'im miss'," she imitated the man's deep tone and rustic accent. "You were tenacious and stayed in the stable with him day and night. Soon, the little animal was trying to stand because you saved him. You nursed him back to health. You refused to give up when all others had."

Charlotte kept her head down, but her tone was mingled with lightheartedness. "I really hope this story is a metaphor for Bentwick and not Matthew."

She heard the smile in Catherine's voice. "He's the most suitable match for you. Quite honestly, I'm so very happy about your marriage. I wish financially we had more to offer him, but Matthew will be just as good for Bentwick, if not better, than a stuffy peer who only offered money."

Charlotte could not help but think that Matthew would not have proposed if she had not fallen into serious trouble with the Duke. He had clearly felt honor-bound to save her from what the Duke's actions had almost done to her reputation, regardless of everything he had said.

And, now, he was chained to her ruined estates. S he could not shake the disillusionment that the only reason he had asked her to marry him was his honor. His character as a gentleman had prompted him to help her out of a dangerous situation. She was well aware that she had chosen to pursue money over love, but the thought of having only Matthew's honor instead of his heart was uncomfortable, disagreeable and terribly disappointing.

Except, how could she demand his heart when she did not know if she could ever offer hers? Matthew had been her dearest friend, and his kisses proved there was some kind of fire between them. Beyond that, she was completely uncertain about the kind of marriage they would have. At least in a match to someone like the Duke she would have been completely clear about her role. She would have known the expectations. A marriage to Matthew was past anything she had prepared for and it quite simply terrified her.

"Mama," her voice broke. Catherine's eyes widened at hearing the name she had stopped using for her very soon after her father's death. They had not spoken about Henry since he had died, and she knew Mother had suffered greatly due to the demise of the marriage and his subsequent death, but she needed to know. "Was your marriage to father one of love?"

Catherine's pause seemed interminable. Her shoulders rose and fell with several prolonged breaths. Her gaze fell to their intertwined hands. Without raising her eyes, she finally answered.

"Yes," her voice was a mere whisper. "I loved your father from the moment I met him. He was lively and fun. He had many friends and everyone adored him."

After another long pause, her brows furrowed. When she lifted her head, Catherine seemed to be looking beyond Charlotte, to another world and time.

"Henry was also quite mysterious. Every so often I would catch a glimpse of hidden darkness and it was alluring to me that he had this other side unbeknownst to all those around him. We married fully in love," her voice was wistful. She was silent for a long time and Charlotte instinctively knew to allow the story time.

Catherine's voice became heavy and lost its whimsy. "Your father's mystery was nothing more than extreme sadness." Irony clouded her tone and brought a shadow to her eyes. "He began to retreat a few years after you were born. He stopped coming to London for the Season. Then, he started to shun the company of friends and family. With each step his world became smaller, but he kept me within it. He clung to me as though I were the air that filled him with life. It was during that brief time when he revealed his plan for his Earldom. I believe that ensuring you would inherit his title, thereby making you a peeress of the realm and ensuring your welfare gave him the will to live as long as he did. While I was honored by his necessity of me, I was also weary of the responsibility for his life," tears fell upon their tightly clasped hands.

"I began to falter in my duties to him because I was overwhelmed. Very soon afterwards, he shut me out. He spent all of his time in his study and soon never left his room. But, on the last day I saw him, he smiled!"

At last, she looked at Charlotte squarely, tears streaming down her face. Her voice ragged and rough. "'It is done. Charlotte is my heir,' was all he said to me. Two days later, the sadness finally overcame him and I lost him forever."

They were blanketed by silence and Charlotte knew she could not be the first to lift it. She watched Catherine struggle with the weight of her memories.

"It did not begin painfully. We were happy for a while. And Lady Adelaide and the Earl were very happy as were many others whom married for love. Love matches do flourish my darling," Catherine gave her a small smile.

Charlotte cringed. If only Mother knew that her marriage was not one of love, what would she say to that?

"If you love Matthew, it is the best reason I can think of to marry. We have been able to manage the financial strain under your leadership. Imagine what you can do with Matthew by your side?" A wider smile broke through the tears showing an iron strength.

What couldn't she do, indeed? Charlotte was very well aware of Matthew's qualities. He wouldn't stop until Bentwick was reclaimed. In that respect, her choice of a husband had been a complete success. Her worries lay in whether or not love would form a part of their marriage. Either response left her chilled. If he did love her, would she have the courage to give him her heart? Clearly, such an act had left her mother in shreds. And, if he didn't, she might live the rest of her life with a heart in pieces because marrying Matthew for his money was, simply put, not right.

She returned her gaze to Mother. " Thank you, truly. I love you."

"And, I love you. Now my darling, Adelaide and Lady Elmvale will arrive soon. We're preparing for your engagement ball and wedding. Make sure you're here for luncheon," she exclaimed sunnily. Almost too sunnily.

For a brief moment, she had been privy to Mother's most intimate feelings and memories. Charlotte gleaned a deeper understanding of her strength and prayed that she had inherited such a quality to lead her own life since at the present moment she had lost complete control of where it would lead.

CHAPTER 17

As soon as the initial interrogation about the engagement ball and wedding was over, Charlotte fled, with her maid, Riley, close behind to the park. She appreciated Lady Elmvale's insistence on perfection, Lady Adelaide's affection for her soon-to-be daughter, and Mother's joy at a love match. So much happiness about her engagement to Matthew kept reminding her of the trouble which had led to it in the first place. She couldn't admit to them Matthew was acting honorably, merely saving her reputation and saving her from Ellis. She swallowed the truth, hoping they mistook her tight smiles for nerves.

Sitting in the shade of a generous elm, her hands moved effortlessly over the page. The instant her fingers gripped her pencil and hit the page, all tension eased away. She forgot why she had run to the park in the first place and became absorbed in her sketch of the soft grass, dignified trees and gentle sloping paths framed by verdant bushes before her.

"I really hope marriage won't change this aspect of our relationship," she heard the smile in Matthew's voice and her fingers stilled. Looking up, her cheeks were suddenly burning in his presence. It was inconceivable. The boy with whom she had shared every childhood adventure had matured into a most handsome, desirable man. He took a seat next to her, one knee up, arm casually slung over top of it, looking far too dashing for his own good.

"Like you interrupting my sketching?" She turned to him with a smirk and stilled when she noticed his intense study of her face.

"I don't think I'll ever tire of seeing your cheeks compete with the hue of roses."

"It's shameful of you to point out my coloring."

"What's shameful is I can't take advantage of it in a very public space," he said under breath and a current ran through her at the memory of the softness of his lips, his hair amidst her fingers, his hands upon her skin. She bit her lip as each recollection sent shards of pleasure running through her.

"Rendered you speechless, have I?" He smiled mischievously. "I'm glad to see you didn't leave your maid behind." He nodded toward Riley whom was in a cluster of ladies' maids at a careful distance.

"Was there a point to your interruption?"

"Yes, but I'd much rather discuss strawberries."

"Strawberries?"

"And rose petals."

"What?"

"I taste strawberries each time I kiss you. The hint of the luscious red berry taunted me for five years."

"You remembered," a soft smile appeared on Charlotte's face. She didn't know why the revelation brought her such joy, but it did. She was saturated with it.

"How could I forget? It was the memory of that kiss which spurred me to become a better man."

"One kiss from me prompted all that?" A raised brow challenged him.

"It was the purest kiss I'd ever experienced. The memory of you, your soft lips so innocently offered…it always reminded me of your dedication to your estate. You inspired me to take my roles seriously," he smiled the real, private smile she knew he only showed her. "Imagine that, Lady Charlotte?"

"I didn't know you thought of me in such admirable terms," she said looking a little shocked. "I didn't know you thought of me at all."

The blue of his eyes darkened as he stared at her. Without a single word, he made a tingle run through her until her toes curled. She bit her lip as his gaze and smile became predatory.

"I also can't seem to escape the scent of roses," he casually returned to his original flirtatious manner. "I'm wondering if you taste and smell the same everywhere. Or, will I find new and exotic scents, new flavors when my mouth travels over every part of you."

The pencil dropped out of her hand, and she was immediately thankful Riley was out of earshot, gossiping with the other maids down the path.

"Different parts…?" was that even possible?

He leaned closer, his warm breath reaching her ear and meandering down her neck. "Oh yes, my dear. My mouth will go everywhere. Unless, of course, you don't want it to."

"No! Yes!" She jumped, then narrowed her eyes when she saw devilish joy in his eyes. "Matthew!"

"Yes, darling. That's exactly how I wish to hear you cry out my name, but with slightly less anger."

"Horrid - "

"It will be everything but horrid. I promise."

"Matthew," she said with such warning in her voice, his predatory smile became victorious. "Was there something else you wished to discuss? If not, I'd like to get back to my sketch."

He was smiling fully now. "Sketching doesn't seem quite so exciting after strawberries and roses, does it? If you must return to it, I won't keep you, but I do promise to find the answer to my question soon."

There was nowhere to hide, and the way he was devouring her with a simple gaze, the last thing she wanted to do was hide. She recalled all the times he had challenged her and she refused to be bested by an insupportable boy. So, she rose to his challenge and levelled him with smoldering grey eyes.

"I can't wait to hear what you discover," despite her embarrassment, she couldn't help but try to beat him at his own game. A satisfied smile spread over her face when she saw him swallow, and for a moment, be rendered speechless himself by her light teasing. Taking a look around the park, she noticed a few pointed looks in their direction.

"It seems we're doing a good job of maintaining the gossip that we're a love match."

"Gossip?" His brows furrowed and Charlotte couldn't help but notice the slight disappointment in his tone.

"Yes," she said after a pause, "According to Lady Elmvale, the *ton* is abuzz over our epic love story. Apparently, the gossip is that we've been deeply in love for years and only just discovered it."

"Who knew I would be so good at romance?" he quipped, winking at her and laughing when she rolled her eyes. Despite his casual attitude, she knew there was something he was keeping from her . If only she could find a way to draw it out.

"For the first time since my father died, I'm not in control of my life. Ever since I knew I would become a Countess, I meticulously planned every move. The decision to marry you, arguably the biggest decision of my life, was made without the usual methodical analysis I've always preferred."

"Let's try to make all of our decisions like we made this one," he lowered his voice, referring to their kiss in the library.

"I'd rather not."

"It wasn't so bad, was it?"

"Matthew!" she laughed softly, "I'm trying to say thank you because somehow, without so much ado, everything seems to be falling into place. You've done your job quite well in saving my reputation. Are you afraid your perfect reputation as a rake will now be harmed?"

"To hell with my reputation," his tone and eyes grew serious. Warmth enveloped her as he leaned closer, his breath a caress to her face. "Perhaps I don't mind what the gossips are saying. Marrying you isn't some grand act of honor."

"Why did you ask me to marry you, then?" She jumped on his answer and watched him carefully. For fraction of a second, a look of raw vulnerability passed over his face. And, then it was gone. He had stopped himself from divulging something important and true. A light wave of disappointment surged through her belly. She cleared her throat and her voice became pragmatic, "We both know we wouldn't be engaged had it not been for - "

"Ellis? I won't give him the satisfaction. Let's pretend he wasn't there last night. And, let's go on as if my every intention was to ask you to marry me."

She willingly fell into pools of clear blue, basking in being his sole point of focus. She stopped wondering how bothersome Matthew Harrington could have such an effect on her. Instead, she allowed herself to be swept up by the lopsided grin, the warm breath reaching the exposed skin below her bonnet, the velvet voice assuring her she was more than a duty.

He reached behind him, producing two packages. He handed her the larger of the two and winked at her. "A gift for my future bride."

She received the gift with a curious grin. A small gasp escaped her lips when she opened the box and her eyes fell upon a beautiful volume about modern farming techniques to improve yield and safeguard lands for generations of farming.

"It's beautiful! Thank you," the whisper was directed at the hard cover. Her hands traveled the length of the spine inspecting the thick book.

"You like it, then?"

"I love it," she smiled through tears, noting the relief on his face.

"You know," he drawled, "it's nothing more than a promise of the many hours we shall spend apart because of all the work we'll be doing."

"We're not even married yet and you're already planning ways to be rid of me?" She teased lightly. "Only you know the importance of such a gift. Thank you. I promise to be a good wife to you. I promise to honor my duty."

She noticed Matthew's smile did not reach his eyes and wondered why he looked as though she had just pierced his heart. His jaw clenched when she gave what she believed was a meaningful vow. He was in some kind of internal battle, but she could not fathom what it was. If only he would tell her. They had never kept secrets from each other, but it seemed engagement had already begun to change the openness of their relationship.

It burned her because as long as she had known Matthew, he had run from the prospect of marriage with unparalleled swiftness. He despised weddings, engagements and anything to do with the institution - he had been late to his own brother's wedding! Why wasn't he just a little upset that his cavalier lifestyle would soon come to an end? Why was he not saying what he was feeling?

Perhaps, he wasn't planning on allowing it to end. He had changed deeply since his return, but any opportunity to reclaim his former lifestyle, to travel, to live the life he had once said he craved, would be denied him. Wouldn't it? He wouldn't dare continue a bachelor's lifestyle once married, she hoped. And, why wasn't he the least bit preoccupied about marrying a penniless woman? She had been flabbergasted at the amount of his fortune and his response had been a noncommittal shrug.

He broke her conflicting musings by lifting her wrist and silently clasping a diamond bracelet around it. Her eyes widened at the precious rope.

"Oh, my goodness! It's beautiful!" Her words were a whisper. She admired the bracelet and didn't stop to think about her next statement. "It looks terribly expensive."

She inspected the glittering stones tied to her wrist with awe and failed to notice Matthew had yet to respond. She inspected it closely, and before truly thinking about her words, she asked, "Are you sure the expense was wise?"

A few moments passed and the only response was stone, cold silence. She was forced to take her eyes from the bracelet. Matthew had straightened and was eerily still.

"Let me make one thing perfectly clear," all sense of play vanished and his voice was barely loud enough to reach her ears. "And, I'll say this only once. I may not have a Dukedom, but I have more than enough to care for and spoil my future wife."

At first, she thought he was teasing, but the seriousness in his eyes told her he had been deeply offended. She nearly scoffed at his audacity to be angry.

Arching a brow, she despondently straightened her spine with frightening rigidity. "I've spent my life weighing the validity of every expense. And, if that's something that'll make you immediately bring him up, when you just so eloquently stated we should forget about him, then let me make one thing perfectly clear, I won't stand for it."

"I've known for a very long time about your goal of marrying someone with the sole intent of saving your Earldom," he continued as though she hadn't spoken, "But, I didn't realize your desires for money ran so deep."

"If that is what you believe, then you know nothing about me."

"Evidently, it doesn't matter what I believe," he replied crisply.

In the time it took her to blink, Charlotte was facing the cold reality of a loveless match and witnessing the beginnings of erosion to her cherished friendship. All loveliness evaporated in the stark wake of Matthew's purposeful steps away from her. She was left utterly confused, sitting perfectly still under the elm tree.

CHAPTER 18

Charlotte rode out early the next morning as far as she could in desperate need to think. A quick glance back showed she was alone. She had stolen out of her stable with the swiftness of a thief unbeknownst to her groom whom would have obstinately escorted her to maintain propriety and ensure her safety.

To hell with propriety. Should she be in danger, she would ignore etiquette and outrace any criminal wishing to do her harm. Fortunately, the park was still, without another soul at so early an hour. She gently squeezed her heels inward urging her beloved steed just a little bit faster. The fresh air of dawn bathed her. The rich smell of dew-soaked grass and saturated soil cleansed her.

She meandered down the lane and even ventured off path to inspect some of the blooms. She dismounted and wandered into the foliage. A cool breeze danced upon her face, luxurious silence broken only by the rustling of leaves. Slowly breathing in the symphony of scents, her body ceased to tremor.

"Good day, my lady. Is there a reason you are out unaccompanied this morning?" Matthew's velvet tone wrapped itself around her.

Out of the corner of her eye she saw him dismount, unforgivably handsome. The cold fury she had witnessed yesterday was apparently gone. And, though happy to see his return to normal, she was also perplexed. She fully turned and found him standing within an inch of her.

Inhaling hints of sandalwood, her breast rose, nearly touching his jacket. A glint of amusement greeted her as his dimple appeared from a widening smile. Heat rose up from the tips of her toes, refusing to stop despite her attempts to keep a deep blush from spilling across her face. Good God, why had he stopped being annoying, bothersome and arrogant?

"Good morning," she stammered. "I rode out alone this morning. It was too early to bother the groom."

Brows furrowed over endless blue eyes. "Of course," his tone was clipped. "Well, it's a good thing your patterns are familiar to me. Charlotte, you're going to be my wife. No more gallivanting without a proper escort. Better yet, since you insist on riding every morning, I'll come along too. London is a dangerous place for a lady to not bother her groom or companion or maid, or even the cook."

"Did you just call my morning ride, gallivanting?" The changes in her friend simply because he was about to become her husband were dizzying. "You practically dared me through all of our childhood adventures, or at the least refused to be bested by a girl younger than you and now you're patronizing me?"

Her nostrils flared when his only response was a smirk. "I'll ride when and how I wish. My morning rides are essential to maintaining my estate. You're sadly mistaken if you think you'll be imposing more rules on me."

A stern scowl suddenly overtook his handsome features,

and Charlotte caught a glimpse of why he had fared so well in the military. "We aren't on your estate. You may be safer in Bentwick, but we'll evaluate that then. There are more dangers in London than you can dream of and I'll not have you exposed to them." He waved his hand in the air as if showing her the currently non-existent dangers lurking behind the bushes to prove his point.

"And, you won't limit my freedom to ride. I'm independent and can take care very good care of myself. Or, have you conveniently forgotten that? You will also stop judging me or throwing Ellis's name about each time you're affronted. And, you certainly can't make damning judgments about my character in moments of unreasonable anger." She met his impassioned gaze with a straight back, face meeting his, ready to defend.

She was disarmed nearly instantly by the slight drop of his head, his sudden change in tone, the subdued fire in his eyes. "I shouldn't have mentioned the Duke. You deserve better. Every time I think of Ellis and the way he almost hurt you…"

"Yes?"

"I'm sorry. I was - "

"An idiot."

"Yes," he smiled, "I seethe when I think about the Duke being anywhere near you. I remember how close he came to… Charlotte, I know what you've lived through. I don't know anyone stronger, or more intelligent and capable. Believe me when I say that is what I believe. It's no excuse for my behavior, or my words yesterday."

"No. It's not!" Charlotte huffed, trying to hang on to her indignation only to find it had evaporated.

She threw him a sidelong glance. "I hate to admit it, but that was a good apology."

"Yes, I rather thought so," he looked smug until she

pierced him with a smoldering look. "All of it was true," he said rapidly.

"So, why restrict my freedom to ride? You may as well restrict my freedom to draw."

His hand ran through his hair. "It's my duty to protect you. I almost failed once and it won't happen again."

"I've been protecting myself for years. Why is it that every man seems equipped with the capability of curtailing a lady's independence the moment he proclaims her his property? Do they take you aside at Eton for special instruction on how to manage us?"

"To answer your question in short, no. Although I know many a gentleman who would love instruction on handling the fairer sex, but not for the reasons you're implying," he smirked. Then, the gentleness she recalled him reserving only for her resurfaced. A finger lifted her face. "Is everything alright?"

"I knew the moment I accepted a gentleman's proposal I would be submitting my independence to him, and in addition to Countess, I would be wife and manager, and eventually, mother. Everything had been crystal clear – I was going to marry for Bentwick. But, ever since you proposed my world has been turned upside down and inside out. My best friend is about to become my husband and is commanding orders expecting me to obey. Everything is not alright."

Matthew released a long breath, his hand falling down the length of her arm until it captured her fingers in his own. "Are you going to cry off?"

"I'd never go back on my word."

"Of course." He exhaled loudly. "I was rather hoping everything would continue as always. We remain friends even though we'll be married."

Charlotte felt every fear about his intentions for their marriage unfold deep in her stomach. She nearly choked out the words, "With the exception that you can tell me what to do? Or, you may continue your bachelor's activities when you're a married man? Your vision for our marriage is for us to act like we're not married?"

"No. I don't want our friendship to end because we're married."

"Me neither," she sighed. "You're aware that means I wish to maintain my freedom." She rejoiced when he slightly winced. "I promise to remain safe, but you must promise to trust me."

"I've never not trusted you."

"It's different now Matthew. You keep behaving like a sermon-happy governess whom expects me to follow all the rules, but there will be none for you."

"What do you mean?"

She raised her brows in disbelief. "I've known you my entire life and even though you despise my saying so, you're a well-known rake. You may not be indulging in the same lifestyle now, but once you grow weary in our marriage, if you think I'll tolerate a parade of mistresses because we're friends -"

"There are no mistresses."

The words quietly and precisely cut through her tirade. His strength and warmth emanated through his gloves as the hand on her arm moved to gently cup her face. His face moved closer and for a moment she thought he would kiss her. His lips a mere breath away. Hints of soap and sandalwood from his skin mingled with the earthy freshness of the park enticed her as his words took hold of her.

"There haven't been any for a long, long time. I haven't been with a woman in years because I couldn't. I had no desire left." After a long look, he released her face and stepped back.

"Dreadful. Ghastly. Brutal. Horrendous. I can't find

enough words to describe what I saw of the living conditions, the disease, the war. There was no solace in casual encounters. I needed so much more than a physical moment to help me cope, to help me forget what I had seen and done. So, I committed to a life very opposite of what rakes are renowned for doing. When I returned home, every lady I met was obsessed with herself or her need of a husband. I knew the *ton* would not offer me a relationship of any substance. So, I remained true to my commitment of celibacy promising to break it only with the right person. But, I let everyone believe the opposite because I needed someone who knows me, not my name, not my position, not my supposed heroic acts and not my fortune. Now that I have her, I would never dishonor our marriage by bringing a mistress into my life."

The air grew thick with his confession. She had misjudged him. Cavalier attitude and charming smile hid a man who truly understood the importance of commitment, sacrifice, and loyalty. He had stripped himself bare by admitting his needs and fears, it would only be fair to reciprocate in kind.

She was too afraid. Admitting her fears, voicing her worries, confessing her failures was not what she had in mind for marriage. Her eyes lowered knowing she could not give him what he needed or deserved.

And then, he kissed her.

Feather light fingers raised her face and warm lips claimed her own with a velvet caress, promising infinite softness and spreading heat through her throat, through her chest, through her legs. Her hands slowly curled at his neck and her toes slowly stood on end, reaching for more. As she rose, her lips parted for him and she felt her mouth being worshipped by warm, moist, luscious strokes of his tongue.

She gave him what he sought, offering her mouth, positive that his kiss would surely make her melt. If this was what Matthew could do to her with a kiss, imagine when he did more? She couldn't help but notice how very well Matthew was kissing her and realized she didn't have a clue what she was doing. She understood the basics of the physical act due to the amount of time she had spent on farms. But the intimacy of it was something she had never known about. She was simply responding to him and following some kind of instinct he had awakened within her. He was Matthew Harrington, the most handsome man she had ever known. He was a charmer of women, was well-travelled and far more experienced than she. She was far from charming or flirtatious, what on earth could she offer him?

She felt his hands travel down her body and settle on the small of her back. He pulled her close as though sensing her hesitation. All space between them eliminated, she felt the hard lines of his body beneath his riding clothes. Her heart fluttered. She felt like the most beautiful creature on earth from all of his attention. Melting into his embrace, she allowed her fears and insecurities to float away. As each soft moan was safely caught by Matthew, her inhibitions were slowly stripped until she was courageous enough to be seduced by an epic rake. An epic rake whom would soon be her husband.

CHAPTER 19

"You're beautiful." Words vibrating between their lips, he kissed her again. "I'll surely die of impatience for the right to bare you nude."

Another kiss with deep, insistent caresses of his tongue trying to show her she was his fantasy and his future. The warmth of her mouth, the velvet of her lips ensnared him. He deepened his kiss, his body hungry for her skin, hungry to feel the glories of pleasure once again, and he wanted to feel everything with her. Only her. His need of her had grown exponentially since their engagement. He knew he was playing a dangerous game, but resistance was futile when his every cell called for her.

His legs parted hers and he pulled her close as his hands moved down to her bottom, pulling her up, towards the evidence of his desire. He was nearly driven to distraction when beneath her many layers he felt the very tentative tilt of her hips as she pushed towards him.

"You like this?" He heard the innocent question through a voice hoarse with desire.

"I think that's rather obvious."

"And you have done this before?"

"Isn't that the question which started all of this?"

"Did you like it then, too?" Steady grey eyes waited on edge for his response.

Very, very slowly his lips moved to her ear and his words were a whispered caress delicately wrapping itself around her.

"Nothing comes close to what I feel when I'm kissing you and I can't wait to do more." The tip of his tongue ran along the tender skin of her ear lobe. He saw the flesh of her throat erupt into tiny bumps of pleasure and felt her shiver as his hot breath travelled down her neck.

She tilted her head, pushing her hips further into his. He happily accepted the offering with a deep moan which was cut short when he heard a slight and very satisfied giggle.

"Are you laughing at me?"

"Is it shameful to admit that I like making you sound like that?"

"Evil vixen," Matthew said with a devilish grin.

With a whirl, he moved her to a more secluded spot. His lips never leaving hers. Hints of rose petals and strawberries invaded his senses. Once they were safely hidden from view, he held her firmly up against a tree. Doing away with his gloves, he slowly collected the hem of her gown. His lips devoured hers, his tongue explored every inch of her mouth and his fingers deftly lifted her petticoat and gathered up the hem of her chemise. All of her layers were slowly moving upwards. He froze above the edge of her stockings when he came upon the silkiness of her thighs.

This was Charlotte; his best friend and the woman who owned his heart. She had been everything, always. And, now his hands were freely roaming her warm, soft skin. His entire being sizzled. Moving expertly up, into the folds of her crumpled dress, against the silkiness of her inner things, he found the source of her fire.

He felt her startled jump when his hand cupped her most intimate place. He held her for a moment applying soft pressure, promising safety, promising pleasure. The tension left her body and she relaxed into his gentle hold. In true Charlotte fashion, her fire to learn more prompted her hips to move against his hand demanding a firmer hold. She made him burn with desire and it was torture to proceed slowly. His fingers ventured further, locating the gentle lines of her folds. Slowly outlining the soft skin of her entrance, carefully easing it open, he found the warm moisture hidden inside.

Gently exploring fingers were urged on by gloved hands digging into his shoulders. He dipped his tongue into her parted lips as his finger slipped inside her smooth, silky heat. His finger gently slipped in and out and Charlotte writhed beneath him. He wasn't sure whom was experiencing more pleasure, more torture.

His free hand found her gown and stays, easily releasing both. Abandoning her mouth, he took the time to love her breast until he heard Charlotte's soft mewls falling close to his ear. She encountered physical intimacy with the same passion she did everything else, the same curiosity and it made him certain he would die if he couldn't satisfy his desire, but he had to exert self-control. His own release was unimportant. He had to prove to her that she was the only one he would ever desire.

He felt her back arch against the trunk of the tree. His mouth left her breast and found her mouth once more absorbing her cries knowing she would lose control soon. His thumb located her most intimate point. Swirling gentle circles, producing more heat, more moisture. Her breath came more rapidly, matching the incessant motion of her hips into his hand.

In one last swift moment, his tongue sweetly caressed hers and he felt her contract, and for a moment he thought she would stop the wave, but it was too strong and he felt her let go. He held her close, absorbing the shudders of her release, offering a haven for her satiated body before falling limp in his arms. He waited for her to descend, for the last throes of pleasure to move through her before fanning light kisses over her face. He lowered the hems of her under-clothes and dress and placed the gown and stays in their proper place.

It was impossible not to stare, not to take her in. She smiled languidly. Her ivory skin was flush, her eyes glossy from the release of her desire and strands of her black hair swirled about her.

He grinned. "Seems our married life will be far more exciting than I let myself believe marriage could be. You should know I've just decided to have you in this state as often as I possibly can."

Her smile did not fade, but her brow furrowed with sudden concern. "Are you alright?" It was evident he would be rather uncomfortable riding back through the park.

"Don't worry about me," he assured her. "A few minutes discussing these blooms and I'll recover."

"My observations on favorite flowers are less than scintil-lating?" She asked wryly.

"I have a feeling that we could be observing soil being turned and I'll wish to continue what we just started." His voice held the promise of pleasure and her blush deepened. He didn't know when it had happened, but the sight of her coloring skin had become pure joy being shot through his veins.

"As much as I'd love to fire up your cheeks even further, we should return." He forced a relaxed smile ordering his body to ignore the frustration for he had no intention of taking Charlotte's virginity in a hedge at the park.

They walked back out to their horses once she pinned stray locks back in place and firmly set her hat. She was the picture of grace and Matthew couldn't believe that only moments ago she had trembled so fervently in his arms.

Just before they mounted, he gently held her face. Their eyes steadily looked into the very soul of each other. "Only you Charlotte. Only, ever you."

I love you.

The words stubbornly remained in his heart and would remain so until he was certain she loved *him*, not his wealth, not what he would do for Bentwick, not that he had saved her reputation. Because beneath the cavalier attitude towards marriage and the mature man whom had returned a war hero with enviable wealth was a frightened boy. A boy whom believed those he loved could readily disappear. His father had gone too soon and his undesired though fortunate future depended on the loss of his beloved brother. It seemed, to Matthew, that too much of his life had been defined by death regardless of how charming he had been. Admitting his love to Charlotte meant he would never survive losing her. So, he kept the words locked up inside where they would safeguard his heart.

The great paradox of this course of action was his desire for Charlotte to love him in return. He wanted to show her that their marriage could be about so much more than convenience, hard work, or passion. The rub lay in the fact that his dear friend would run from love as swiftly as he once claimed he would from marriage.

They were quite the pair, he scoffed mildly and pretended to sneeze when Charlotte gave him a quizzical look.

He ignored the nagging doubt suggesting Charlotte would not love him in return. She had witnessed his darkness and had helped him through with complete calm. She knew every part of him, commendable traits and not; yet, only moments ago, she had given so much of herself to him he was almost humbled by her fearless passion. It was clear that physically at least, they were very well matched. Using passion to get to her heart was certainly an added bonus, he thought slyly.

He grinned, aware of the challenge he had set for himself. He had to somehow find a way to overcome his fear and help her overcome hers in order to achieve what they both believed to be impossible, a happy marriage based on love.

CHAPTER 20

Charlotte stood in a corner of the ballroom trying to catch her breath and admire the beautiful ball the Earl and Countess of Elmvale had thrown for her engagement to Matthew.

The room was draped in white flowers. White linens trimmed with gold reflected light throughout the room casting every one present in dreamy softness. The scent of roses enveloped every guest in thoughts of romance and love. The food was exquisite, the music delightful and all were giddy because her marriage to Matthew was a love match of the most romantic proportions. Imagine spending your childhood living next to the boy who would one day become the man you married, not because of parental agreement, but because of love.

Evangeline, Isabella and Julia were doing a fine job of ensuring the gossip remained in that vein. Charlotte ensured to maintain the story for it benefitted both her and Matthew, and the Earl's toast to their happiness had everyone swooning, solidifying their belief.

With a stolen look at her future husband, she wished he

would spend more time next to her and not showcasing his charm to all of the married ladies and widows whom received his polite attentions with a distasteful overdose of excitement.

Her observations were forcefully interrupted when the very air surrounding her chilled. The Duke of Ellis casually stood by her side. His eyes were black holes which promised torture. He fixed them on her.

"The lady of the hour! I was surprised when I received the invitation to your engagement ball."

"The Countess of Elmvale wouldn't dream of offending your grace."

"She's an intelligent woman. Perhaps, take a cue from her my dear. I trust you are enjoying a ball in your honor, Lady Bentwick."

"Thoroughly, your grace."

"My wife would have enjoyed this ball. She was an avid supporter of *love matches*," his voice curdled the air. "Ours was one. But, she left me far sooner than expected and since her passing I have been forced to attend these horrid functions alone. I am left to devise my own forms of entertainment since she is no longer with me."

After what seemed an interminable silence, he spoke again. "It is unusually warm for this time of year. Could I interest you in a breath of fresh air? I believe the Countess takes great pride in her gardens."

Inwardly, Charlotte nearly choked, on what she did not know for she had no drink in hand. He had repeated the exact statement of the infamous night she had boxed him. Outwardly, however, there was not a speck of discomfort evident on her face. She should have been awarded for retaining her cool demeanor in the face of such insult. "I'm afraid I must decline your kind offer, your grace, I feel a bit of a cold coming on and I don't wish to encourage it by taking cool air at this time."

"Oh, my dear Lady Bentwick, you should be afraid." Ellis lunged at her choice of words and his voice was a sharp blade slicing towards her. "I am owed for what you and your Honorable intended did to me."

Charlotte took a deliberate pause. She refused to let him feel he had the upper hand, deciding the less she said the better she could control the timbre of her voice. "Pardon me, your grace?"

"Oh, I believe Lady Bentwick comprehends more than she admits," he snarled. "I could have ruined you, both of you, but I am a kind-hearted man and decided against it. I believe that as a consequence of my goodness and failure to report you," he stared at her with hard black eyes, "you are indebted to me. We would have had a lovely time in that garden Lady Bentwick, but I believe we will have an even better time when you willingly come to me. Married or not, you shall give me what was denied me that night and you shall do so of your volition as a form of redemption for your injuries upon a Duke of the realm. I will call upon you the day I wish to collect payment for your debt and you will abide. If you do not, your honorable husband will pay the price with his life," Ellis finished with a deadly glare.

The words coiled around her constricting her breath, almost squeezing the will out of her. Almost.

"I highly doubt Margaret would approve of your form of entertainment," Charlotte spat back, holding her ground when fury sparked through his eyes at her audacious use of his late wife's name.

"She left me. She abandoned me and our sons. Her opinion is meaningless now."

"Then stop invoking her and leave her in peace."

"You'll pay dearly for your stupidity. Be ready, dear

Countess, when I call. It would be a shame to widow so young. Trust me, I would know."

To the untrained eye, the Duke was merely enjoying a chat with the honored bride-to-be. They ended their exchange with severe politeness and no one was the wiser to the Duke's blackmail. Or, at least, Charlotte hoped no one was.

Later that night, Matthew sat in the library unable to finish his drink. The Earl's guests continued in delightful revelry celebrating his engagement. He had slipped out once Charlotte departed on the excuse of a head ache, which everyone charmingly allotted to nerves. Matthew suspected otherwise for she made her escape only moments after Ellis had left her side.

From the opposite side of the ballroom, he had witnessed every second of their interaction and he knew it had been torturous for Charlotte, despite her cool, controlled exterior. His knuckles whitened around the glass in his hand. He had had little respect for Ellis before his attack on Charlotte, but now he would gladly rid the *ton* of the most despicable peer it had given birth to. Ellis had remained in the ballroom after Charlotte's departure and he was certain he had seen a disgusting smirk on his face when she had. Out of deep respect for Robert, he had exercised great restraint not to call the Duke out and meet him in the morning. Every one of his instincts yelled that Charlotte was in danger and he needed to discover why.

His body was suddenly filled with intense desire to see her. If the Duke had threatened her in any way, she could not spend the rest of the night in fear.

He left by the back door and kept to the shadows. Within ten minutes, anyone watching the garden wall of Bentwick

House would have missed a peculiar shadow stealthily going over it because it moved with such swiftness, it was gone before it was even noted. He deftly unlocked a garden door and made his way upstairs hoping to remember the location of Charlotte's bedroom based on the window she had pointed to on one of their walks. Within moments, Matthew was standing in front of a door hoping Charlotte would be on the other side, lifting his hand he knocked ever so gently.

CHAPTER 21

Charlotte's eyes stubbornly refused to close because the memory of Ellis's face loomed, waiting to taunt her with his threat.

Come to him or Matthew dies.

She whipped the bedcovers off, grabbed a soft blanket and fell into the chair by the window. Angrily undoing her braided hair hoping the lack of constriction would somehow help her to think. She ran her fingers over her scalp, prompting the solution forward.

A long sigh escaped her lips. She wrapped the blanket over her shoulders, protecting herself from the cool night air and from the memory of Ellis. Each time the dark abyss of his eyes flashed in her memory her stomach clenched with need to empty its contents. She would outwit him because one thing was absolutely certain, she would never betray Matthew. She had already placed him in the impossible situation of marrying her and therefore becoming responsible for Bentwick, she could not add infidelity to her list of undesirable gifts.

Underestimating Ellis had been a grave error in judgment

she would not repeat. If he was not satisfied, he would force Matthew into an illegal duel which he would ensure to end with Matthew's death. Her head fell into her hands. Matthew's ability to duel honorably was unquestionable, but she knew Ellis would seek a satisfactory vengeance to appease his bruised ego. If she did not submit to him as he desired, the man would ensure Matthew be killed.

The thought of danger coming to him forced her head up. Ellis fully believed she would go willingly to him, like a lamb to the slaughter, because he had threatened to injure Matthew. Her jaw clenched. Her hands clenched into fists and she swore by everything she held dear that her best friend would remain unharmed. She would never go to Ellis and she would protect Matthew at all costs.

Fortunately, the Duke underestimated her. Her hands trembled as she lit the lamp on her desk. The dark bedchamber was pierced by a soft glow. Slowly, the answer came to her. A plan to outsmart the arrogant, sinister Duke became clear. She would need the help of a few powerful peers whom also considered Ellis a stain on the peerage. If she could convince them to help her, she could finish the Duke. She would wait for his call, and whenever that would be, she would be ready to destroy him.

Bloodthirsty readiness to destroy a Duke of the realm in order to protect Matthew?

Clearly, her feelings for him ran deeper than she admitted. He had always been dear to her. He had been her only friend. He knew her the way no other person ever had. Certainly, that closeness was reason enough to be vehemently ready to plot the annihilation of another human being, wasn't it? She shook her head. There was no point in assessing the truth of her feelings because thinking could lead to dangerous revelations.

She could not love him. It was impossible to ask her heart

to put down its shield and allow love to flourish when all she had known as a child was isolation, sadness and pain because the man whose love she had most wanted was never available.

She couldn't willingly put herself in the same situation with a husband. Imagine, loving Matthew, a man who had scoffed at marriage for as long as she'd known him. Imagine, waiting for love as an adult in the same way she had waited for it as a child. The thought made her ill.

No. They had friendship and a deep history and obviously, passion, she reasoned, with a leap in her belly. But, she couldn't fool herself into thinking there would be love. Hoping for love had been foolish, at least the fates had given her the chance to marry someone whom brought out so many other good feelings – she should be grateful because she could have ended up with someone like the Duke. That thought made her ill, too.

In the meantime, she had to ensure the true nature of her encounter with the Duke remained hidden. Matthew would surely become all male about it, pontificate about his duty to protect her and then do something stupidly honorable like challenge the man to a duel, which would play right into Ellis's plot.

Her thoughts were interrupted by the softest of knocks. Her head turned sharply in the direction of the sound listening for it again. It could not possibly be her maid at this time of night. Charlotte walked very slowly to her dressing table and took hold of the first thing she could find to defend herself with, a comb. She approached the door quietly and froze when she heard a man's whisper.

"Charlotte! Charlotte! Don't be afraid, it's me. Open the door."

Matthew? What on earth? She held the comb firmly in her right hand and very slowly opened the door to a sliver with her left. She glued herself to the door and peered out into the dark corridor. Her eye widened when she recognized the disheveled brown hair. She immediately stepped back and let Matthew into her room.

He closed the door behind him and locked it.

"You look like you've seen a ghost," he said as though he were discussing the latest gossip.

"You're in my bed chamber," she said in a stunned, matter-of-fact voice. "In the middle of the night."

It suddenly dawned on her that she was wearing nothing more than a sheer night gown. She quickly brought her long black hair forward to cover up as much as she could. The action seemed to have helped her regain her voice for she asked in no uncertain terms, "What are you doing in my bed chamber in the middle of the night?"

"Isn't it obvious? I had to speak with you."

"Now?" Her eyes widened. "It couldn't wait until a decent hour?"

"No," he replied swiftly, "It had to be tonight. Right now." He suddenly eliminated the space between them in one smooth stride.

In her bare feet, Charlotte found herself face to face with his broad chest. She looked up and saw his blue eyes had darkened. He stared at her with fierce intensity, his gaze travelling over her as if to ascertain her well-being. His thick brown hair was wild from the night time breeze. A Greek god sailing passionately through the night. The effect of his good looks, however, vanished the moment he spoke.

"What did Ellis say to you?"

"What?" He had risked life and limb, alright maybe not life, but he could have broken a limb, to discuss the Duke. In her bedchamber. In the middle of the night.

"I know with every fibre inside me that he wasn't merely

offering his congratulations after what happened in West-mount's garden. What did he say?"

"We really must address the use of your military tone on me. It won't work, so stop bothering."

"Did he threaten you? Did he insult you? Charlotte, if I'm to protect you, I need to know what he said."

"You would've known what he said if you had been by my side instead of graciously conversing with other ladies all night." Her words were meant to distract; however, they left a rather bad taste in her mouth along with a sharp stab to her heart. It seemed she was more bothered than she was ready to admit.

"What other ladies?" Then, he shook his head as though refusing to be diverted. "What precisely did Ellis say to you?"

"It's unimportant," she tried a casual shoulder shrug.

"Charlotte," the warning tone, the hands balled at his side told her he was grasping thinly at self-control.

She pursed her lips knowing she needed to get him out of her home before scandal fell on them both. She paused to remember the Duke's words and used them so that what she told Matthew wasn't a complete fabrication though she did mutter her way through the words she inserted feeling utterly guilty at voicing them. The only feeling stronger than her guilt for lying was the need to keep him safe.

"Very well. He said…he said that we owe him *an apology* for our treatment of him that night, that he was kindhearted and good in his failure to report us. He said that our debt to him will be paid by me, in the form of a *heartfelt apology,* and that no harm will come to either of us when I do. So, I shall *write* him this *letter of apology* promptly and I'll deliver it to him when he calls upon me to do so and not before that because he still needs time to prepare for the, uh, *apology.*"

Matthew crossed his arms and fixed her with a hard stare. "A letter?"

"Yes," Charlotte replied primly, her fingers running lightly over the comb. "Now can we please stop talking about Ellis in my bedchamber in the middle of the night?"

He fell silent. Turning from her, he paced the room with hands clasped behind his back. His thoughts assessing, balancing, analyzing the situation were almost audible. "I can't believe that's all he's demanding. He's playing a game and his real demand is yet to be revealed."

Fiercely controlled facial muscles masked the daggers of accusation striking Charlotte's chest. She had to lie. She had to prevent him from seeking out Ellis and possibly be killed in an illegal duel.

"We can't know that nor can we surmise it. I can't keep discussing a man I would rather forget for the rest of eternity." Finally, a pure, utter truth.

She watched him deliberate carefully. His hand ran through his hair and she was able to breathe again. He would let it go, for now. Hopefully, he would be too distracted by their marriage and the restoration of Bentwick to think about the Duke again. So, by the time Ellis came to collect his *apology*, she would be ready to eliminate him from their lives forever.

Matthew hung his head slightly, giving her one of his sheepish looks. She smirked and rolled her eyes.

"Really Charlotte, what had you planned on doing with a comb?"

She looked down, realizing the comb was still firmly in hand and laughed aloud. "You'd be surprised. Riley does a fine job of showing me the dangers of a comb each time she jams it into my head. A good hard poke in the eye and I'd have a criminal down before he could say comb."

After a shared, hushed laugh, Matthew sobered. "You need a weapon. I'll teach you how to use it and where to keep it. It'll be my first husbandly duty."

The moment of playfulness ended when she saw the change in his gaze. He looked at her with a mixture of tenderness and possession. Feather-light fingers cupped her face. "If I'd been by your side, Ellis wouldn't have had the chance to be anywhere near you. I won't let anything happen to you."

"Nothing will, I promise." She leaned her cheek into his palm, his thumb lightly caressing her face, feeling the endless comfort and security he had always given her. She looked into his eyes and made a silent promise to protect him as fiercely as he had always taken care of her. A small smile came to her face when a lopsided grin appeared on his.

And that was when he realized how deliciously alone they were.

CHAPTER 22

Every beat in Matthew's chest was a command to make the beauty materializing before him, his.

Charlotte's lush silky black strands fell all around her, adorning her body, and framing a wispy night gown. He inched closer, without thought, like a magnet finding its pole. Blue eyes darkened by unfulfilled passion, by fear for her well-being, by the very primitive need to keep her safe, and focused solely on her. He was consumed by the desire to possess her, to make her his. He needed to feel her beneath him trembling with desire for him and forgetting her damned duty.

Each step led her tentatively backwards until she bumped into her dressing table and had nowhere to go. He extended both arms to lean so very casually against the table and essentially caged her in. A sly, languid grin and predatory eyes hovered breaths away from her face.

"Did you actually feel my absence?"

A provocative purr over her lips. Every rise and fall of her breast told him her blood was pumping as quickly as his.

Intoxicated by her warmth, by her sweet breath falling onto his neck, he knew it was time for his vow of celibacy to come to its end. He noticed when she gingerly placed her fingers on the table behind her, seeking support for the heat between their bodies threatened to make them melt. He waited patiently for her response, eyes drinking her slowly with a heavy-lidded stare.

"Did you really sneak through the streets of Mayfair in the dark of night, scale walls and infiltrate my home just to ask me about Ellis?"

"Can you ever answer my question without one of your own?" His lopsided grin softened the mocking tone. He felt her warm sweet breath sweep over him as she exhaled and knew the fiercest army could not tear him away from her.

"Partly, yes," he answered with an unwavering gaze. "But mostly," he paused and the air around them grew heavier. His voice was a rough whisper, "I had to do this."

He lowered his face, happy to see her raise hers to meet him, and kissed her. The warmth of her lips gradually seeped into his body. Infinite softness soothed away worry, doubt, fear. Her hands left the security of the dressing table, curling themselves around his neck. Sinking deeper into her warmth, feeling her breasts rise to meet him sent a myriad of sensations to every region of his body, especially when he felt her kiss him back.

Butterfly wings moved tentatively over his mouth. Curiously searching lips became impassioned and shyness gave way to need.

He gladly gave her what she sought. Tender, insistent, worshipping of her mouth. The woman he loved was kissing him, trying to show him her passion and desire for him. He was humbled by her innocent curiosity and knew he wanted her more than anything he had ever wanted in his life. He ached to make her his, but he remained rational enough to know he had to do it right. A soft groan of hardship escaped his throat when his lips released hers.

"It was a very worthy idea," Charlotte said thickly, wearing a playful smile. "I can't believe we're going to be married. You're the boy I raced across the meadows and the boy who helped me down from trees when I realized I was too high off the ground," she gave a short laugh which soon became rueful. "You're still saving me."

He raised his brow and cleverly opted to ignore her first admission that his proposal had avoided a near disaster to her reputation. The way the proposal had transpired no longer mattered. Sour events had merely precipitated what he had wanted.

"I'm not saving you," his voice was thick with desire, "I'm marrying you."

Because I love you. The words remained in his throat because Lord knew he wasn't ready to be rejected by the only woman he had ever loved. Voicing his feelings would only make him vulnerable because if anything ever happened to her, he would be lost. As he had been when his father died; perhaps, even, as he would be whenever Robert would die.

However, the present moment wasn't exactly the time to be pondering his dread of love and loss. Pushing all fears aside, he showed her how deeply he cared. He kissed her hungrily. His warm tongue claimed her, teasing, cajoling, caressing her mouth, promising more. His lips took the time to devour and consume, and he joyfully felt her surrender to his soft command. Words of love could not be spoken yet, but his body would happily express his love until he knew she was ready to hear it, until he was certain she loved him too.

The evidence of his desire grew harder between them. Charlotte broke their kiss, looking at him with infinite trust.

"We're in a precarious situation, don't you think?" Her

smile bathed him in a very different kind of warmth than their kissing had produced. He raised his brow in assent.

She bit her lip. He wanted so desperately to do the same, he forced his eyes back to hers. "What shall we do about it?"

"We've always been honest with each other, and, well, I think all it would take is one word from me and you would become my husband this very night."

"While that idea is a very worthy one. And, I have to admit I'm in agony and hoping for such an occurrence – dearly – I can't expect, nor will I force you to do something –"

"Yes." She smiled with such radiance all arguments, which were counterintuitive to his every desire, vanished.

"Matthew, you're going to be my husband – under circumstances which were out of my control. I came to London for a husband, under pressures which were not my creation. I'm tired of being a slave to my Earldom, to society's expectations of me. I want this part of my future marriage to be on my terms, since no other part of my life has been."

The mixture of tenderness with the steel of her conviction told him she was prepared to offer herself before they exchanged vows. It was an unparalleled gift. He kissed her deeply, capturing her moan in his mouth. Remaining rational and controlled after years of celibacy proved to be excruciating.

She was worth it. She deserved a slow pace, even though it would surely drive him mad.

His lips remained firmly on hers, his tongue loving her mouth as fully as possible. His hands found the lush ocean of raven strands falling all around her. His fingers roamed its silky waves, fragrant roses splashed up to greet him, bewitching him further under her spell. Nearly drunk with sweet torture, he lifted his head and studied her intently. Her grey eyes darkened and her lids heavy with desire were barely able to lift to meet his eyes. The flush of her cheeks and her swollen pink lips told him he could spend the rest of his life making love to her and it would not be enough. Still, he needed to be sure she was ready to join in their intimacy as a willing participant.

Charlotte saw what he was looking for and her lips formed the words but she could not find her voice. She smiled languidly and tried again.

"Yes," she whispered hoarsely with a dazzling smile.

Matthew carefully ran his fingers through her long soft locks sweeping them aside leaving nothing but the sheer fabric of her night gown as a barrier between them. His hand could no longer resist and he let it free to roam her lithe, taut lines as his lips returned to hers. Her soft curves slid seamlessly between breast, waist and derriere. Slowly, his hand moved down and up. Gentle strokes, tender hugging, intoxication in the palms of his hands while his tongue caught more of Charlotte's tiny moans.

He slowly untied her gown, loosened it and ever so gently, draped it over her shoulders until its own weight caused it to slip down her body pooling at her feet. He breathed in sharply as he took in the shock of black hair at her center and its contrast to her porcelain skin complimented by pink buds on small breasts and pink swollen lips, a mass of raven tresses tumbling around her, falling down to her waist. Matthew stared at every curve believing he had surely died and was being visited by a siren.

"I don't think I'll ever tire of having you look at me like that," Charlotte said, a small shiver quivering through her body.

"As a gentleman, I should be offering protection from the

night air brushing your body, but that would mean covering up a most beautiful work of art." His voice vibrated with insatiable hunger, eyes roamed every inch of her

"Really? I'm an imposter. I lack elegance and my body is far too strong to be a lithe lady of the *ton*," she said. All complaints ceased when she was in his arms once again and felt his hand slip around her waist.

"You're gorgeous," he said with complete seriousness as he lowered his mouth to her neck and continued exploring downward.

She dropped her head back and he feasted on her offering. His mouth suckled, teased and lapped, giving loving attention to each breast and feeling her writhe beneath him.

"Matthew," an urgent whisper. She gently tugged at his waistcoat and then lifted her brow at the obvious discomfort his clothing was causing.

He gave her a cat like smile and divested his garments as quickly as he could. Charlotte giggled when he struggled with his boots while he silently cursed. Hearing her laugh at that particular moment was not quite what he had in mind.

"You're amused by my discomfort." He finally stood wearing nothing more than his white linen shirt, his tone indicating that he was anything but amused.

"Well, you're amusing." Charlotte grinned. "I'm also quite nervous. Besides, do we have to stop teasing each other because we're in my bedchamber?"

"No. We don't," he cupped her face. "And while I'd much rather hear you cry with desire, I adore your level of comfort with me right now."

Everything inside him stirred when she smiled brilliantly at him. Evidently a little laughter would not dampen their moment. Despite his immense effort for self-control, he had reached his limit and could not wait any longer. Lifting her in his arms, he carried her to the bed and gently laid her down.

Sitting next to her, he took her hand in his. "Charlotte, are you sure?"

"Yes." She leaned up on her elbow and kissed him. It was all the invitation he needed. Pulling his shirt over his head, he laid beside her.

Mouth instantly finding hers, hands slowly caressing her stomach, her hip and moving inwards finding silky porcelain skin on fire everywhere he touched. Until, he found her. A deep moan rumbled through his throat when he was greeted by her hot slickness.

She writhed in response to his exploring hand, offering him wider access. Charlotte balled the sheets beneath into her fists, and her beckoning mewls encouraged him to delve deeper.

He explored her fully, tracing the delicate skin of her womanhood and finding her point of singular pleasure, teasing it until the wave was too strong and she shuddered fully, fighting to keep from crying out her desire.

Her skin was glorious silk, her hair ribbons of velvet and her mouth delectable. He held her and kissed her and told her he wanted to give her such pleasure again.

Matthew positioned himself above her, gently pulling her closer. He lowered himself onto her and gently began his entry. It took every ounce of self-control he had left to ever so slowly, join them. As every inch of her warm silky skin made contact with his, he knew this would be the most special night of his life. He had been with other women, but no experience could compare to this moment. He was sharing his body with a woman he loved and he intended to make it absolutely perfect for her.

Passion gave way to curiosity, he saw as Charlotte watched with baited breath.

"This might be easier if you relax darling. Am I hurting you?" he asked.

"Not quite. I'm wondering if you'll fit."

Despite the unrelenting need for release he stopped and nearly laughed. "Darling, that is truly the most complimentary thing you've ever said."

Before she could ask another question, he pushed in a little further. Her brow furrowed but he couldn't stop. Glorious tight heat welcomed him, beckoned him further. He pushed through the incredibly soft, tight space finding the proof of her innocence. He came down closer to her, leaning on his elbows, his face above hers, his thumbs brushing her flushed cheeks.

"I'm sorry my darling, I'm trying to do this as slowly as possible. It will hurt a bit, but will feel better soon," Matthew whispered – hoping this was true, but too far gone to care. He had never bedded a virgin and had heard the soreness subsided. He hoped it was true because he couldn't stop and she looked at him with such deep trust.

In one swift thrust, Matthew buried himself inside her. She cried out once and he stilled until she nodded once the initial pain and shock subsided. Matthew tried to contain himself, to make it pleasurable for her, but he knew after years of self-imposed celibacy, he would not last long. He moved his hips slowly into her and his senses were overtaken by her exquisite tightness holding him, enveloping him. It was sweet torture.

He began to move slowly, pushing deeper into her with each thrust. She held her breath until sheer necessity forced her to exhale, her breath moved through her, pushing her hips towards the delicious pressure.

"Again, darling, again," Matthew urged in a pained breath.

She moved upwards again and began to match his slow

movements, raising her hips up towards him, rhythmically meeting him. Her breath quickened as she urged him deeper. Her body moved beneath him bringing him into the most profound parts of her.

He fell further into her as she kept pace with him, ragged breaths, deep moans, hot skin, wet mouths and he knew they would not last much longer.

Matthew felt his explosion begin to erupt but he had to make sure she was with him when it did. Just a little longer, he nearly ordered himself aloud. He bit his lip and clung to the sheets with both fists ordering his body to control itself. He looked down and saw Charlotte's eyes full of desire for him and was nearly undone. Kissing her deeply, her warm mouth received his, her arms wrapped around his neck.

Arms, legs urgently forcing him deeper, entangling their bodies together to fully become one. He felt her begin to tighten around him. Deep inside her, there was a contraction and a slow explosive heat began to greet him.

He buried himself inside her feeling her mounting heat finally burst and the overwhelming flood of satisfied, sweet desire sweeping through her took hold of Matthew, sweeping him into his own outburst. A fierce contraction gripped his body and he exploded into her. The intensity of their heat drowned him, filled her. His love, desire and sheer need of her all released, and he joined her in the throes of passion.

They floated down, remaining locked, one within the other. Deep breaths, gentle kisses and words buzzed all around them. Moments later, Matthew settled himself behind her, holding Charlotte in his arms, running his fingers through her long black hair. She was his and he would care for her with his life. Nothing would ever happen to her because he would never allow for the pain which had attacked him when his father died to occur again. Losing her was unthinkable.

He had broken the chain of celibate nights with the woman he loved, his best friend. Holding her tight, he knew his life would never be the same again.

CHAPTER 23

Charlotte moved into the warm cocoon of Matthew's embrace. She was supposed to have married a wealthy peer of the realm, a man she had never met, and fulfilled duties to protect Bentwick and her family name.

Instead, she was marrying her best friend, who though wealthy, was not as rich as Bentwick needed and not a titled man, and the only duties she was fulfilling were those to her wanton body.

She suppressed a giggle because she had never been happier. It suddenly dawned on her that the happiest memories of her life had always included Matthew, so it seemed somewhat appropriate that these new memories of passion she had never known should include him also.

A kiss on her shoulder interrupted her thoughts. "Did I hurt you?"

"No. I feel wonderful," stretching languidly, she turned to face Matthew with a private smile hoping many future nights would be precisely like this one.

"You may be sore in the morning, darling. In fact," he looked around and stood.

"Where are you going?"

"I'll be right back," he whispered moving towards her dressing room and returning with his arms full of strips of linen, a basin and jug. "This will help with the soreness."

"And, what do you think you're doing?" she asked stunned when he laid her back, dipped and wrung the linen in the basin and moved his hand to her sorest spot.

"Relax and allow me," he said softly. With the lightest of touches, he gently dabbed the cool cloth on her. "This should help you feel better in the morning," his brows furrowed with utmost concentration as he slowly cleansed her. Light, tender movements of the soft linen soothed and cooled her. Once he finished, he lay next to her again, and lightly brought the blanket up to their shoulders.

"Thank you," she said, feeling her face blush profusely, "after all which has transpired, that felt oddly intimate and a little humiliating. But, it did make me feel more comfortable."

"It won't always be painful," he assured, fingers lightly stroking her hips, stomach, arms, as though he could not keep from touching her. "I do have a question about something you said."

"Mmmm?" Charlotte replied dreamily.

"Why were you so upset about my social interactions this evening?"

"I don't think it's in my best interest to answer that."

Matthew laughed. "And why is that?"

"Regardless of what's happened tonight Matthew Edward Harrington, I've known you for an age. You'll tease me mercilessly at every turn if I confess."

"I'll tease you mercilessly if you don't and I'll pester you with questions until you do," he pointed out, "So, it's in your best interest to admit it."

Charlotte groaned. "Very well."

He smiled wickedly. "I believe I enjoyed your groans from moments ago better."

"Evil man! It's abominable to point out my shameful wanton cries!"

He stopped her tirade with a kiss. "I loved your shameful, wanton cries. In fact, they are an expectation henceforth, so don't stop evoking them in future. Now, tell me."

She sighed. "Those ladies are widows or married, unhappily I'm sure the way they were watching you." She blushed profusely at the admission. "From my vantage point, on the other side of the ballroom, I felt they were far too liberal with their smiles...and well..." her voice trailed off.

"I was being polite to my brother's guests. Besides, those women don't interest me."

"But if there is one that does?" Charlotte challenged.

"I'll never betray you," he said vehemently. "Unlike many marriages of the *ton*, our marriage will remain closed to all others."

"Forever?" Her voice was feeble as her fears about Matthew's past slowly disappeared.

"For always."

"So, the world will know that you belong to me and I'll never share you. My annoying, bothersome, arrogant husband will be all mine." Charlotte's eyes sparkled with mischief.

"All yours. I see you realize how lucky you are," he teased. "If I hadn't been playing the part of the good, honored guest, and accepting far-too syrupy felicitations, I would have heard every word Ellis spoke to you. And, I can't shake the feeling that he'll seek retribution for our actions that night."

"I can handle him." She swallowed down the fear creeping up her throat.

Matthew raised a brow, clearly doubtful of Charlotte's handling of His Grace, Lord Ellis.

"I'll never underestimate him again. You must believe me when I say I can handle him. He'll never hurt me."

Matthew's arm reached for her waist, pulling her close in a firm embrace, molding her form into his, making their bodies one. "You're the most capable woman I know. Still, I can't erase the nagging doubt about Ellis. You must promise me that if you ever feel there is any threat or danger from the Duke, you will - "

She stopped the words with a deep kiss, knowing that she could not make the promise. Such a vow would be broken in the same breath with which it was uttered. It was now her duty to protect Matthew from the unforgiving Duke. If there was one thing Charlotte knew how to do well, it was to abide by her duties. Under no circumstance would she do anything to put Matthew's life in danger, even if that meant keeping information from him. Like a blade being honed by the fiercest of fires, deep inside her very soul, she knew he was now hers to protect.

Her hands moved lightly to his chest. Hard muscles beneath smooth skin tightened in the wake of her touch. Matthew was powerfully built, in his nakedness she was able to appreciate it all the more. A groan deep in his throat urged her to continue and the intention to distract him soon turned into intense desire.

She forgot about the Duke as Matthew's mouth and hands roamed. Dreamy, gentle caressing made her molten. Her only duty at the present was to enjoy her future husband as thoroughly as she could before his departure - a duty she would happily fulfill.

He made the slow, gentle entry and held still.

"You're barely moving," she whispered.

"You'll be sore in the morning. I don't want to hurt you," he leaned onto his elbows and whispered in her ear.

Her eyes widened at the subtle sensation of being entirely

filled by him. Pulses. Shivers. Tiny eruptions of promised pleasure fired her need for him. "More."

The tortured syllable commanded his hips to move with supreme gentleness. Slow rhythmic thrusts matched the gentleness of each kiss. Each moment of contact was gloriously measured and tender. She quivered and moaned feeling him deep within her. Her hips met his lingering rhythm until she was hypnotized. Every part of him covered her, loved her, languished in her and she wanted more. Tingles and shivers clamored for more of him until the ache became too strong.

The familiar contraction began to collect deep inside and the heat of promised euphoria mounted. Her hands held him firmly keeping him profoundly within. When the wave became unstoppable, she held herself aloft as it engulfed her and drowned every inch of her body. Throwing her head back, tears sprung from her eyes and a cry escaped her lips. Upon her release, Matthew pushed in the same, slow rhythmic movement, until he buried himself to the hilt; he had no choice but to meet her in kind.

They clung to each other in the throes of their simultaneous release until all that was left was the quiet contentment of their leveled breathing and the slick wetness of their beautiful, fiery pleasure.

"When is the wedding?" Matthew asked, once able to coherently form words.

"Six weeks, in Bentwick," she replied as he positioned himself behind her and protectively draped an arm around her waist.

"I can't wait that long," he buried his face in her neck. "Six weeks without you in my bed will cause my imminent death." He nibbled gently creating a stir in Charlotte's belly. She laughed softly.

"We really must do something about your need to laugh at me when I'm attempting to be romantic."

"Then you must really do something about your sense of humor and stop making me laugh." Her smile would become a permanent state if this was what marriage would be like.

"I'm not trying to make you laugh. I'm trying to obtain your sympathy for the suffering I shall endure for the next six weeks." He kissed her to mute her laughter. She returned the kiss sweetly.

"That's more like it. Would you object to a special license?"

"No." Her sly look made Matthew laugh.

"I see I'm not the only one who will suffer from a long wait."

"No need to be pompous about it."

"I'll never fall in danger of that behavior around you darling. Would Lady Catherine object to a more hurried marriage if I speak with her in the morning?"

"I doubt it. Sorry to say, but you're nothing more than your fortune instead of a son to Mother right now."

"Perfect," he pulled her towards him, lying face to face and lowered to nuzzle her neck. "I hope to change her sentiments, but at the moment they suit me just fine. And, speaking of morning..."

"I know."

Matthew dressed and gave Charlotte one last, long tender kiss. With promises of seeing each other soon, he slipped out of her room, out of her house and into the night.

Just as quietly, he had slipped into her heart, but she hushed away all feelings other than friendship, gratitude and quite obviously, passion. Any other emotion would be disastrous. Her mother's dissolution due to her father's illness and death proved love destroyed people. She was too afraid of what loving Matthew might do to her.

Fear encroached and her heart thumped loudly in her ears. Despite the steely securing of her heart, she yearned for love. She had hoped so desperately to marry for love instead of money, to allow the magical emotion into her life and finally feel what all the commotion was about.

The possibility of her wish coming true terrified her more than she had expected. She would not survive a broken heart at Matthew's hands. S he would not survive losing her oldest, dearest friend. She pulled the blanket over head avoiding any exploration of what Matthew meant to her, but she knew he was more than the man who would save them from ruin. He was more than the man who inspired unbridled passion within her. He was more than her best friend. Her fingers trembled as she covered her eyes, forcing them to close, shutting away all thoughts. She breathed deeply and fell into a restless sleep in what now felt like a large, lonely bed.

CHAPTER 24

"You look happy," Charlotte said to Matthew after their dance.

The *ton* was in full celebration mode for Viscountess Merriweather's annual birthday ball. She stood next to Matthew, watching him move confidently, looking gorgeous in full evening dress. His manner hadn't changed. He continued being charming and affectionately complimented her appearance admiring her swept-up, raven curls and the way her gown of ice blue moved effortlessly around her. Yet, she couldn't help but look for signs which might confirm the gossip about his intentions.

Tea at Hexbrook House had been difficult that afternoon. Apparently, Julia had heard Matthew was marrying her for her Earldom.

"Ridiculous!" Isabella had scoffed. "He can't have the Earl-dom, Charlotte is the peeress."

Evangeline had intervened thoughtfully. "Yes, but with Elmvale neighboring, it will make him a very powerful man."

Charlotte hated to admit that the rumors answered the

one question about Matthew's sudden change of heart about marriage.

"I'm in a state of relief," Matthew's voice brought her back to the ballroom. "My wish has come true, I will soon be an uncle."

"Oh!" her eyes widened. "That's wonderful news!"

"The title is safely in Robert's lineage. Elmvale will remain with a Harrington, but not me," Matthew said softly, breathing a sigh of relief.

"That piece of news has made you rather happy, hasn't it?" She looked deep into his eyes trying to decipher how much of the gossip she had heard was true. His blue eyes glowed with sheer joy. Clearly, his desire for her Earldom was nothing but awful assumptions being spread by hateful people. Still, the fear in the pit of her stomach remained.

"You've no idea," he looked at her far more intimately than polite society permitted even engaged couples.

The heat rising to her cheeks was checked immediately by the dreadful voice of Lord Ellis. Her blood turned to ice.

"This is our dance Lady Bentwick," he said with severe politeness and escorted her away. Charlotte glanced quickly at Matthew and saw his features darken with fury.

"You feel unusually tense this evening, Charlotte," Ellis lowered his voice to a dangerous whisper and tightened his grip.

She breathed in sharply when she heard her name upon his lips. She straightened her shoulders creating a greater distance in their hold because any one of the guests dancing next to them could have heard him, create a delicious piece of gossip about Ellis's daring intimacy and hurt Matthew. The man was taunting her, toying with her as one would with prey.

"Your Grace, forgive my forwardness, perhaps the late hour or your age might be the culprit behind such an oversight, but I am Lady Bentwick." Every word was succinct and her voice remained even.

"There is nothing to forgive, Lady Bentwick," Ellis retorted with renewed appreciation for Charlotte's pluck. "I simply thought I might be of service to help ease your anxiety. Many ladies feel quite relaxed after some time with me." His lips moved into a leer, matching his salacious tone.

She fought every instinct to push him away and pour the nearest bowl of punch over her head to clean away his filthy breath. "I assure you I'm well and this time spent dancing with you is more than I need."

"The lady has claws."

"The Lady will defend herself."

"Tut, tut, Lady Bentwick," Ellis grinned wickedly, "It is I who has been wronged. Have you already forgotten your path to redemption? I assure you, I have not. You will come to me and your Mr. Harrington will remain unscathed. Do not and...well, the consequences will be dismal indeed." He bowed on cue as the dance finished and stealthily slithered out of view.

Charlotte walked away from the dance floor smoothly. She was the model of cool confidence using every ounce of control to stop her hands from pleating her perfectly smooth gown. She saw Matthew walk towards her and her heart sank knowing the lie had to be continued. They greeted each other formally, standing side by side on the perimeter of the dance floor.

Bringing a glass to his lips, his voice was a murmur masked by the noise of the ballroom. "Stop trying to convince me that Ellis isn't a danger to you."

"I thought we had settled this," Charlotte replied. She hoped her voice didn't betray the tornado in her stomach, wishing desperately he would drop his investigation.

He grinned as though she had just made the wittiest of

observations, but his knuckles whitened as he gripped the glass in his hand. "Not to my satisfaction. What did he say?"

She turned sharply at the growl reverberating through his chest. Before a word escaped her lips, Matthew put his drink down on the nearest tray and took her by the elbow. He was suddenly leading her out of the ballroom and she kept a calm demeanor for all to see everything was fine. Once alone in the dimly lit corridors, she countered his tight grip with a futile struggle to be released as he madly tried to unlock doors. Ignoring her protests, he dragged her into a drawing room, slamming the door behind him.

"What do you think you're doing?" She yanked her elbow out of his hold, her voice a shouted whisper.

"What did Ellis want?" Fury vibrated through gritted teeth and she knew his fragile veneer of self-control would soon break.

"You can't do this every time he comes near me. I can't just turn him away, deny a dance, he's a Duke after all. This obsession with Ellis has to stop. You need to trust me!" Charlotte moved to the door, but he prevented her exit.

"A man like Ellis doesn't take what we did lightly. He's clearly a threat and I can't believe you keep denying it. The mere thought of you in his clutches makes me see red, and your refusal to admit he's a danger makes me seethe. What are you not telling me?"

She watched him brood. The storm of memory and fear was beginning to take over. She tried to lightly touch his arm as she spoke, to bring him back, but it was evident he was on the brink of being washed away by the horror of his memories.

"Ellis has not threatened me," she said carefully and as truthfully as she could. After all, the Duke had saved his biggest threat for Matthew. With each carefully enunciated word, she saw his jaw clench until the grinding of his teeth could be heard.

His voice, deadly calm, was barely audible. Each word a whisper loaded with angry terror. "He is a serpent. He's venomous and will bite when you least expect. Men like him are of the worst kind, without honor or scruples," his voice became hollow, his eyes almost glazed and she knew he was gone. He wasn't seeing her anymore. He was seeing what had happened in war.

"There were young ladies of the upper class in the pile of bodies. Armed, ready to fight – following the orders of unscrupulous, bloodthirsty men. They were young, beautiful, stubborn and strong, like you. And, they died horribly. I can't let you die, Charlotte. I can't let you die." He took hold of her shoulders. With an implacable grip, he shook her, repeating the words, over and over.

"I'm not going to die!" She cried out, putting her hands over his, trying to ease the tension, but he was too strong, his grip too tight. Instinctively, she placed one hand on his heart, the other on his face.

"It's me, Matthew. Look at me. It's me," she said as soothingly as she could, over and over, until the wild gaze of his eyes began to calm. He released his grip on her shoulders looking positively horrified at himself.

"Please tell me I didn't hurt you. Please," he begged through a rough throat.

"I'm fine. I promise," she said still holding his face.

"I thought I'd asked you to leave me anytime I'm in this state. I can't trust myself when I'm lost in the horror."

"And, as I informed you, I'm not very good at doing as I'm told," she reminded him with a tender smile. "If it hadn't been for me, you'd still be lost."

He grimaced when he saw the marks peeking out from under the sleeves of her gown, pink from the strength of his grip. "We can't stop this marriage. But, you should be far away from someone like me. Let me shield you from me, let me safeguard you from Ellis."

"As you can see, I'm fine. I don't need protection from you. These episodes don't scare me and they don't define you. I'm not crying off or abandoning my husband because of the side effects of war when all it takes is a touch and soothing word from me to calm you."

His hand covered the one she still held at his heart, and his searing look of somber blue told her he was ever grateful for her strength and determination.

"I also don't need protection from Ellis. He'll never hurt me. I swear."

The Duke's name brought fire back to his gaze. "Why do you keep defending him? Tell me what Ellis said. Why does he insist on maintaining contact with you?"

Charlotte took a moment to absorb the meaning of his words. After a drowning pause, she released him. The tone of his question told her he suspected her of breaking her vow to him before they were even married. She took a step back and stared with cold defiance. "After everything we've shared, how could you possibly suggest I might be entertaining a liaison with the vilest man in England? You obviously have a very low opinion of my character and think very little of my honor."

"It's not what I meant," he moved to hold her, but she sidestepped out of his arms. "You would never...it's not even a possibility. I know that whatever he wants, and you're hiding, is worse. Let me help."

"There's nothing to help," she insisted, feeling tired of the deception, wishing desperately he would stop. "Perhaps you're afraid that another man is courting your Countess?"

He ran his hand through his hair. "There's one thing we agree on, you're my Countess. And not for the reasons the brainless gossips of the *ton* are suggesting. The foregone conclusion seems to be I'm using you and I'm nothing more than a peeress hunter."

"So, you know?"

"Of course, I know. Just as I know you Charlotte Asbury, from the deepest part of your soul to everything which elicits your melodic laughter, I know the woman I'm marrying would never betray me. But, I also know that you're fiercely stubborn, and to my undoing, I'm sure, hellishly independent. Let me in. Tell me what Ellis truly wants and we can fight him together."

She stiffened. The desire to flee became as palpable as the loud beating of her heart. She struggled with remaining before him, their eyes connected to the innermost parts of each other. She wasn't ready for this. In the sudden awareness of the vulnerability intimacy gave way to, escape became the only option.

"I gave you my body," she whispered, "I gave you my word and I'll never betray my best friend. There isn't more I can possibly give you. Let me be, Matthew. I can't give you more than I already have." With a sweep of her gown, she ran out of the library without stopping to see the shocked faces of those she swept past. She ran out into the cold air of night. She ran and ran, until she couldn't run anymore.

Matthew watched her move farther and farther away from him feeling like a brute. He had been unable to control his fear and had let the terror overtake his mind. He had grabbed her. Grabbed her! He scoffed at himself with disgust. How could he have possibly believed loving Charlotte would have been enough to erase the torments of his past. His worries about death and love seemed infantile compared to this awful reality of becoming a different man each time he was in terror. He swore loudly.

Except, Charlotte had courageously seen him through.

Anyone else seeing him in the lost state of horror would have fled, but not her. In fact, she chose to flee when things became too intimate for her. She owned his heart and he would be damned if they lived a life without her feeling how deeply he loved and needed her. He would prove the *ton* wrong about his suitability for Charlotte. He would prove Charlotte wrong about fearing love. He would prove himself wrong about being a danger to her. He wasn't too damaged and the one person who had shown him that was Charlotte.

He groaned realizing their conversation wasn't over. Cursing again, he slammed the library door behind him and ran after her.

CHAPTER 25

Charlotte succumbed to her heaving chest and stopped. Wiping the tears from her face, she looked around relieved to see her feet had brought her home. She remembered flying through streets full of carriages, brushing by lords and ladies walking animatedly to their respective social engagements and keeping her head down to avoid being recognized and therefore the topic of next morning's gossip-hungry *ton*.

She walked slowly to her study, holding her surging stomach and trying to resume regular breathing. Tea was immediately delivered as though the housekeeper had been aware that Lady Bentwick had been running through the streets of Mayfair in the middle of the night. She turned to pour herself a cup and froze when Matthew stormed inside. She nearly dropped the cup, turning to exit through another door.

"I'm not interested in a game of hide-and-go-seek. And, don't even get me started on the perils of running through the streets of London past midnight," Matthew's tone of mingled anger and fear froze her. "I'm however very curious about why my future wife feels she needs to run away from me."

She turned to face him. "You couldn't possibly understand."

"Really?" He walked slowly towards her until he was a mere caress away. "There was nothing we couldn't discuss. No topic off bounds. Now that we're going to be married we're creating limits on what we can talk about? I don't believe you, Charlotte. And I know you don't even believe yourself."

His blue eyes singed her with their sincerity. His hair moved about him in wild brown waves and his breath ran through him as he tried to settle it down. She breathed deeply, inhaling his essence, filling herself with the mingled scents of Matthew and midnight. It could be so easy to let go, to be swept into his warmth. But, she couldn't. She froze because the kind of closeness Matthew was seeking led to dangerous feelings which left a person conspicuously unarmed, open to the kind of wounds only love could inflict. She swallowed back the burn of tears.

"You asked me to let you in. Do you understand that I've never let anyone in? You're the closest I've come to baring myself, and most of the time we were racing horses or climbing trees. More recently, I literally bared myself to you, but I can't give you more. I don't let others in. I manage my affairs on my own, and up until now, I seem to have done quite well."

"You don't have to do it on your own anymore," his hands found hers, gripping them softly. "This isn't easy for me either."

Of course, she thought miserably, he had committed to marry when he wasn't ready to marry.

"I'm not used to this infernal fear of something happening to you," his voice thickened with emotion. "I've experienced grave loss, I've witnessed too much loss…to lose you too…" he suddenly cleared his throat, "I won't let it happen."

"You told me you preferred to be alone and happy than married and miserable. We're not married yet and I'm already making you miserable. I didn't want our friendship to be affected by our marriage – we're not married and things are already so different!" A shiver rolled through her, revealing her fear of so much intimacy.

The longing in his gaze consumed her. His hands began to shake. For a moment, she thought he was facing the pit of memory again, but his voice was too present. He wasn't lost in the past, he was struggling with his present. "You must know, I would do anything for you…Charlotte there's only one reason why I asked you to marry me."

Every nerve in her body fired because his tone was too serious, his manner too intimate. So, she stopped him from telling her why. Her fear prevented her from hearing the one explanation that would put her worries to rest.

"To save the reputation of your dearest friend," she interrupted gravely, almost regretting her words when she saw his eyes harden and his jaw clench. He had been about to divulge something, something important. But, her fear had stolen the moment. Her brows furrowed as the uncomfortable silence continued.

"Well," he finally said, "as your best friend," he sounded as though he was choking on the words, "I suggest you allow me to help. Confide in me. Tell me the truth about the Duke's intentions, I promise we'll rid him from our lives forever."

His tone dropped and the very air between them grew warm. Charlotte suddenly found it difficult to breathe. A mere brush of his gloved hand transfixed her and his bare skin had driven her wild. Ever since his proposal, he had commanded every waking thought. Matthew had become so much more than her best friend. The thought of losing him, of any harm coming to him ignited severe pain in her core. She had to protect him at all costs. And, at the present moment, protecting Matthew meant keeping Ellis's blackmail secret.

"I want to," her voice quivered, "but I stopped being vulnerable the day Father died – weakness was not what Bentwick needed. I yearned for love but I also knew I wouldn't give my heart away because I wouldn't survive the ache of a broken heart with the same tenacity Mother showed. Confiding in others is something I'm just beginning to learn. But you truly don't need to worry because all the Duke wants is an apology. There's nothing more to it."

She swallowed down the guilt of lying to her best friend as cold filled her stomach. Engaging in any and all protective measures to keep Matthew safe from the Duke was her only goal. She was not going to risk hurting him with fabricated and humiliating gossip or losing him in a duel Ellis would ensure to win. He was hers. It was her duty to protect him and she would do anything to see it through. Except, she hadn't prepared for the fracture it would create in their friendship.

Matthew cleared his throat. "To be clear, you refuse to tell me Ellis's exact words and you reject all avenues which could lead to a true marriage?"

"Ellis wants an apology, there's nothing more to tell. And a true marriage leads to heart ache. We have friendship and loyalty – so much more than what others base a marriage on. I would never forgive myself for ruining our friendship because of trying to have something neither one of us is any good at."

"Of course," he said succinctly and stepped away from her, taking with him all warmth. She suddenly felt like a boat without a harbor.

He ran his fingers through his hair, turning away from her, stepping farther away from her.

Her fingers twitched at her side, needing to reach out, to touch his shoulder and bring him back. Fear rooted her to the spot. She remained frozen, the terror of telling him more seized her throat, making her voiceless.

With one last look, he gave a grave good night and quietly closed the door after him.

She stood staring at the closed door for what seemed an interminable amount of time. The echo of his words rang through her study. Confide. Trust. Together. A true marriage. The meaning of each word mocked and pricked her, daring her to believe with Matthew it could be possible and she would be safe.

Endless streams left her face wet with salt water full of fear as she stood on a precipice she had unknowingly proclaimed off-limits years ago. She supposed Matthew's words would have been a balm to soothe any lady's fears. Her mind wandered to her dear friend, Lady Westcott. How wonderful would those words be for her, if spoken by her husband. Then, why, oh why, was she so contrary and they couldn't be enough for her?

CHAPTER 26

Lady Julia Bexley, Countess of Westcott, sat in her office contemplating the world through her window. Every minute forced to sit in her office was spent day dreaming because she hated everything inside. The room had been decorated by Westcott. It was rich and luxurious, draped in gold and scarlet. Julia preferred more soothing tones of mint and heather grey, but her husband had ignored her because powerful colors would induce stronger thinking. The volumes on her bookshelves included several tomes on mathematics, housekeeping accounting, home furnishing, and gastronomy. She had requested volumes of poetry, botany, art, the most current novels and periodicals about ladies' fashions. All of which were noticeably absent from her reading selections. Every item in the room had been designed and selected with the express purpose of helping her to run the Westcott estates. All they induced in Julia, however, was the intense desire to flee.

Thankfully, Mrs. Morrison, Westcott House's house-keeper was an absolute treasure. The woman was a force. She meticulously maintained Westcott's London abode and even his closest country estate in Hampshire with immaculate precision. If a mouse sneezed in Westcott House, Mrs. Morrison would know of it and rid the home of the creature within the hour. She dutifully prepared such detailed accounts that Julia could indulge in her favorite past-time fully confident of passing said accounts to the Earl without fear of being questioned.

She sighed. At the very beginning of their marriage she had tried to complete the offices of a Countess. She had prepared the accounts and had attempted to oversee Westcott's residences. Her reports had made the Earl smile, then smirk, then roll his eyes, then set his lips grimly until he finally ignored them and simply said to leave it to the housekeepers because he always ensured to hire excellent staff. Julia knew she had never done very well in maths, but how could she improve if never given the chance?

Busy yourself with the same things other ladies do, the Earl had advised without looking up from a very important document. She had left his office, eyes downcast and retreated to her rooms.

So, on most mornings when she was in her office maintaining the façade of running a home, she sat and stared at the world beyond her. Occasionally, she would pull out her journal and write a verse or two to keep up the pretense of working in her office, which was especially helpful when maids delivered tea or the butler announced a caller or brought the post, or the Earl walked in with his daily lectures. It was a sad ruse which all the staff was privy to, but out of deep admiration for her (for they all loved the sunny Countess) and deep respect for the Earl, every person employed there, from the butler to the scullery maids, all pretended Lady Westcott actually knew everything Mrs. Morrison knew.

She was scribbling in her journal when the door opened

without a knock. Her fingers froze because only the Earl walked into every room with full authority over it, and everything within it, because it was all his. She looked up and held her breath for the daily list of social events to accept, to decline, what to wear, who to call upon and a few notes on the successes or failures of any recent social interactions. Regardless of the myriad of little cruelties she had suffered, her traitorous heart still leapt each time she saw him.

Lord William Bexley, Earl of Westcott, was a tall, powerful man. Every part of him exuded such authority and control it was difficult not to be simultaneously drawn to him with fascination and to be slightly cowed with fear. His ice blue eyes were always calculating, measuring, evaluating and deciding. She ran her hand over her honey blonde hair ensuring it was smoothly in place and dared to meet his eyes.

"I don't like the way your eyes shimmer with fear each time I walk into a room in my own home. You shiver each time I'm near and not in the ways one would hope one's wife would shiver by one's presence."

She blinked at the sentiment behind his statement as the meaning of his words took root. Heat crept up her throat and she was positive the pink patches which appeared along her neck each time she was unnerved were revealing themselves. They never spoke about marital intimacy, or lack thereof. Westcott never showed sentiment, at least not of the kind which indicated concern or care. She swallowed hard hoping the moment would pass and managed to quietly say, "I'm sorry my lord."

"An apology isn't necessary, Julia," he said looking at her in a way he never had and making the effort to soften his coarse, deep voice. "Your creamy complexion looks far better with confident green eyes, not mousy eyes ready to jump as though I were a terrifying villain. I would never hurt you. I'd protect you with my life. You belong to me and everything that belongs to me is fiercely safeguarded."

Julia pursed her lips, eyeing her husband with great confusion at his sudden noticing of both her eyes and her complexion. And, did he just vow to protect her?

"You must know," he continued roughly, "I would never force myself upon you, especially after your discomfort during our wedding night. We'll have to produce an heir of course..." his voice trailed off and then added, "Besides, what will callers think?"

The little bubble of hope deflated quickly when he reminded her that their marriage was all for show. "There's no one here but us, my lord."

"Right." He pursed his lips and stared at her.

She squirmed under his assessing gaze. She started to feel the peculiar sensation that he was seeing her for the first time, which was preposterous for he marched into her office nearly daily with orders or suggestions. The intensity of his icy gaze nearly consumed her, but it didn't stop her from noticing that there were dark circles under the light blue eyes. His clothes were unkempt, as though they had been slept in and his black hair had been quickly swept back. There was a shocking air of disorder about him.

"I dislike seeing you sitting at your desk, looking so fragile and so afraid of me," he said, breaking their held gaze.

"I'll ensure to look less afraid, my lord."

"That's not the point, Julia."

"It isn't?"

He turned again to face her. Why did he look as though he was in pain? Her eyes widened as she watched him pace the room, one hand rubbing the back of his neck. His size, breadth and sheer force of his personality took over the room as he ruminated. Taking advantage of his distracted pacing, she studied her husband. He did not have the delicate lines of handsome men. His face was formed by a strong brow and straight nose. He was hardened by what was most certainly a stormy past for there was a faded scar along the left side of his face. She caught a glimpse of the silver line which travelled from his chin to the outer corner of his eye wondering, as she often did, how he had obtained it.

She spoke without thinking, "What's wrong?"

"Pardon me?"

Normally, his raised brow over a cold blue eye and the tinge of derision in his tone sent her scurrying. But, not today. She straightened her back and spoke clearly.

"You don't look like yourself and you are acting less so."

"Sleepless night." His eyes dared her to ask more questions.

"Of course," the hint of irony in her voice revealed her full knowledge of what his sleepless nights entailed. The club. Drink. Women. Except, he was behaving so differently she couldn't escape the feeling that he was hiding something. Lots of things probably, but she wasn't strong enough to ask or to confront him.

The corners of his lips drew slightly upwards, as though in appreciation of her tone. Then, he cleared his throat. "I actually came in here to tell you that Lady Bentwick's wedding might be sooner than we believed."

"Really?" Julia's eyes widened, fixing her bright green eyes on him.

"Uh, yes."

She smiled at his rare lapse. Westcott never stammered, he was never at a loss for words and was always in control. Every so often she noticed that her reactions confused him and he failed to have an immediate response. It was one of the very few joys she could take from her marriage to him.

"Yes," he said more firmly as his lips continued their upward pull. Julia realized it was the first time she had ever seen him almost smile. "I know how you love having information before anyone else."

"You do?"

"Don't look so stunned. I do know things about my own wife. You're a notorious gossip – but not a malicious one. Though I still haven't gathered why you're enamored by other people's lives."

"It helps me to stop thinking about my own-" she stopped, feeling the burn along her neck sharpen and bit her lip.

"About your own life?" He finished for her. The smile was gone, but he watched her. The sadness in his gaze travelled the length of her body and nearly brought tears to her eyes. She saw his jaw clench.

"Harrington and I were supposed to meet this morning and had another appointment next week to discuss both my bill and an investment in an overseas shipping venture, the Asian market is looking rather profitable, although we were also considering another company in the Caribbean..." She smiled softly when she noticed he was babbling. And, then, as though he caught himself in the act of speaking without thought, he quickly said, "Not that it's of concern to you –"

"It is!" She interrupted eagerly. "I like hearing about what you do."

Apparently, it was the wrong thing to admit. Instantly, she saw his eyes cool with mistrust bringing the fragile moment to a screeching halt. "No woman is interested in a man's affairs unless it suits her in some way."

"That's not true," the words were released through a brave whisper.

"The sum of my experiences has proven it so."

She glanced down at the few words she had begun to string together willing any tears away. After a few moments of silence, during which she was sure he was gritting his teeth, he spoke again.

"Harrington cancelled both appointments. I believe he is off to see the bishop today –"

"Which means Charlotte will be married in a few days," Julia finished with a rueful voice. "She must be so pleased and excited. The way he looks at her, you can tell he is absolutely in-love."

"Your eyes are never brighter than when you declare your faithful belief in love. Perhaps, one day I can elicit such a look."

Julia's stomach caved with the strangeness of his words. She bit her lip wondering what had brought on a statement which was completely unlike any she had heard from him in their short marriage. Then she saw icy eyes fall to her mouth and her heart beat faster as he devoured what he saw. The air grew thick when his eyes moved back to hers.

He rubbed the back of his neck breaking their moment and she knew he was in discomfort.

"My apologies, I shouldn't have been so excitable over the rumor of a special license," she said quietly.

"A special license isn't always about love," he warned soberly, "And, I doubt much romance is involved in this case. Rumor has it Lady Bentwick is in dire need of funds and as heir to Elmvale, Harrington is making the wise decision to become lord of both Earldoms."

"Marriages aren't always business contracts and partnerships between unfeeling individuals. Regardless of how naïve you think me, or silly for having such fanciful notions about the real world, I'm right." He had silenced her for far too long, and really, what would he do? Ignore her? Chastise her? He had already done all of those things and she had survived. She didn't know where the fire had come from or why she was suddenly emboldened to speak up.

He grunted in response and Julia's eyes widened. "You don't believe it can be about love? He can't possibly be hurrying the date of their marriage because he loves her deeply?"

"Marriage is never about love. And, with Harrington's reputation, I doubt it's love for one woman motivating him," his tone matched the hard ice of his eyes.

She saw his surprise when she sat straighter. She always retreated when he used his tone of power and authority. She always cast her eyes down whenever he dared to speak of scandalous or impertinent matters. Not today. "I suppose not. Some men believe marriage shouldn't hinder the social activities they kept while bachelors, though by the way Mr. Harrington looks at Charlotte, I highly doubt he'll be one of those," she looked at Westcott squarely, her eyes revealing her full knowledge of his social activities.

He remained silent.

"There are some things you'll never understand and it makes me sad for you." There was iron behind her soft tone and she saw him nearly take a step back.

"Some men wouldn't have to keep up those activities if they were welcomed in their wife's bed." His voice filled the room with ice. "Some men wouldn't bring themselves to seduce a woman who fears them."

Her green eyes hardened. "Some men try to make their marriages work beyond the initial business transaction." She challenged him despite the intense beating of her heart. This was not the usual morning conversation they shared daily. Something else was happening. She had no idea what was transpiring between them, but she knew in every corner of her being that she could not back down despite his evident desire to embarrass her by speaking about topics one would never address in a study in the middle of the morning.

"Some men also don't comprehend the folly of willfully

making themselves vulnerable to the charms of a woman and to false declarations of love. Save your pity Julia. I don't need it. I merely thought it might give you something to look forward to – you'll have a mid-season trip to the country. They'll marry in Bentwick."

After a few moments of silence, during which neither flinched, nor moved their eyes from each other, she asked, "You're not attending?"

Regardless of so many disappointments, she maintained the little seed of hope that one day he would become the husband she desperately wanted. And each time he failed to meet her expectations, she became more keen at protecting herself from her own desires for love and her husband's complete unwillingness to truly feel the power of it.

"No. I have delicate business matters in the city," he said, avoiding her gaze.

Hiding. She couldn't escape the notion that he was hiding.

"Very well then." Her face was a mask of politeness to conceal the throbbing lump in her chest. She looked down at her journal hoping he would leave before the water pooling in her eyes spilled down her cheeks.

Westcott whispered good day and quietly closed the door to the gold and scarlet study contemplating how on earth he could have such a gentle, beautiful wife and still feel so utterly miserable. He was a cad for not accompanying her, but her safety depended on it. He needed her away from the city for a while. Besides, his entire life's experience had taught him that women were untrustworthy. If he opened himself to Julia, she would surely obliterate what little the others had left behind.

CHAPTER 27

Two nights later, Charlotte brushed out her hair and arranged the sheer, silk trimmed so-called night gown to fit around her bosom perfectly. In a moment of madness, she had blurted out to Julia her fear of her wedding night. Julia mistook her terror of seeing Matthew for the first time since he left her study for virginal embarrassment. To help her, Julia had sent a gift box to her room the morning of her wedding. Inside it was the sheer, lacey affair bordered by silk trim. Though it fell to her ankles, it was by no means demure. Thin ropes of silk held it at her shoulders and the sheer lace fell so low on her breasts, they nearly spilled out. The bodice clung to her waist, falling into a full skirt with a generous slit which parted right up the middle exposing most of her legs. She had shrieked at the sight of it. Julia's note mentioned she hoped it would help. She had never worn it but believed someone should on her wedding night.

Charlotte's black hair fell smoothly to her waist and contrasted sharply against the ivory ensemble. What a difference to the bride dressed in a rich plum silk gown with her hair upswept in an intricate band of braids and curls. She had felt beautiful as Matthew's bride. And, now, thanks to her friend, she felt sensual and alluring. Perhaps, a little cold too. She slipped into her dressing gown, trembling in anticipation, waiting for her husband to knock at her bedchamber door.

She glanced around the bedchamber noting what she could do to make the room hers. A few pillows here and a blanket there, perhaps she could rearrange the furniture or bring the drapes from her old room and the bedchamber would lose its association with Mother. Catherine had moved to another wing of Bentwick Manor until the small cottage – small compared to Bentwick Manor – at the south side of the estate was ready for her. Charlotte now occupied the Countess' bedchamber – a room she had refused to take, until tonight.

She released a long, heartfelt sigh thinking about Matthew. Her husband.

They had not spoken a word to each other after his quiet exit from her study. In fact, when she had walked down the aisle on the arm of the Marquess of Pembrooke, Evangeline's father, it was the first time they had seen each other since their disagreement.

She remembered smoothing down the silk skirts of her voluminous gown when a sudden urge nudged her face upwards. She saw Matthew standing at the altar waiting for her. Her breath caught. He was so tall, so strong, so absolutely gorgeous. Every inch of him poured into his breeches, waistcoat and boots. His brown wavy hair was neat, but not so neat that he did not look like himself. He gave her the slightest of winks, meant only for her, telling her everything was alright. The unrelenting terror which had seized her the night he had closed the door to her study, gave way to relief as she stood before him, and locked eyes with the only person who had ever offered a haven, somehow knowing that they would be alright.

It had been a beautiful ceremony in Bentwick's village church. All had attended, honoring their Countess with strewn flowers. Charlotte repaid their kindness and loyalty with a lovely breakfast in which she and Matthew partook for a little while before going back to Bentwick Manor.

The day had floated by so that she could only remember it in moments. The moment she walked up to him. The moment they said "I do". The moment Mother and Lady Adelaide offered a warm embrace. The moment Lord Elmvale affectionately welcomed her to the family. The moment Julia (without Westcott at her side) offered warm congratulations. The moment Evangeline and Isabella grinned excitedly about her wedding night. The delectable feast which had extended itself throughout the day due to the merriment of all present.

The magic of sharing their union with those closest to them had created momentary amnesia. She had indulged in the splendid feelings of the day preferring to ignore their last exchange and succumbed joyfully to the celebrations. It was clear that Matthew had opted to do the same.

Would it be appropriate to address it all tonight or should she just let it be brushed off by the fine feelings of the day?

Her stomach fluttered and she pursed her lips. Despite the way their last interaction had ended, her traitorous body couldn't wait for Matthew to join her. Her husband was on the other side of that door and would shortly enter to claim his husband's rights which, she admitted, she was anxious to offer him. But, what was taking him so long?

She stood, tentatively walking towards the door. Full sheer skirts moving about her bare legs as she walked, sending shivers of anticipation to all regions of her body. A palm rested gently on the door, she leaned forward as though trying to feel what was occurring on the other side.

"Good evening wife." Matthew opened the door. He caught Charlotte in one arm as she fell onto him with a loud yelp and balanced a bottle of champagne and two flutes in the other. The sight of him keeping everything from breaking turned her cry into nervous laughter.

"We really must stop this persistent need of yours to laugh just before intimate moments," he said while placing down the champagne and glasses. He attempted a stern tone which only prompted more laughter from Charlotte.

"Then you have to stop making me laugh." Happiness spread through her every limb, followed closely by relief because there was still laughter. Perhaps, not all had been lost in that study three nights ago.

Matthew grew serious, though his eyes still danced with unshed amusement. "I want your eyes to sparkle like that forever. I'll gladly spend the rest of my life making your eyes sparkle like they are right now."

Her heart leapt and she bit her lip as he stepped toward her, his hand cupping her face. "I promise to do everything I can, every day of my life, to bring you happiness," he took a deep breath, "We need to discuss the other night - "

"Do we have to?" A small, fearful voice.

"Yes," he said gently. "I'm sorry. I shouldn't have pushed you. I know better than anyone what your childhood was like and what that means for your expectations of marriage. Charlotte, I l- " he stopped. S he watched him deliberate, her chest filling with anticipation, fear, excitement.

"You?" She prompted, sensing him maneuvering away from something.

His brows furrowed before continuing. "I'll never hurt you. I trust you with my life and I vow to work every day of my life to ensure you feel safe and cared for. I don't ever want to feel like I did three nights ago again. I don't want to lose my best friend, ever."

The warmth of his hand seeped into her cheek and went straight to her heart. Though they had exchanged their solemn vows that very morning, this promise Matthew made for her alone embedded itself in her soul.

"I'm sorry, too. I know I have much to learn about intimacy and truly sharing everything with you – at least more than just racing our horses."

"We can still do that. But, be warned, I won't let you win anymore."

"You mean I'll ensure to beat you soundly," she raised her brow at his smirk. After a pause, "Thank you for easing the pressure of expectation. I'm so happy you're still my very best friend in the world."

She was lost in a sea of blue. Her eyes moved across the planes of his face and landed on his lips. Full. Delicious. She glanced back up with a small smile, "Now that your place in my life is righted once again, all that's left is to make sure we're, um, married."

Matthew's eyes narrowed matched by a predatory smile. His hand slowly moved to her shoulder and Charlotte felt the heat of his skin burn through her dressing gown. She breathed deeply as he slowly untied it and slipped it off. Her very confident husband froze, mouth gaping, at the sight of her in the barely there lacey, sheer, night gown.

A mental note to send Julia a heartfelt thank you. "Do you like it?"

"Ahem," the words were lost, but Matthew's eyes devoured every inch of what they saw. "You, my dear, are either toying with me in a most cruel way or are planning my imminent death on my wedding night."

Charlotte giggled as he yanked her into his arms, his mouth making immediate contact with her neck. His warm lips, tongue, mouth nuzzled and kissed up to her ear. Slowly, his tongue outlined the small lobe. Hot breath elicited a tingling sensation she didn't know could be harnessed by having her ear so lovingly kissed.

He groaned. "I'm torn between the need to disrobe you and take you or to keep you dressed like this forever, and still take you," he continued a loving assault of her lobes and neck with whispers promising his fullness deep within her.

A throaty laugh reverberated through her pausing his exploration of her skin. "Do I sense a bit of mocking? Or, perhaps, playfulness?"

"Maybe I'm enjoying the effect I'm having."

"Let me help you enjoy it some more."

A trail of warm moisture from her neck to her bosom shot shards of pleasurable anticipation deep within her belly. His mouth kissed every inch of exposed skin and sent wondrous sensations everywhere inside her.

Gingerly standing straight, her fingers easily undid the sash of his dressing gown and as it fell to the floor her sudden attempt at being the elegant temptress was momentarily interrupted with a sharp gasp when she saw that he was stark naked and fully erect underneath. He offered a shrug and lopsided grin. "I didn't see the point in more clothes to take off."

She grinned slyly and her boldness returned. Her gaze followed the lines of his strong shoulders, muscular arms and powerful legs – a flutter of delight to be taken to her marital bed by him moved through her. Her hand outlined the hard lines of each muscle and moved down towards his hip bones sliding across to that slip of skin under the navel that holds the promise of more. Matthew's subtle intake of breath encouraged the exploration of his body, before she could stop herself, she giggled.

Really? His eyes asked.

Her only response was a playful shrug.

Her stomach tightened with the primitive need to feel him. Her roaming hands elicited a sharp gasp from her husband. She should have been shocked by her wanton desires, she should have been repulsed by behaving in a manner so unacceptable for ladies of her ilk, but she was drowning in sensations seeking release. Every breath, every touch was a powerful elixir propelling her toward her husband.

He closed his eyes, jaw clenched, as she continued her tentative exploration. Her hand found him, encircled him and her eyes showed the wonder of feeling his hardness, so vulnerable in the palm of her hand. She felt every inch of him, curious to discover exactly how to touch him, how to drive him wild.

It seemed he had allowed her exploration for as long as he could when in one swift motion he lifted her with supreme gentleness and carried her to the bed. Setting her down, sheer fabric draped alluringly about her legs, he lay next to her. His mouth found hers, his hands moved to her stomach, fumbling with the lacing of the bodice until it came off. The night gown floated off the bed as he pulled her close singeing her with his hot skin.

Feather-light fingers returned to her body, slowly tracing her most sensitive spots, until finding her centre. Welcoming his intimate touch, she writhed as he gently opened and filled her. He kissed her deeply. His tongue insistent, yet slowly devouring her mouth while his fingers matched the intensity deep inside her and she became liquid fire.

He released her mouth, his heavy lidded stare telling her how far gone he was by her. His lips found her neck, collar bone, breasts, and he trailed a hot, moist path down her body until nestling in between her legs. He lifted her hips slightly upwards. Charlotte's eyes widened when she saw his smile disappear, his head lower and he kissed the very center of her being. She scrambled to her elbows. He eased her back down with a whispered, "Trust me."

She bit her lip in utter disbelief that such a thing could be done yet was soon so very happy that such a thing was being done. Her body tingled with each soft stroke outlining the tender folds. The pulsing, malevolent tongue entered her followed by the slick interruption of teasing fingers made her ball the sheets into her hands. He lingered and lapped, filling her, leaving her empty. Then he concentrated his efforts on the small, sensitive bud. His incessant caressing mounted each sensation higher and higher until she began to feel the wave commence.

His mouth was relentless, as he held her firmly by the hips forcing her to stay, to feel each caress. It was unstoppable. Crying out her pleasure, her entire body sparked at the peak and it overcame her. She shuddered in her surrender until all was sizzling calm.

He slowly kissed his way back until they were once again face to face. He paused over her for one moment.

Ivory skin flush with desire, her eyes a darkened grey, ribbons of black hair floated all around them. "You're positively the most beautiful woman I've ever seen and you're mine. You have erased everything. Only you Charlotte, only ever you. Now, I want you to do that again for me," he said gruffly, his mouth finding her breasts with more force as his hands separated her legs.

Words eluded her. The fire in her belly stirred again, the urging in her skin told her she needed him again, more than ever. Arms curled around his neck as he found her lips, bringing him closer to her and she kissed him, fully, passionately, avoiding frightening words.

He joined their bodies. Her hips rose to meet him, revelling in feeling every part of him touching her bare skin. She held him close wishing they could melt into each other. And, as they moved together in perfect synchronicity, the rising tide began again and was ready to overtake her. Each moan, each breath, each thrust pushed her further and further into the sweet agony of pleasure only he could help her find.

The rhythm of their breath took them further into their own pleasure, faster and deeper thrusting took them just a bit further into each other. Matthew drove into her until he was buried to the hilt and Charlotte clung to him as the wave overtook her. Her release was met with his contraction and cry of pleasure. They held each other tightly until every spark of desire was satiated.

Once the last ripples of pleasure rolled through them and they lavished soft kisses upon each other, Charlotte cocooned herself in Matthew's arms. They fell asleep peacefully. But, in the moments just before sleep enveloped them, she was almost certain she heard him mumble something. Though she tried to convince herself she heard wrong. It could not have been what she heard. It was not possible. He had started the night promising not to place undue pressures or expectations on her. What was she supposed to say in return?

Matthew fell into the delicious lull of deep relaxation, the kind which numbs one's body moments before sleep claims one's consciousness. The woman in his arms had been his best friend for as long as he could remember. She was the woman who had stolen his heart, she had become his wife, his lover and would one day be the mother of his children. All was as it should be. He sighed contentedly brushing his lips across the top of her head while she slept, and in the same moment in which sleep overtook him, he whispered, "I love you."

CHAPTER 28

I love you. The words had vanished with the whispered utterance and had haunted Charlotte every day for the next two months.

She rode with Matthew daily. She sketched during a free moment and he loved to interrupt her in a more daring and delicious manner than when they were younger. He made love to her every night with passion and tenderness. A blush began to creep upon her cheeks as the memories of their lovemaking inundated her. She broke the erupting giggle with a short cough and continued pouring tea for her husband. A small smile of admission came to her lips. She was behaving like a green girl by being completely infatuated with her husband, a man she had known since childhood. She couldn't help it. Every thought of him, every whiff of him or sight of him made her absolutely giddy. After spending years preparing for a marriage based on nothing more than monetary gain, Charlotte was stupefied at how much more Matthew had given her. Nonetheless, she was plagued by the three words which had escaped his lips on their wedding night and had remained unspoken, elusive ever since.

" – doing great work."

"Pardon?" Charlotte's cheeks burned because she had not heard a word he had said. They sat for tea in Bentwick Manor's outdated and shabby parlor which, along with the rest of Bentwick Manor, would be renovated once Bentwick was in a much healthier state. Matthew promised their home would be fully and tenderly restored and had honored her request to help the people living on her lands first. She handed him a tea cup, milk, no sugar and a plate of biscuits.

Matthew received both, placing them on the table next to him and offered a lopsided grin. "I'm boring you already? We've only been married two months."

"Already? You assume you didn't bore me before?"

Matthew arched a brow as though he was being rather ill-used. "I was telling you of the deep gratitude expressed by Mrs. Miller. Our young vicar has a formidable wife in Mrs. Miller."

"There's something I never expected to hear you say."

"I was always too busy helping you out of trouble to make heartfelt observations about the people on our estates."

I love you.

Charlotte nearly groaned. Regardless of their banter or their most tedious of conversations about the farms, lumber production or thatched cottages in need of repair, the words loomed. They hovered, just out of reach, but daring enough to despondently display themselves in her memory at the most inconvenient of times.

"You've that faraway look again," Matthew drank his tea, blue eyes studying his wife over the rim of his cup. "What's robbed your attention?"

"Jealous?" She bit into a biscuit, playing, flirting, hoping to distract.

"Extremely. I enjoy being your sole focus of attention and despise anything which takes it away."

If only he knew how much of her attention he had. Asking him to repeat what he had said the night of their wedding made her shrink. Besides, he had practically been asleep, he had probably forgotten all about it. Or worse, what if he hadn't meant it? What if she had imagined the three little words?

His support of her and Bentwick, his dedication to their marriage, to their home and estate was more than Charlotte could have ever dreamed. Did three words really make a difference?

Her voice shook. "I'm still considering using the profits from our latest investment to repair the main roads instead of installing the irrigation systems on the farms at the east end." Though she did think about the estate a lot, she wasn't obsessed by it as she was by *I love you*.

She flinched. Heaven help her, there it was again.

Matthew swallowed his tea and contemplated his wife. " You realize our profits are enough to do both. Or, have you already forgotten this morning's celebration? I can gladly remind you of the way my...what did you call it? Oh right, my reckless investing tripled its yield within a month, so we can repair roads and work on the farms." His velvet tone shot through her chest and dove straight to her toes.

Charlotte bit her lip. She blushed remembering the kissing and lovemaking which had occurred in his study that very morning when they had celebrated their triumph. Her memory easily conjured the feeling of Matthew's presence within her body sending tiny ripples of pleasure through her.

I love you.

"No!" Her voice broke. "No need," she smiled, more to calm herself than soothe Matthew's worried look. "Uh, will you accompany me to the village later today? I'll be seeing some of the shop owners."

"I'd love to, but I won't see you until dinner. I'm meeting with Mr. Brown and a few other farmers precisely to discuss the irrigation system. Charlotte, are you sure you're well?" He dropped the friendly banter and looked her over with a furrowed brow.

"Yes. Yes, I am," she assured with a wide smile. "A lot on my mind I'm afraid." She added under breath.

"You're doing too much." With infinite softness, he passed his hand along the side of her face. "I can imagine how tired you must be. We have spent nearly every waking minute working for Bentwick, and what we've accomplished is nothing short of miraculous. But, we can't continue like this at the expense of your health. Stop protesting. We have all the time in the world to rebuild – I'll never forgive myself if I let you fall ill in the process. Stay home and rest today darling. The shops will be there tomorrow and the day after." He kissed her forehead, her nose and very gently, her lips.

She opened her eyes, drowning in a sea of sky blue. "I feel fine. It's just a quick trip to discuss new inventory with our shop owners."

"Wasn't I supposed to have an obedient wife?"

"Really? I don't remember that part of the ceremony."

"Of course, you don't," he smirked. One more kiss and he departed.

She sat on the sofa waiting until the last possible moment to hear him say the words. Not until she heard the soft click of the door closing did she exhale.

Disappointment clouded her parlor. How could she hope for love? Love had brought her mother nothing but pain, neglect, abandonment and abuse. Could she love Matthew and risk losing him to the unknown darkness to then be left essentially a married widow, heartbroken and alone?

Except, she understood in the deepest part of her that Matthew was the opposite of her father. In the past two months, he had been free from haunting shadows of war. His easy nature, his charm and sense of humor, his spark for life followed him everywhere once again. He had shown her he was capable of rising above wretched darkness.

He had found his purpose and therefore, terror and fear could no longer entrap him. It was not within him to succumb to anger, self-pity or the weight of the pressures upon him. He greeted every problem with a smile and the confidence that there was always a profitable solution. A man like that could not possibly give into sadness or moroseness. She would not lose him the same way her mother had lost her father to drink and darkness – of that she was almost sure.

She bit her lip. If there was no danger of losing Matthew, then what was holding her back from loving him?

I love you.

Perhaps the words were not as terrifying as she had originally thought. She groaned. Such turmoil over three little words. Surely, Matthew's dedication to Bentwick and the nightly passionate devotion of his body to her pleasure should suffice.

Perhaps, a few months ago, all of Matthew's actions would have been sufficient. Except, she knew what she had heard. When the words had reached her ears on her wedding night her life had changed completely, though she had been too much of a coward to acknowledge or reciprocate them. But if she was being honest with herself, she craved to hear the words again and again and again.

The lump in her throat dissolved and her eyes shimmered with tears of joyful insight. Marriage to Matthew meant she needed to hear him say that he loved her.

Because when he did, she would be able to tell him that

she loved him too.

Tears spilled from her eyes, landing softly on her wide smile. She did not know when her love for Matthew had begun. No, she shook her head, it was untrue. She had always loved him. She had been too afraid to hope that the charming boy with the blue eyes and cute dimple would in any possible way be interested in her, the serious girl with more than her share of financial problems. It was easier to prepare for a loveless marriage than it was to hope for one with Matthew which might not ever exist.

She permitted herself a little laugh and even a playful shrug as she sat alone in the shabby parlor as though she had managed to outmaneuver fate by marrying the exact man she had privately always wanted to marry. Then she mused that perhaps marrying Matthew had been her destiny all along. Had her life been completely in her hands, she would be in a much more dire predicament.

The Duke of Ellis came to mind making her shudder. Each day had brought her greater security in her position as the Countess of Bentwick and as Mrs. Matthew Harrington. It was probably why she had not given Ellis a moment's thought.

Nonetheless, time and distance had not completely erased the man's threats. Her fear of him had not completely vanished. She prayed he had found another source of entertainment, had forgotten her, and would never find her to claim her redemption, as he called it. She shivered at the thought of the despicable Duke's hands on her and became downright furious that he had threatened to hurt Matthew.

She jumped when she heard a loud commotion in the great hall, making her forget Ellis and his threats. She pursed her lips when the shouting became louder. She stood, opened the doors and was absolutely shocked by the sight of the Earl of Elmvale, clearly in his cups, shouting for Matthew.

CHAPTER 29

"Lord Elmvale?" Charlotte rushed to the Earl, leading him by the arm to the parlor.

"Robert," she said, hoping the use of his given name would help him focus on her. She motioned for the servants to leave them. "What is it?"

"I need tuh theee Mafew." Robert leaned heavily on her. She heaved him towards a sofa.

"He will be home shortly," she replied practically, furrowing her brow at his slurred speech. She remembered all too well the pointless endeavor of speaking to a man who could barely focus or pronounce words. Her nose crinkled at the smell of him and she nearly vomited, reminded of her father in such a state. She controlled her body and squeezed her eyes shut to trap the inevitable salt-water which would surely fall down her cheeks. Composing herself after a few measured breaths, she took charge the way her mother used to.

"Let us ring for some tea or some broth. Perhaps both," she said under her breath eyeing the extent of his drunkenness. "You may rest while you wait for him."

Robert grabbed her hand, stopping her from gathering and fluffing cushions. Charlotte paled, staring at her brother-in-law in complete shock. Her heart pounded. It was like being a child again and at the mercy of her drunken father in one of his tirades against society and its stupid laws. She fought hard to remember that this was Robert, not her father.

"Mafew shoulda married you yearz a-go. I alwayz knew he loved you, he jus' didn't know it. Sometimes…sometimes we take longer tuh understand what women ha've known fur yearz." He caught sight of the iron grip on Charlotte's arm and released her looking horrified by his actions. "You'll be a good mother to the next Earl,' he muttered and hung his head.

Charlotte nodded and placed a cushion under his head, fighting back tears. "Thank you."

She felt rather relieved that he closed his eyes and essentially ended any further conversation. Matthew came into the room moments later and looked at Charlotte over Robert's head inquisitively. She moved to Matthew's side and lightly kissed his cheek whispering in his ear.

"I believe he's foxed."

"One of the stable hands alerted me to Elmvale's arrival and his state. Are you alright?"

"Yes, a bit unnerved, but otherwise alright," she admitted freely when his arms came around her.

She looked up with a small smile, "He said I'm the best thing that ever happened to you."

He smiled, kissed her lightly and watched as she slipped out of the room leaving the brothers of Elmvale to their privacy.

Hours later, once Robert left Bentwick Manor much sobered

and well fed, Matthew marched into Charlotte's office and closed the door.

"Clara has lost their fourth child," he said without preamble. "I had no idea this had been their fourth child."

His beautiful wife looked up sharply from the ledgers in front of her.

"They have been ordered to cease all attempts of procreation because her life could be in peril. They are both devastated." He crossed the room and stood at the window looking out onto the lands he was bringing back to life. He ran his fingers through his hair.

"Oh, Matthew," she said rising from her desk and coming to his side. "Poor Clara. To be told she can't be a mother. And, poor Robert," she added quietly.

"It will not be me," he said. "The next Earl of Elmvale will not be me." He placed his hand on her stomach, "But it will be him."

Charlotte's eyes widened, "How did you..." she could not finish her question for it was stopped by his kiss.

"Robert will live for a long time my darling. My destiny is tied to yours, my life is here, at Bentwick." He held her close, resting his chin upon her head, the drum of his heart a strong assertion of his devotion to his family. "Our son will have two Earldoms. Or, our daughter." He paused and allowed the words to sink in. "I've suspected for several weeks. I'm surprised, quite frankly, that it took this long," he said slyly.

"I'll know for certain in a week or so."

"Well then Mrs. Harrington, we can never be too sure," he said suggestively.

"Are you sure?"

"I want you. Now."

In one swift movement, he placed her atop her desk bringing the hem of her skirts up around her waist. His hands moved up the creamy skin of silken thighs until they disappeared under the gathered dress. Fingers found her most intimate place, and he groaned because she was ready.

He gladly accepted the offering. Standing before her, freeing himself from his breeches, he possessed his wife. A deep groan filled with need, with fear, with the need to escape reverberated in his chest. He kissed her roughly. Holding her back with one hand, his other found her breasts. He felt her legs tightly wrapped around him, bringing him deep inside her warmth. With each strong thrust he tried to bury himself, to escape the horrific details of his brother's experience, in her.

The need to be one with her, to ascertain she was his and nothing would ever happen to her was relentless. Her heat, her hips matching his pace, her mouth receiving his enveloped him in blind desire. He powerfully buried himself inside and released his need, finding the peace his body sought and was surprised to feel Charlotte meet him in kind. She joined him in a meeting of passionate lovemaking full of need, fear, desire, and did he dare to believe, love.

His pride prevented another slip. Remembering the words sliding out of his heart just before he had fallen asleep on their wedding night made his stomach clench. She had frozen in his arms and feigned sleep. Surely, if she wasn't certain of her feelings then, she had to be now. He had given her everything. His pride stopped him from saying the words again until he was certain that her feelings for him were more than mere gratitude for saving her and for helping her to save Bentwick. He knew he was being unreasonable. Her nightly passionate surrender should have been enough. The way her grey eyes lit up every time she saw him should have been enough. Her response to a mere caress, their easy conversations and laughter, their daily rides and sought-after excuses to spend time together should all have been enough.

But it wasn't.

He selfishly, foolishly, childishly needed the words and didn't wish to say them first, or again, he corrected, without knowing that his feelings were reciprocated.

"Matthew, are you alright?"

"Yes, of course," he grinned sheepishly at being caught lost in his thoughts. He kissed her softly and helped her off the desk. They both put themselves to right, adjusting and tucking clothes and hair pins.

"You're not alright," Charlotte said softly once they sat in chairs by the windows which they had moved closer together so they could hold hands.

"How well you know me," he smiled wistfully. "Darling, witnessing Robert's pain today proved to me how fortunate we are. I already knew I was lucky in marrying you, our life so far has already surpassed my wildest imaginings," with the exception of the unsaid words which hovered like a teasing bee, but he refrained from saying so. "And today I was reminded about...by God, Robert cried in my arms like a babe just an hour ago. I was reminded how very fragile life can be."

"Life is fragile. And, it is short. And, perhaps, sometimes we take things for granted," Charlotte said, her fingers lacing in and out of his. He felt nervous moisture begin to cover her palms.

"I'll never take us for granted. The dark memories of war no longer taunt me because I've found my purpose by your side. I'll protect you with my life, I..." his voice faded.

He saw her waiting in anticipation, grey eyes searching his. Asking for something. He clenched his jaw, forcing the one word which would scare her off to remain unsaid.

"As will I," she smiled. Her hands tightened around his. After a deep breath, she spoke again, "You're the most important person in my life, and we may have started a new life," one hand flew to her stomach, "Our family will be complete.

I can't imagine doing any of this with anyone else, Matthew, I...I - "

An impeccably timed knock by the butler nearly drove him mad. The bubble of intimacy burst when he delivered an urgent note from Elmvale Park, sent by the Dowager. It appeared that their presence was requested. Immediately.

Matthew instantly felt a blanket of mourning envelope him when he entered his former home. The blanket tightened as he crossed the threshold into the Countess' sitting room. They weren't greeted by Clara but by an ashen-faced Lady Adelaide.

"Mother?" Matthew's voice cracked with emotion, willing his mother to apologize for the hurry, to make her say there was no reason for it. Except, he knew there had to be and it was directly out of his deepest nightmare.

"Robert is dead." Lady Adelaide's voice was a ghostly whisper.

Matthew nodded vehemently. "That's impossible because he left Bentwick Manor in perfect health. He's probably still out riding. He took a longer route home. He was naturally quite upset today," he spoke with urgency, rationalizing Robert's delay to keep the horrid truth at bay. He moved to the window hoping to catch a glimpse of his brother returning home.

Lady Adelaide continued speaking as though nobody was in the room with her. "The gardener found his body not far off."

"Mother." A growl of warning.

"They brought him home. But he was without breath when he was found and it never returned." The grief-stricken mother buried her face in her hands.

"No! It's not true - Robert was in my home a few hours ago." Matthew's desperate whisper insisted.

The Earl of Elmvale, a most respected and beloved man had shockingly died far sooner than anyone expected. Reality seeped into his bones. Matthew ran his fingers through his hair. Wild with despair, he stormed out slamming the door behind him. He had been wrong. His fate was to be the Earl of Elmvale after all.

Without a word, he marched directly into Robert's study. The once comforting smells of leather bound volumes sitting on shelves and comforting sights of the large mahogany desk, rich velvet drapery and voluminous upholstered chairs, did nothing less than attack every single one of his senses until his body was a wretched ball on the ground wracked by heaving sobs.

Losing Robert was like losing his anchor. It was losing his father all over again when he was six. Except he had known and respected Robert far deeper than life had allowed with father. The darkness of the room was seductive and the darkness in his mind became a skilled temptress. Matthew unwittingly fell under the pull of the dark because it was easier than to remain in the present where too much pain promised to undo him.

His mind wandered to the memories where more death awaited. Bodies laid before him at differing stages of decay and the stench of mortality infiltrated his nostrils. Then he remembered, holding a weapon, using the weapon and taking life. Taking life to save his own life. And, now, Robert was dead. Fate had an interesting way of finding balance. Shouldn't it have been he, dead as retribution for all the lives he took? Robert had not pulled the trigger or wielded sword. Breath should have been strangled out of his pathetic lungs, not Robert's.

No. This was life's cruel irony. He would live a long time

to suffer for all the suffering he had caused and endured and witnessed. He would watch all those he loved, die, he was sure.

Charlotte? Never Charlotte. He would die before anything happened to her. His hands shook. His stomach trembled. His chest burst with the ache of his racing heart. His head throbbed with the onslaught of memories until they were too powerful and his body thrashed around on Robert's rug in Robert's study.

Suddenly, his face was being held between two hands with a soft, warm yet firm touch. His eyes opened wildly.

"Go!" A throaty growl escaped his lips ordering her to leave him because he would never hurt her. "I need to be alone! Go!"

"Never," tears streamed down her face, but her voice was soothing and resilient giving him the life-saver he needed with one hand firmly planted on his heart. "No. You will not drown. I won't let you. Come back to me. You're stronger than the memories. You're stronger than the grief. I promise."

Her body heaved with sobs too. Sobs filled with grief and fear, but she didn't let go. "I'm here. Always. Come back to me."

The hand on his face wiped his tears. He hadn't even realized he had cried. He breathed deeply until air was no longer shaking the very core of his body and he was able to sit on Robert's rug, in Robert's study. Shaking hands found hers and took hold of them, pulling her to sit beside him.

"I can't do this," he admitted, "I can't without Robert."

"I'm so sorry my darling," Charlotte said softly, "I know this was never part of your plan, but neither was marrying me or becoming a father. If there is anyone I know who can navigate new waters, manage difficult terrain, it's you. Your humor and charm and intelligence make a success of every endeavor you take on. You can do this, of that I am absolutely certain. And, you'll be able to mourn Robert and say goodbye to him too – no matter how painful. But, you have to do it without letting the awful memories of war take over."

The pain shooting through every part of him each time he recalled his beloved brother was gone was bone breaking. However, her words were a balm to his soul and almost convinced him she was right. She reminded him of all which he had accomplished when abroad to help people in a different land, reminding him all of his experiences abroad had not been horrific.

"How do you know I can do this and I just won't run away, like I did when I ran to India?" he asked, doubting this strength she seemed to believe so blindly he possessed.

Her cheeky, half-smile in such a somber moment brightened the consuming darkness of Robert's study. "Because you have me, of course."

A short, rueful line appeared on his lips. Almost a grin. It was enough to show him that he could face a life without his brother and be the man Robert had somehow known he would become. He would never dishonor Robert's memory and would do right by Elmvale. He would do it all with Charlotte by his side. He held her fiercely. His harbor. His life. They remained so in utter darkness for several hours, whispering of how they would overcome the heartbreak and the challenge of steering both Earldoms.

Together, they left Robert's study ready to take on this new challenge and to accept a world in which Robert no longer moved.

CHAPTER 30

Matthew read the document three times without retaining a single word. He sighed. The paper in his hands floated back to the desk unread and unsigned. Perhaps, he should have gone riding with Charlotte. He turned to survey the vast expanse of land through the windows of Robert's study in Elmvale Park and privately cursed.

His study.

He glanced at the document mocking him from the smooth surface of Robert's desk.

His desk.

The turn of events in his life were almost incomprehensible. In a mere four months, he had returned from India, married Charlotte, was expecting his first child and had become Earl of Elmvale.

He swallowed hard. The room in which he sat could only be referred to as Robert's study. He was an impostor in Robert's home. Every time he heard the name Elmvale, he expected Robert to walk into a room before him. He winced each time he was announced as such, and receiving his writ of summons to the House of Lords had nearly undone him.

Robert was the Earl. He was just Matthew. He breathed deeply to deter the sadness.

"You're troubled." Charlotte's voice caressed his cheek and was quickly followed by the light brush of her lips. "You didn't even hear me enter your study."

"I'm not Elmvale." He replied with a rueful breath.

"You're not Robert." She corrected slipping onto his lap.

He instantly wrapped his hands around her waist and held her close. His eyes crinkled with joy as her hand softly came to his face.

"No one knows Elmvale the way you do. Well, except for me, of course," she smiled mischievously. "You've been riding these lands for as far back as I can remember. You know the people. With all due respect to Robert, for he was a wonderful Earl, you are more Elmvale than you realize."

"Robert's entire being was tied to Elmvale...I can't, I won't give up who I am for the estate."

"Then don't. Do things your way."

"Then I want to make Bentwick our permanent home."

Charlotte smiled. "Are you sure?"

"With every breath inside of me. I promised you I would rebuild Bentwick, that includes your – our home. We can't leave it."

"Can we live here until that happens? You need to learn Elmvale as well as I know Bentwick. We'll abide by our duties to both Earldoms together. But, perhaps, we should remain here for a while longer."

He nodded, contemplating his wife. She had given him the space to grieve and learn to become a new version of himself with unwavering support. Since the day of Robert's death, the awful memories and tide of darkness had been kept at bay. He had found the strength to move daily as Elmvale without succumbing to nerves or fear or torment and each night he went to bed feeling stronger. Perhaps one day it would become instinctual being Elmvale and fear of the memories would be in the long distant past. With Charlotte by his side, it was all possible.

"As you wish Lady Elmvale," he said. After a deep kiss, Matthew cleared his throat. "Speaking of riding, you were out too long my dear, we agreed on ten minutes."

"I called on Clara. She was subdued but very glad to show me her new home. She seemed so lonely. She's never been the most forthcoming with her emotions, but I believe she truly loved Robert."

"This new reality which does not include my brother has us all in a bloody haze. In my wildest dreams, I truly believed I would live as anything other than Earl of Elmvale."

"Yes, I know," Charlotte said without a flinch. "If I may, without dishonoring how much you miss him, dwelling on our loss will not help us move forward. We must take Clara's practical example and focus on the present and future. It was how I survived ten years of hardship before marrying you."

"So, tell me Lady Elmvale, was it worth the sacrifice, the wait?"

"Every second," she said as though imparting an important secret.

"You accomplished your goal. You saved Bentwick," his voice held no malice, but his greedy heart prompted her for more. He felt ridiculously infantile at needing to hear her say she loved him, for she expressed it in every action. But, his soul needed all of her.

"We did, Matthew. All I did was get myself into trouble," she said ruefully. "I'm so very grateful for your support and protection and money. But it's not all I'm thankful for."

"What else are you thankful for?"

"You. Just Matthew Harrington."

"Just Matthew Harrington?"

"Yes. Arrogant, bothersome, annoying Matthew. My

Matthew. Anyway," she quickly changed the subject, "I think Clara will be happy on the estate left to her, it is absolutely lovely."

He watched as she pleated and unpleated her skirts. Nervous fingers hiding and revealing something. His hand fell to hers, stilling the incessant movement. A lopsided smile came to his lips when her clear gray eyes focused on his. He couldn't push. She still needed more time. A nd, as impatient as he felt, he would give it to her. He would give her all which she needed because she had done the same for him.

"You didn't mention a visit to Clara before leaving, and we agreed on a ten-minute ride," he repeated, accepting the change in subject and watching her breathe with ease.

"I agreed to none of your restrictions and left before you ended your sermon. I had a fine ride and an even lovelier time with Clara," Charlotte stated sweetly, her hands resting easily in her lap.

"Nothing will happen to you or our unborn child," his hand found Charlotte's still flat stomach. His voice was coarse with emotion and his eyes bore into hers. "I'll protect you. Even if I have to protect you from yourself."

"Really? Tell me Lord Elmvale, how are you going to protect yourself from me when you keep insisting on limiting my freedom?"

"Charlotte, please. It's too soon for mocking. Robert was in our home one moment and the next I'm signing documents as the Earl of Elmvale."

"It was an unfortunate and terrible accident. But, I can ride our lands blindfolded in a rain storm and you well know it. In fact, didn't we try that once?"

He was not dissuaded by her attempts at playfulness. "Promise you'll be careful. Promise you'll take care of yourself and our child always."

She held his face in her hands, leaning closer towards

him. "You've nothing to fear. And you must remember, I'll take care of you also." She kissed him sweetly.

Their kiss was interrupted by a knock on the door. Charlotte stood and smoothed her skirts, waiting as the butler entered the room.

"The Duke of Ellis has arrived in need of help for a lame horse," he announced. "Tea has been served. His Grace awaits you, my lord and lady, in the drawing room."

CHAPTER 31

Charlotte was positive her already porcelain skin dropped several shades. Despite the sharp pain in her abdomen, she stood even straighter, squaring her shoulders and stilling her pounding heart with a deep breath. "Thank you, Cole. Notify His Grace that the Earl and Countess will be with him shortly."

She noticed Matthew's eyes had not left her face, calculating in his assessment of her. The instant Ellis was announced, his emotions changed in chameleon-like fashion. All traces of sadness or fear, were gone. His eyes blazed as he raised his brow. "This man shouldn't be welcomed in our home."

"We can't do that and you know it," she said tartly, "But, we can be polite in the extreme. We can show him that we're not to be trifled with."

"I should've called him out in London," Matthew muttered while tracing his index finger along the letter opener.

"That, my darling, is exactly what I wanted to avoid."

He let the opener go and immediately took hold of her wrist. "Explain your meaning."

"I didn't want you to call out a dangerous man over a situation we salvaged." A deep pink hue appeared on her cheeks, and she spoke with perhaps more force than necessary. "We're happily married. I'm expecting. He'll see that we've moved on and so will he."

"Why would he need to move on? What are you keeping from me?"

"I thought we had settled this on our wedding night," she said through gritted teeth.

"On our wedding night, I apologized for behaving so beastly and I promised not to pressure you. But the very man who instigates the fires of hell to run through my body has materialized in my drawing room and I want to bloody know what he wants with my wife!"

Anger coursing through Matthew was a rare sight indeed. Charlotte swallowed, steeling her nerves. "He's likely ready for his apology. We should go. We shan't keep His Grace waiting." With a sweep of her skirts she left the room before Matthew could say another word.

"Your Grace," Matthew stalked into the room following his wife. He crossed to stand by the fireplace directly opposite to where the Duke sat.

"Elmvale," Ellis replied as he rose to greet Charlotte. "Countess."

The Duke of Ellis was politeness incarnate as Charlotte neared to greet him. "Breathtaking," he whispered so only she could catch the undertones of his word. She forced her hands to still and sat on the chair next to where Matthew stood.

When tea arrived, Charlotte regally poured it for both men. She proudly controlled her shaking fingers as tea cups and saucers were passed around. In between long pauses to sip tea, there was clipped conversation about the weather, local and international affairs and mundane gossip. Charlotte was severely polite, excruciatingly graceful and downright frosty. She needed Ellis gone, out of her home and life forever. Ellis glanced at her with an arched brow every so often reminding her that he hadn't forgotten his claim. Charlotte's stomach tightened.

"Your new circumstance came at a great loss," it was as close to condolences as Ellis would offer. "I'm acutely aware of the former Earl's reputation. He was a worthy peer."

"Yes, your grace. Lord Elmvale was a great man," Matthew said through a tight throat.

"It will be difficult to transition when you were not schooled to become Earl. But, I am sure the Countess will assist you," the Duke said.

Charlotte nearly dropped her teacup. It took every form of muscular control to keep her mouth closed. How dare he enter her home and insult her husband like this? She saw Matthew clench his jaw. Evidently, he chose not to take the bait, unfortunately she could not let his insult pass.

"Elmvale is an accomplished man who handles himself expertly," she said smoothly.

"I do not doubt that. A shrewd character is necessary when one is a peer. It is important to take opportunities when they arise," the Duke sipped his tea as though he had not just implied that Matthew was a peeress hunter.

"I'm honored to be the caretaker of my family's legacy," Matthew replied with seeming ease. Regardless of his offhand tone, he glared at the Duke with such open hostility it was a wonder they didn't push the sofas aside to break into a duel.

Ellis pursed his lips. Charlotte remained coolly silent. Matthew glared. The only sounds heard were teacups hitting saucers, spoons twirling against the fine bone china and the occasional crunch of a biscuit. Finally, Ellis cleared his throat.

"Speaking of legacies, I was travelling to tend to one of my estates and am concerned for the well-being of one of my horses. I fear if I do not care for the animal properly she will not be able complete the trip. Will you permit me use of your stables and groom?" The Duke was polite enough to make the request knowing full well they could not deny him.

"Certainly," Matthew said without a beat. "You'll find our stables and groomsmen the finest in this part of England. Your horse will be in perfect hands," he assured. It was not the creature's fault to have a detestable master, Charlotte noted in appreciation of her husband's instant offer to help a wounded animal.

"Excellent." The Duke smiled far too devilishly for Charlotte's comfort.

She immediately called Cole and Mrs. Lovett, instructing the butler and housekeeper to prepare a set of rooms and all that was necessary to attend to the Duke of Ellis for he would be remaining at Elmvale Park for a few days. Her eye was unwittingly caught by him when Matthew moved to give further instructions to be sent to the stables. The Duke looked at her as the most heavenly dish presented to a starving man. She felt a deep stir in her belly and ordered its contents to remain where they were. She would need to steel her nerves and finally put an end to the threat he had made in London.

Matthew paced his bedroom late that night. Every instinct fired telling him the Duke was a menace to his family. His sudden presence in their home brought with it the shadowy bitter taste of threat. His nostrils flared as he ran his hand through his hair. He hated waiting for Ellis to make the first move. He hadn't succeeded abroad by being passive.

What was the Duke's game? And, why was Charlotte hiding it? Because he knew his wife well enough. She wasn't being completely forthcoming about Ellis's supposed letter of apology. The question was, why. The magnitude of their accomplishments during their short marriage was nothing less than miraculous. Her tremendous support during a horrific time had solidified their relationship on a level Matthew did not know could possibly exist. Then what was the Duke plotting, how did it involve Charlotte and why was she keeping him in the dark? He strode into her bedroom determined to find answers and froze when he discovered that it was empty.

He marched through the corridors until he found her in her study.

"What exactly are you doing?"

"Writing a letter," Charlotte answered in an *isn't it obvious* tone.

"I can see that dear wife," he replied impatiently. "What are you doing wandering in the middle of the night with Ellis in residence?"

"I'm in my home Matthew and therefore perfectly safe. How did you know I was here?"

"You weren't in your room."

"It took until past midnight for you to notice," she observed in a clipped tone.

"That's beside the point - "

"It's precisely the point. The Duke is here and you turn into a growling man that prowls the corridors."

"With due reason!" How was she maneuvering the conversation?

"Without any reason, whatsoever. I'm the Countess of Bentwick and of Elmvale. This is my home and the Duke is a guest. He won't misbehave here, or anywhere else for that matter. You, on the other hand, must trust me." She rose to her full height, though several inches shorter than him, her squared shoulders and set face created a daunting effect.

"And you, dear wife, must stop underestimating him. If that man even dares to touch a hair that falls off of your head, he'll answer for it with his life. I won't let anything happen to you. I won't lose you too," he held her tight vowing to discover the true reason behind the Duke's presence in his home. With sudden fire he took her hand and led her to his study.

"What are you doing?" she asked.

"Something I promised to show you months ago but have been too busy to do," he said, producing a leather case holding a small knife.

Charlotte's eyes widened. Then her brows furrowed with understanding, "Now?"

"It's the perfect time. A weapon to defend yourself in case that fiend tries anything when I'm not near you – even though I intend to be by your side every second while he's here. It's small enough to keep in your boot, or it can be tied around your leg if that's more comfortable," he gently lifted her foot onto his knee, pushing the night gown up and revealing her calf. Gently he pulled the leather strap around the widest part of her leg and tied it firmly before bringing the night gown down. "All you have to do is reach for it swiftly, discreetly because surprise is the best element for a lady against a viper whom won't expect it and then wield it with such authority he'll retreat."

"And, if he doesn't?"

"Then you'll use it. Strike hard and fast for it to penetrate the skin."

He saw her swallow hard but continued his hurried lesson with military precision. "Here," he said pointing to the sides of his abdomen under his ribs. "Here," he repeated pointing to his lower back on either side of his spine. "Or, here," he pointed to his throat.

"Matthew, I can't - "

"If you hit his arm it will only enrage him and cause him to come at you with more strength," his need to keep her safe made him ignore her protest, "if you strike his leg, you'll have enough time to flee. I know you're quick, but you can't look back."

"I don't think I'll need this. I won't be able to..." she was dazed. He took her by the shoulders and spoke firmly.

"Yes, you will. Only if you have to. I'm not leaving you defenseless," he said. "I know there's something you're not telling me. I know in every single bone Ellis is up to no good and for some reason you feel the need to keep me in the dark. You're frightened and I won't have that. We'll wave good-bye when he leaves our home and you'll remain unscathed. I promise. Now, let's practice."

"Now?"

"Yes, now," he said, preparing himself to attack her.

She laughed. "Matthew, this isn't necessary. His horse is lame, he'll leave within a few days and I'll be completely fine."

"Your stubbornness is truly infinite, my Countess. Now if an attacker comes at you, you must swiftly bend, reach under your skirts and pull out your blade. If he is being stealthy, keep it behind you. If he is being aggressive, use it immediately. Wield it in front of you if he gives you space. Or, in the most dire of circumstance, hurt him with it instantly. Then, of course, run."

He saw her shoulders drop, as though finally accepting that this was happening and she would learn how to use the small, yet sturdy weapon, whether she wanted to or not. Both were breathless after several hours of lunging, maneuvering, positioning and learning to hold the blade firmly despite being shaken or pushed or knocked about.

"You're stronger than you know," Matthew said through ragged breaths in a tone of admiration.

"Funny, I said the same to you not too long ago," she responded with a small smile, her lungs also searching for air.

"We're quite the pair, aren't we?" he said ruefully, knowing she always had been and always would be his balance.

"Yes, we are," she reached over and kissed him, long and hard and soon breath began beating about them once more, except breath filled with desire, passion, love intermingled with the need to protect. "Thank you for your lessons."

"I will keep you safe forever, you must know that," his was voice gruff, his hands unable to stop touching her.

"And, I you," she said and kissed him again.

He carried her to his room, the blade in its leather case in her hand. They did not leave until late in the morning well after the Duke had broken his fast by himself.

Charlotte strode through Elmvale Park's gardens in the afternoon. She was deep in thought when she walked by tall shrubs which encircled a private alcove boasting the most beautiful late summer blooms, a spot in which she loved to sketch. A spot which Ellis discovered and also seemed to be enjoying.

"My dear Countess," his smooth tone stopped her. "How lovely to have a few moments of privacy with you."

Charlotte took a deep step back as though she were on the verge of touching a most poisonous plant. "I trust all is well."

"I could do with a warmer bed," the Duke said suggestively.

"I'll ensure the maids heat it properly for you this evening," she replied practically.

"That will not do my dear Countess. My goodness the country air suits you. You have blossomed since marriage. In fact, you have bloomed fully," the Duke did nothing to hide his appraisal of her full breasts. His eyes lighted with recognition. "But, of course."

"Your state makes our predicament all the more delicious. There is no worry about a bastard at all! I am looking forward to your submission to my demands." Ellis laughed diabolically.

"You'll refrain from any further comments," Charlotte said firmly, unable to hide the disgust in her voice. "In fact, you will finish your business with your horse, leave my home and never return."

Ellis's eyes narrowed. "That would suit you. It would not, however, suit me. You see my dear, there remains the little issue of the grave disrespect performed upon my person by you and your husband. You are aware of my terms. Come to me and all will be forgiven and forgotten," the Duke reminded her of his horrific blackmail. "If you do not meet my terms, my dear Countess," the man's eyes were alight with malicious intent, "I will let it slip that you are a woman who does not turn away other men because your husband was not man enough – in age, title or wealth – to satisfy your needs and that is why you strayed to me in the hopes that our affair would assist you. It will even put your child's parentage into question. You will have every liberated man of the *ton* at your door." Ellis's smile was pure evil matched with black eyes promising pain.

She didn't waver. Privately, she prayed that Evangeline

had received her letter, while outwardly she was the icy Countess.

"We'll meet in the gardener's cottage at the west end of Elmvale Park in two days. I'll send notice about the time. No one will interrupt us there. It's a secluded spot." She left before Ellis could say or do more.

Once safely in her study, Charlotte read Evangeline's quickly penned note and smiled in relief. S he wrote to Mrs. Parker, Bentwick Manor's housekeeper, informing her to prepare for the arrival of guests. She informed Matthew of her departure to meet Catherine the next day. Although surprised, he was grateful for the excuse to remove his wife from Elmvale Park and out of Ellis's reach. With everything in place, Charlotte breathed deeply, secure in the knowledge that her actions would save her family from the threats and actions of a very dangerous man.

CHAPTER 32

Charlotte stepped out of the carriage very early the next morning. Meeting Mother at Bentwick Manor had been the perfect reason to leave Elmvale without rousing Matthew's suspicions. She despised lying to him but was without another option. The fib was necessary for the successful removal of the Duke from their lives.

"My Lady," Lloyd, Bentwick Manor's trusted butler entered the peaches and cream parlor in which Charlotte sipped tea, "The Marquis and Marchioness of Hexbrook have arrived with the Earl of Carters and Lady Evangeline."

"Please have them shown to their rooms so they may rest and wash from their trip," Charlotte said looking up from the note she was writing to her mother.

"Also, Viscount and Viscountess Vale and Baron and Lady Redding have arrived," Lloyd added. Charlotte's eyebrows furrowed. Evangeline had brought her sisters and their husbands too.

Lloyd cleared his throat. "They are also accompanied by Viscount Wynthorpe, The Honorable George Wynthorpe and Miss Wynthorpe."

Her mouth dropped. Evangeline had brought a veritable army. "Offer tea and sandwiches in the drawing room immediately and instruct Mrs. Parker to ready rooms for everyone. Ensure they are well housed and provided with every necessity and luxury."

Lloyd nodded and left immediately to help accommodate the added guests. She had never spoken those words before. She was in the position of being able to spare no expense because Matthew had helped her to save Bentwick, and that was before he had inherited an Earldom. He had entrusted his life to her, his child to her and his heart to her – even though he had not said so since their wedding night. Clearly, it was her duty to protect him.

Except she felt it so much deeper than a mere duty. Matthew was not an obligation or a responsibility. He was her life's breath, her beating heart, and in these few short months, the boy who had ridden wild across the countryside with her had become the man she could not live without. Charlotte would vehemently protect him and their unborn child with all of the passion which had consumed her when she was ensuring Bentwick would not fall to ruin.

She smoothed her black gown, for she was still in mourning and ran a hand over her black hair which sat at the nape of her neck in a neat bun weaved of two long braids. Only her grey eyes betrayed the storm within as she prepared to convince her friends and their family members to help her entrap the Duke of Ellis. She needed their help to eliminate him from their lives forever.

"Charlotte!" Evangeline cried out, embracing her immediately.

Isabella was close behind and offered the same greeting once Evangeline finally released her.

"We convinced our family to greet the Countess at dinner. Our mothers understood our need to see you privately first and so dragged everyone with them. My sisters are most excited to see you again," Evangeline explained cheekily. "So why did you need us all here in such a hurry? What was the emergency of grave peril?"

"The Duke of Ellis is at Elmvale Park."

Isabella frowned and Evangeline arched her brow.

"You should sit." She indicated perfectly placed chairs across from the settee where she settled on. "It's not easy for me to reveal what I'm about to tell you. Nor, to ask for your help. But the past few months have taught me much about opening myself to the goodwill of others, and the two of you were instrumental in this lesson because of your loyalty and friendship," Charlotte took a deep breath before beginning her tale.

"The night Matthew proposed, he did so to save me from a very compromising position into which the Duke had lured me. Our betrothal was Matthew's way of saving me from severe misjudgment. Ellis believes Matthew and I wronged him in an awful way and desires retribution for what he perceives as grave insult to his person."

"What did Matthew do?" Isabella asked with great concern.

"It wasn't Matthew, it was I. As I said, Matthew saved me."

"You?" Isabella's blue eyes were wide. "What could you have possibly done?"

"I defended myself from unwanted advances. I may have hit him," she admitted in a small voice.

"What?" Isabella's eyes widened further and her fingers flew to her mouth.

"I boxed him actually. I had to stop him. Perhaps I used more force than intended because I was so afraid…he fell unconscious. Matthew taught me how to do that when we were young. He said something about young women knowing how to defend themselves."

"Seems to me Ellis received what he deserves," Evangeline said haughtily. "I have heard father say many times there is more than one peer who desires to do what you did. I guess it had to be left to a Countess." She smiled smugly. "So, what does he want from you and Matthew?"

"Me." Charlotte blushed profusely at revealing all of these events to her friends. She was running the risk of scandalizing them. It was a horrid story which could ruin them by mere association. They could choose to leave and her fragile plan to stop the Duke would collapse.

"I don't understand," Isabella said. She looked from Charlotte's blushing face to Evangeline's knowing gleam.

"Oh," Isabella said, also blushing once she realized the Duke's crude desires.

"As long as I go to him, he claims he will keep the encounter private and all debts will be repaid. If I don't, he will spread malicious gossip that I strayed from my vow and put my child's parentage into question." Charlotte's hands clenched into tight fists on her lap.

"Oh, my goodness," Evangeline said. "So, you are...?"

Charlotte nodded, her jaw tight.

"And that man wants to....?"

Charlotte nodded again.

"We can't let that happen."

Charlotte agreed.

"No. We cannot," Isabella's voice was the harshest Charlotte had ever it. "But, what about the Earl? Haven't you informed him? Surely, he should know."

"Absolutely not." Charlotte nodded vehemently. "Matthew will immediately challenge him and I won't risk my husband's life in a duel which won't solve anything. It'll also fail to show Ellis that I can defend myself. He cannot view me as a weak woman who needs her husband to resort to illegal duels. I must defend myself and my family on my terms. I can't let Matthew become a murderer or risk being caught in illegal activity. And, I definitely won't risk his life for Ellis is not a man to be trusted and he'll surely find a way to bend the rules to his gain. The Duke has all but said he will find a way to kill my husband. Matthew can't find out. I have to keep him safe, even from his own sense of honor."

"Very well," Evangeline said, and Isabella nodded her consent to Charlotte's terms.

"We must tell my father everything, and brother," Evangeline advised, "Father is a formidable Marquis and Oliver has made many powerful connections. Jacqueline and Emilia will expect no less from Vale and Redding."

"Father will do everything he can to help and so will George," Isabella added. The Wynthorpes were much more powerful, respected and liked than she ever admitted. Charlotte did not know if it was her humility, or if Isabella truly didn't know the power her family could wield. She stared at her friends through water-filled eyes. She would rid Ellis from her life forever with their help.

After dinner, Charlotte gathered her guests in the drawing room, including her mother and Lady Adelaide, and informed them about her predicament with the Duke and her plan to entrap him. The women demonstrated a range of reactions, from sheer disbelief to disgust and complete outrage. The men were dumbfounded and ready to call out Ellis themselves.

"A perfect example of why I taught Evangeline to box, dear mother," Oliver whispered into Lady Hexbrook's ear whom was drinking a second glass of wine to help calm her nerves.

"We can't allow him to get away with this," Isabella said with such vehemence every eye in the room stared at the normally soft-spoken lady.

"No," Oliver agreed and looked at her as though seeing

her truly for the first time, "we can't. Although, I disagree with your decision to keep Harrington in the dark."

"We all do," George Wynthorpe said, his hand motioning towards the gentlemen standing about the room. "There are enough peers here who can take your case against the Duke to a magistrate."

"Yes, but ultimately, it will be Ellis's word against mine. All of you have heard only my version of the story. He will surely find a way to make himself look the victim and in the process, ruin my reputation and Matthew's. He's not the type of man to deal with anything honorably. I have no choice but to beat him at his own game using his tools."

Oliver looked at Charlotte with newfound respect. It seemed he had overlooked the intelligence and bravery of Evangeline's contemporaries, for his sister only used hers to antagonize him. "Harrington won't -"

"Elmvale," Lady Hexbrook corrected, lightly touching Oliver's arm.

Oliver sighed. "He prefers Harrington."

"It's not up to him, is it?" She replied in that knowing and slightly condescending way in which only mothers can.

Oliver ran his hand over his perfectly combed black hair. "Elmvale," he said with emphasis, "must know his wife is being blackmailed, coerced and severely insulted. His honor is at stake, as is yours. It's his duty to protect you and you can't take it away from him."

"I can't let him fall into Ellis's trap because it is a trap. He'll find a way to kill my husband." Charlotte's steely glare and quiet tone left Oliver without reply. "This is very diffi-cult for me...I have relied on no one but Mother my entire life, but the two of us can't do this alone. I understand the enormity of my request – the horror of my story. If anything goes wrong, you'll all be embroiled in hurtful scandal and gossip. Just being in this room, being privy to this story can hurt my dearest friends," she motioned to Evangeline and Isabella, "It can hurt your families deeply. I'm aware of what I'm asking. But, I can't let the Duke ruin my life and in turn ruin Matthew's, and I can't let Matthew step onto a field Ellis has designated as his place of death." Her tears remained unshed though her insides trembled with fear that every single person would walk out and she would be left without a way to bury Ellis.

"It's settled then," Evangeline said barely hiding her smile at watching the Countess of Elmvale handle her brother so effortlessly. "We do this Charlotte's way."

"We have to ensure Ellis is out of our lives forever," Lady Adelaide added in a somber tone. "I agree with Charlotte. My son will only play into his trap. We have to keep him safe."

"Very well," Oliver muttered. "But, none of the ladies should be present."

"Excuse me?" started Evangeline.

"Oliver," Lady Hexbrook turned on him, "Nothing any of you say will keep us from supporting Lady Elmvale. Or, haven't you noticed that it's the men putting up all the arguments and the women who are ready to break Ellis's neck?"

"And other parts of him," Evangeline muttered.

"Father?" Oliver looked at the Marquis, then Viscount whom did nothing but shrug.

"Precisely why I say marriage is an abominable state for any gentleman," he muttered, then sighed. "I also disagree with keeping Elmvale in the dark and I'll be the murdered one when he discovers this plot. He'll kill me for letting you be used as bait, he'll kill me for betraying his trust, he'll kill me for every reason he's ever had for wanting to kill me."

"Sounds wonderful," cooed Evangeline. "We should've kept a secret from Elmvale years ago."

Oliver's less than polite retort to his sister was interrupted by their father, the Marquis of Hexbrook. "I will agree on the condition that this entire plan be revealed to Elmvale upon its execution. Oliver and Wynthorpe are right. His honor is being quite mishandled and he will only forgive us because we are helping you and because he will hear the truth shortly thereafter. We all feel as they do," he motioned to Matthew's closest friends, Oliver and George. "Well, we do dear," he said under breath to his wife when she harrumphed loudly.

"On my honor," Charlotte replied to the Marquis. "Matthew will be aware of everything the instant Ellis leaves our home and life forever."

"And, how do you plan on ensuring that dear?" Viscount Wynthorpe asked gently.

Charlotte revealed her simple plan. While the men continued to voice their discontent about keeping Matthew in the dark, all agreed it was a solid plan. Once all knew their roles, from Matthew's distraction to ensuring Charlotte's safety, they retreated to their bedchambers. They needed a good night's rest for tomorrow would be the day they would collectively bring down the Duke of Ellis.

CHAPTER 33

"I didn't expect you so early," Matthew rose when he saw Charlotte enter the dining room. He kissed her deeply and neither regarded the footman discreetly leave the room. He couldn't help but notice the slight shake of her fingers and uneasy smile on her lips afterwards. "How was your visit with Lady Catherine?"

"Lovely. We made a solid plan for the future," Charlotte's voice increased in pitch.

He raised a brow. "Are you alright?"

"Perfectly fine," she said. "My visit with Mother was most pleasant and satisfying."

Matthew pursed his lips. She seemed herself. Perhaps the pregnancy was behind the strange behavior, he rationalized pushing away his concern and remembering how much he had despised being without her.

"I can't bear my bed without you in it. In fact, my day has just been cleared of any and all appointments," he began to move her towards the door.

"Matthew, no!" she cried through light laughter.

"No?" He didn't bother masking his disappointment. "Is this how it starts?"

"How what starts?"

"What my married contemporaries warned me about. A wife's priorities magically reorganize and without warning one finds himself always last."

Her teasing smile did little to assuage his fears. "No wonder you were always so afraid of marriage with counsel like that. We're expecting our mothers' regular morning call. Will you promise to clear any and all appointments tomorrow?" She drew close to him looking sweetly up into his eyes while her hands wandered down the side of his hips and lightly encircled his bottom. His fears evaporated with a well-intoned groan.

"You, Mrs. Harrington, are a vixen of immeasurable proportions. I'll clear all appointments for a lifetime as long as each day starts like this."

He kissed her again.

"Your mother is coming today even though you just spent two days together?"

"She likes the company and she'd love to see Lady Adelaide again," Charlotte replied quickly. Too quickly, he thought.

"Ellis is still here," he said pushing aside his concern as they sat for breakfast. His features darkened. The very thought of him making his blood boil.

"I can't imagine his horse is ready for travel yet," Charlotte noted and the slight shaking of the fork in her fingers was noted by Matthew.

"I tried suggesting leaving the mare here and assuring him we would safely return her to London so he wouldn't have to delay his trip. I offered one of our own horses for his use. Of course, I was only interested in hurrying his departure before your return. He obstinately refused. I was almost insulted when he rejected our care for his animal, but I think the horse is an excuse to stay."

Charlotte's napkin fell out of her hand. He slowly picked it up and put it on the table studying her reaction.

"What makes you say that?"

"Mason, our head groom, came in to see me shortly after you left. During a conversation with one of Ellis's footmen who happened to be in his cups, Mason discovered the footman's lack of surprise for the mare's pain. It seems that very mare which Ellis forced to travel across our lands, was barely recovered from injury a few weeks back. In fact, his own groom in London had warned against travel. But, he brought the animal with him all the same. I asked Mason to keep this information to himself and help the mare as best he could, which we both know will mean he will be up caring for her round the clock. I didn't believe it was possible, but Mason's tale lowered my opinion of Ellis even further. Imagine such a horrid disregard for an animal in his care. It's as though he planned for this to happen."

"Dear God. We have to find a way to keep her. She can't go back to him. He's – he's an absolute brute!"

"We'll find a way to keep the mare, I promise," his hand moved to cover hers. "Do you have the gift I gave you before you left?"

She raised the hem of her skirts revealing the pearl handle of the knife firmly in its leather case strapped around her calf.

"Good. He'll leave our home soon and all will be back to normal," he said, watching his wife closely, hoping to discover what it was she was keeping from him. He was certain Ellis was in his home to harm her. And, by everything he held holy, he would make sure to stop him.

. . .

Matthew noticed Charlotte's hands were tightly clasped in front of her when they entered the drawing room. Perhaps it was because their mothers had arrived unusually early. Her tension visibly eased when she greeted Lady Catherine and his mother. However, her steps faltered awkwardly when her eyes landed on a third lady.

"Lady Clara decided to join us," Lady Catherine explained, a little shrilly Matthew thought but he put his judgement aside assuming they were all feeling awkward due to Clara's first appearance for tea in a home which used to be hers since widowing. She was draped in mourning clothes and her light brown hair was severely pulled back. None-theless, she attempted a small smile.

"Lady Adelaide invited me to tea. And, I finally said yes," Lady Clara said through a rigid throat. The look his sister-in-law exchanged with his wife was beyond strange. Regard-less of his long friendship with Charlotte, women remained a bit of mystery, one which he would certainly never solve.

"It's lovely to have you," Charlotte's voice was nearly a whisper. A whisper raked over cobblestones. Why was his wife so out of sorts? Before he could study her further, the butler entered the room.

"My Lord, Viscount Vale and Baron Redding have arrived and wish to pay their respects."

"Show them in Cole," Matthew immediately said, looking at Charlotte with surprise. "I know Carters' in-laws have relations close to our estate, but I had no idea they intended to travel here."

"It's a day full of surprises," Charlotte giggled nervously.

Matthew's eyes narrowed at her response. Clearly, what-ever ailed her earlier hadn't subsided.

He greeted Vale and Redding with the respect and warmth owed to the family of one of his closest friends. After a few pleasantries, he noticed Charlotte rise. She made her way to the window with Clara, as though pointing to the gardens before her. They weren't discussing the roses or any other blasted flower, he would bet his life on it. Her shoulders were too stiff and high, and her fingers hadn't stopped playing with her skirts since her entrance into the drawing room. Every instinct instructed to march over to his wife and drag her to her room, and not for the reasons he normally wished to drag her to her room. But, he was in deep conversation with his mother and Lady Catherine about the Earldom. His ears twitched with great desire to know what was being whispered in the corner of the drawing room, especially since Vale and Redding had been drawn into the conversation also.

"I can't believe you would agree to be here after everything Adelaide told you," Charlotte said through a small smile, pretending to point at the hibiscus in full bloom.

"Both you and Matthew have been nothing but kind during a most horrendous time in my life. Robert would have gone to great lengths for both of you if he was here. Though I disagree with your tactics, you have my loyalty and help. You are my family," Lady Clara replied with more warmth than she had ever shown while feigning great interest in what lay through the window.

"What are you two doing here?" Charlotte looked up through gritted teeth when they were joined by Vale and Redding. Both men were tall, quietly handsome and had the look of discomfort about them. "You're supposed to be convincing Matthew to take you to the farms to see the irrigation systems being installed."

"We agreed to do this because Carters and Wynthorpe are far closer with Elmvale and couldn't lie to their friend so directly," Vale said as though he was asking about the painting over the fireplace. "But, it doesn't mean we don't feel horribly dishonorable in doing so."

Redding pulled at his collar. "We know this whole endeavor will be over soon and hope Elmvale will forgive our role in the deception. I know I'd be ready to kill the lot of us."

Charlotte's eyes filled with tears. "Please, just a few more hours and I promise, your honor will be restored, I'll make sure of it. We can't give up before it has even begun."

The men nodded gravely, then Redding turned to the garden making a loud and less than witty remark about the lazy look of the roses.

"Do you think it's the babe?" Matthew asked his mother under his breath when Charlotte was stifling a laughing fit, very much afraid for Charlotte's state.

"Perhaps, darling. A woman in Charlotte's state can behave quite unlike herself for no reason at all. But, she is positively glowing with good health. No need for concern my son. Your wife is well as is your child," Adelaide said with a maternal look of deep love as her hand brushed his cheek. While his mother's words reassured him, her demeanor did not. Certainly, Adelaide had changed and sobered severely after Robert's death, but not so much that she had lost her quick wit. Her words were far too warm and maternal to fool him. Something was amiss and he was determined to discover what it was.

"The Countess tells me of the fine work you are doing in building irrigation lines for Bentwick's farms," Vale said pointedly.

Matthew was quite distracted by Charlotte's persistent fidgeting with her napkin and took a few moments before answering. He needed time to care for his wife, but how to derail Vale's obvious intentions to see his fine work for the afternoon.

"The work hasn't been solely mine," he said mechanically

as all eyes landed on him. He squirmed under the group's expectant stare, waiting for the rest of his statements.

"Would you care to see what we've been doing?" Matthew asked tightly hoping Vale and Redding had other business to attend.

"I most definitely would Elmvale, thank you!" Vale replied looking slightly relieved and, Matthew wasn't sure why, quite content with himself.

"Sounds splendid!" Redding added eagerly. The four ladies smiled at the plan and Matthew felt himself maneuvered into a corner.

"Very well," Matthew said his eyes landing on his wife.

"Let us not keep you!" Charlotte nearly shouted. She smiled and sat back down in her chair.

"I mean," she breathed deeply, "We're enjoying your company but we don't wish to delay you. Bentwick is close, but the work being done is extensive. You will have much to investigate," she said with renewed composure.

Vale and Redding excused themselves to prepare for their outing and followed the butler quietly out of the room. Matthew scrutinized Charlotte as she approached him to say goodbye.

"That was a pleasant surprise," she said, lips quivering into an anxious smile.

He frowned. "Somehow, I'm the only one who seems surprised. Do I need to remind you that you can trust me with anything?"

Charlotte laughed nervously.

"Tell me what's wrong."

"Nothing," she answered quickly. Her hands fell to his chest and she tried answering him again. "Nothing darling. Everything is fine. Once you're back you'll see that everything will be just as it should be. You don't need to remind me about anything. You're my bothersome, annoying Matthew and I lo –" she stopped and blushed deeply.

Matthew's eyes widened. Did she stop saying what he thought she was about to say? His heart raced and he wished he had the power to make every person in that drawing room disappear. He heard Cole clear his throat as he entered the room again, looking for him, no doubt. Hell! He had to go explain watering systems when his wife had been on edge all day and had nearly said the only word he had dreamed of hearing from her for months! His jaw clenched as his hand ran through his hair.

"I would drag you to your room this very instant if I could," his voice was ragged. He took a deep breath and looked at her squarely. "But it seems I've been forced to do otherwise today. Make sure our mothers remain until I return and keep the knife with you. I don't want to leave you with Ellis lurking."

"I'll be safe. I promise."

"We'll continue this when I return."

"We will," she said solemnly.

With one last, intense gaze, Matthew closed the door to the drawing room.

"You can breathe now darling," Catherine said soothingly from her chair once the door closed firmly.

"I doubt I'll be able to do that until we're finished with Ellis," Charlotte turned to face the women in her family. "I hate lying to him, but I'll lose him if he discovers the truth."

"Everything will turn out according to plan," Clara reassured coolly.

"That's why we're here," Lady Adelaide said, her knuckles nearly white from her tightly clasped hands. "We shall wait for the men to depart and we will take our leave shortly thereafter. You will take the most direct route and the three of us will travel along the gardener's path to the bend before the old cottage where we will ensconce the horses and meet the others," she repeatedly muttered the plan.

Charlotte moved to the window, watching for the men's departure. She hoped she hadn't made a huge mistake and prayed for the courage to ensure everything would indeed turn out well.

CHAPTER 34

Charlotte rode by the bend before the old gardener's cottage and noted it was vacant. A nervous flutter attacked her stomach.

Where could Mother, Clara and Lady Adelaide have gone? Surely, they knew the estate well enough to not be lost. Charlotte tried to assure herself that they had merely located a better spot to hide their horses. Perhaps, they had traveled a little farther into the woods to ensure Ellis would not detect their presence and would soon surround the cottage as had been planned.

She neared the cottage and it looked completely deserted. A quick walk about revealed her complete solitude. It appeared, her plan had failed before it even had a chance to begin and she would have to find a way to thwart Ellis on her own.

Perhaps, Hexbrook and Wynthorpe had decided she was a disgraceful woman who would bring scandal to their good names and forbade their daughters to continue their friendship. Perhaps Carters had abandoned the deception out of honor and fear of Matthew's anger. Perhaps fear of the Duke of Ellis had paralyzed their good intentions to help. Perhaps, she would have to do this on her own.

The sting of tears attacked her eyes and her throat seized. It was too late. With or without them, she would have to do away with Ellis once and for all. She called upon every ounce of courage she had ever shown in her defense of Bentwick. Every nerve, every sense of cleverness and wit was essential to her survival and the Duke's ruin.

Her fingers shook as she tethered her horse to a nearby tree. The boom of crows harmonized with the echo of her footsteps on the stone foot path, telling her how very remote and alone the cottage was. The occasional bristling of leaves and buzzing bees surrounding the wildflowers broke the quiet, emphasizing her isolation. The door complained with a high-pitched creak as it swung open. She stepped inside, removing the hood of her cloak. Silence swallowed her. She breathed deeply to summon all of her courage and closed the door behind her. The windows were hurriedly opened with resounding thuds to bring fresh air into the cottage and to allow the others unobstructed views and clarity of sound. Beams of light flooded in, illuminating the rising dust from the stirring of Charlotte's skirts. A quick peek out each window showed she was still very much alone.

Where had Mother gone? Of all those willing to help who had abandoned her cause, shouldn't she be waiting by the window? She instructed the dread growing within her to still for she would need her wits to escape unscathed.

She lit and stoked the fire. Then, she placed a bottle of whiskey flanked by glasses on a small table, hoping a few sips might prompt a faster confession out of the Duke. Once satisfied with the cottage, she pulled the hood of her cloak back over her head. She sat in a chair in the corner of the room, checking the knife tied about her calf was within easy reach, and waited.

It wasn't long before she heard a knock at the door, followed by the arrogant entrance of Lord Richard Thurston. He took a moment to survey the cottage.

"I must say, dear Countess," the sibilant sound of his voice turned her stomach, "I was rather disappointed by your request to meet here. I would have preferred the perversion of taking you in the same bed as the Earl. Although, I am forced to admit that the seclusion of this location offers much more privacy for me to truly indulge in the many pleasures I am sure to find in your body."

He stepped authoritatively around the small cottage. "Finally, the Countess of Bentwick will be bare in my arms," he released a low chuckle. "Oh, this will be delicious indeed." She swallowed a horror-filled scream when she saw him adjust his breeches to accommodate the immediate response to his desire.

His eyes narrowed surveying the modest though accommodating furnishings. "I appreciate the comfortable bed. Though I might not need a bed for the various ways in which I wish to take you, dear Countess." His voice became a razor moving dangerously closer. He removed his gloves, placing them on the table next to the whiskey and glasses.

"Ellis," Charlotte didn't hide the disgust from her voice. She rose from the shadowed corner in which she sat. Removing her hood, she stood in the full light of the windows on either side of the fireplace. Her back was as straight as a fiercely wielded blade and her eyes flashed.

"I won't submit passively to your demands." Even though her limbs had turned to ice, she steadied her hands, feigning confidence, refusing to let him smell her fear.

"Lady Bentwick," he said, his voice thick, "You are most fetching this afternoon." He bowed his head slightly and his eyes were glazed as they focused intently on his prey. "You know all too well how I like things. The more a lady protests and fights, the more desire I feel. You are giving me great anticipation to the pleasures we will surely encounter. You will be honored to know, bringing you to submission will count as one of my greatest coups."

Charlotte made no reply, standing completely still and meeting his hunter's gaze squarely with her own unyielding one. The man's dark eyes were blacker than night, it took every nerve in her body to remain immobile. She willed her throat not to seize and forbade her body from casting up its accounts. She had to maintain complete authority and control since they were playing a game which she could not afford to lose.

Ellis gave her a leering smile. Every inch of him showed a man who was accustomed to being obeyed.

"Come now my dear, join me in a drink," he commanded. He poured the amber liquid and tipped his glass upwards allowing it to smoothly travel down his throat. He poured himself another before offering one to Charlotte.

"None for me."

"Then, what was the point of the second glass?" Ellis asked with a touch of irony. "We can enjoy ourselves this afternoon Lady Bentwick. When you surrender to me you'll see that this act of the martyred lady was all for naught," he promised with a malicious grin while he removed his coat and dropped it on a chair nearby.

"Lady Elmvale," Charlotte said sharply. Her eyes widened when she saw he was unbuttoning his waistcoat.

"Pardon?" Ellis asked with a feral smile as he continued to make his way down the buttons.

Though her heart raced she willed her eyes to ignore his intention to disrobe. She arched her brow and set her lips, her eyes had yet to deter from his. "I prefer to be called the Countess of Elmvale."

"Why?" Ellis laughed.

Charlotte fought every urge to box him a second time.

"You are wasting yourself on the new Earl. You my dear are held in very high regard for your tenacity and ability to steer Bentwick out of ruin. The new Earl is such because his older brother, a very fine man, died – but he was nothing more than a second son who never knew his place. Commit yourself to me and you will see exactly the magnitude of our combined power." He stepped towards her, his voice dropped as did his gaze. His waistcoat was open and he began to loosen his cravat.

Charlotte felt desperation creeping into her throat and hoped it would not seep into her words. "Your grace, I'm a married woman and your proposition is both disrespectful and utterly scandalous." She stepped back against a chair. There was no space for escape. She had to make him speak now and pray that someone, anyone had arrived at the cottage by now or all would be ruined.

"I've met your demands and ask that you take your leave and never bother me or my husband again."

She bravely looked him in the face, hoping this was the nudge he needed to spill the terms of his blackmail one last critical time.

Ellis's cravat fell to the floor. He sank onto the bed, his face contorted into an ugly smirk. "Met my demands? My darling, you have not come close to redeeming yourself for your disrespect toward a Duke of the realm. My boots!" He bellowed.

Charlotte jumped and looked at him dazed. She was losing control and from all outward appearances, her plan had failed. Somehow Adelaide, Catherine and Clara had lost their way. The Hexbrooks and Wynthorpes had abandoned her cause, not that she blamed them. It was a fragile plan, completely founded on the willingness of others to put their reputations on the line for her.

She was utterly alone with this man and she had to do whatever necessary to flee unharmed, to protect her child. She slid her shaking hands in the folds of her skirts kneeling before him, and found the pearl handle of the small knife. Holding it tightly, she reevaluated the situation, looking for a way out.

"Remove my boots!" He ordered her again, his voice thick and black as tar. He stood when Charlotte did not move and grabbed her by the arms, dragging her up.

"You must submit your body to me. Those were my demands for leaving you and your little Earl alone, not a little meeting in an obscure cottage. I believe that is why we are here, no? I enjoy the pleasures of a Countess in her own right for your right to an impeccable reputation. If you fail to do as I desire Countess, I will have everyone believe that you came to me before your freshly uttered vows were made complete. I will let everyone believe that your child is not the Earl's, I will have your name dragged through mud before you even exit this little cottage." Each word was laced with venom and he grimaced horridly inches from Charlotte's face.

Suddenly, his face relaxed and his eyes brightened as though he had just come upon a most clever idea. "Except, I believe my demands have changed," his voice became silk and his hand moved slowly along the side of her face.

"That is dishonorable. You cannot change your demands!" Charlotte cried as the fear she had so admirably controlled began to trickle out and coldly take her in its grip.

Ellis sensed her wavering and towered over her. "I believe I will require more visits to this little cottage while the Earl is away. I believe my honor demands more of a sacrifice from you to feel esteemed once again." He glared into her eyes and spoke with utmost contempt. "Why are you making such a fuss over a man who is so worthless?"

Ellis's vile insult was the spark Charlotte needed to overcome the on-coming fear threatening to drown her, to make her submit. She forced herself out of his grasp with strength she didn't know she had. Taking him by surprise, he lost his grip on her arms. She held up the knife, wielding it before Ellis who stepped back with a snarl.

"You're the worthless one," Charlotte's voice was lethal ice. The sunlight reflected off the sharp blade, a warning to Ellis. He stood. His hands in the air proclaiming his defencelessness but Charlotte wasn't fooled. His eyes remained deadly.

"My dear Lady Bentwick, once I'm finished with you, you'll know I'm right about everything."

Her hand gripped the pearl handle. "Stay away from me and from everyone I love."

He lunged at her and she moved quickly to the side, turning to face him, keeping the knife firmly between them. He came at her again and she had no choice but to use the blade. She missed his torso and cut his upper arm. The knife sliced through his shirt and the immediate stain of blood spilled through the tear. The Duke winced, catching his arm.

"You bitch!" he sneered and lunged at her with such force, her ankles nearly gave way. He snatched her by the wrists and brought her arms high above her head trying to squeeze the knife out of her hands. She held on despite his disgusting breath falling all over her face. With one big heave, she kicked her knee into his groin as violently as she could. He released her, doubling over and she stepped away, standing strong.

"Worthless?" She questioned, all traces of fear gone. Her voice was a hoarse whisper that increased in volume until it practically boomed with the full force of her emotions taking aim against the Duke. "My life would be nothing without Matthew. I love him and he's mine to honor and protect! You would be lucky if any woman loved you half as much as I love my husband!"

Her fury was interrupted by a great commotion at the door. It burst open and a flurry of people fell through it. Someone grabbed the Duke by the shoulders, whirled him around and punched him squarely in the face. Charlotte felt herself embraced by two people asking about her well-being with grave concern. She recognized the voices of Evangeline and her mother allowing herself to finally feel the intense danger in which she had been. With great relief, she breathed in and allowed them to sustain her, the knife firmly in her hand. Beside her she noticed that Vale and Redding had their arms around their wives, protecting them from such a hideous sight.

Vale and Redding? Charlotte's mind was in a haze. They were supposed to be surveying Bentwick with Matthew. Her gaze moved to the scene before her, through the bodies of the Marquis and Viscount, and standing next to the Earl of Carters and Lady Adelaide was Matthew. He was standing before the Duke breathing heavily with both hands fisted by his side. It had been Matthew who had taken hold of the Duke, which meant Matthew had heard everything and Charlotte's greatest fear had materialized.

CHAPTER 35

"Leave Elmvale and never return. You'll never be welcomed at Elmvale or Bentwick and you'll never, ever so much as throw a glance in my wife's direction again or I will end you," Matthew growled.

Ellis stood with one hand holding the wound on his arm. Despite the blood trickling from his fattened lip and the emerging purple swell of his eye, his stare was meant to intimidate. "How dare you?"

"How dare I? How dare you disrespect my wife and home!" The rising volume of his voice made the paintings on the wall shake. "How dare you commit such dishonorable acts and still have the arrogance to call yourself a Duke of the realm? You're a disgrace! I'd kill you with my bare hands, but I wouldn't stain my name with your death."

Each heavy breath running through Matthew's body elicited more and more composure, until all that was left was the iron coolness of deadly calm. "You're a vile creature and you need to return to the rock from under which you slithered out."

"You'll pay for such treatment of me, Elmvale," the Duke spat.

"I'm afraid, Ellis, that it is you who must answer for your most grievous words and actions," Evangeline's father, the Marquis of Hexbrook finally spoke, directing the conversation toward a more fruitful end.

"We have all witnessed and clearly heard your dishonorable blackmail of the Countess of Elmvale. We may not be Dukes, but among us there are enough peers and honorable persons to present a very strong case of your coercion and most perverse behavior. It will be your reputation, name and title which will be thrown into the shadows of scandal for generations to come, not the Countess'."

A deep growl reverberated through Ellis's throat, but the Marquis continued as though dealing with a wild animal was a daily occurrence.

"You will make absolutely no attempt to twist this afternoon's events to your favour, to incur pity for the damage done to your face for you deserved far worse. We will not ever hear about a scandalous case being brought against Bentwick or Elmvale by you. Ever. Therefore, it will be in your best interest to disappear for a very long time. A trip abroad would do well right now. If you choose to return, you will ensure to remain distanced from Elmvale, Bentwick and all the persons and their familiars before you here. If you do not, you will meet your ruin. Documents, signatures and testimonies will be presented shortly, but we will only act if you force us to. Think about the legacy you will be leaving your twin sons."

Ellis took a moment to sweep a glance of pure loathing and contempt about the room. His nostrils flared and his mouth moved into a small snarl. He finally acquiesced to the terms with a slight head nod, refusing to bow it low. Vale and Redding finally led the Duke out of the cottage, out of

Elmvale Park and out of Matthew and Charlotte's life forever.

"Thank you," Charlotte whispered to the Marquis of Hexbrook. "I don't have a father, but I somehow feel as though I was just protected by one." He offered a kind smile and a warm squeeze of her arm before departing to ensure Ellis kept his word.

She looked at the people leaving the cottage and her heart swelled. "Thank you all of you," tears ran down her face. "You took the grave risk of being embroiled in a horrendous scandal which would follow your families for generations. Your actions here are both daunting and humbling and I'm so very grateful for the extended family which has somehow become a part of our life. All I can say is thank you."

Smiles of encouragement, whispers of love and support, apologies to Matthew whizzed around Matthew and Charlotte as each person left the cottage.

"Elmvale - " Oliver started.

"Not now," Matthew said to both Carters and Wynthorpe. "For now, I'm grateful my family is unharmed." They exchanged a hard look of understanding, of forgiveness before the two men left.

Silence hugged Charlotte and Matthew as they turned to face each other in the empty cottage. She was within an arm's length from him, but he couldn't move. He looked over every inch of her, noticing the knife still locked in her hand. The lick of flames from the fireplace crackled in the quiet aftermath of what could have been her demise. His jaw clenched at the thought of his wife in danger. He heard the breeze continuing to flirt with the leaves outside the open windows. A symphony of bees reminded him nature had been completely unperturbed by the events in the cottage and was highlighting the palpable tension between him and his wife. Temporary relief for Ellis's removal slipped away as the raw fear which had gripped him sought release.

"Are you alright? Did he hurt you?" His voice spilled coarsely from a tightened chest.

"Yes. I mean, no, he didn't hurt me. I 'm fine. We're both fine," she stammered, a hand over her stomach.

"Thank God," Matthew sighed. He gently took the knife and placed it on the table. Running his hand through his hair, he breathed deeply. Fear turning to anger in his blood when he thought of everything he might have lost. "Why didn't you trust me? You used yourself as bait! Of all the risks you have ever taken, this was by far the absolute worse."

"I exposed the dishonor of the most notorious man of the *ton* without putting you in harm's way. He threatened your life! I had to protect you, can't you see that? I deserve accolades, not reprimands." Tears streamed down her face, but her eyes were steel.

"Accolades? You put yourself and our child in incredible danger! I couldn't believe what Vale and Redding readily admitted. They blurted everything because they were so wrecked with shame for their deceit. I can't believe you made every one of them agree to this ridiculous plan! I nearly broke my neck racing here to save you!"

His rising voice, his angry tone, his speeding heart were suddenly doused when she moved towards him and her hands came up to his face. She looked deep into his eyes and he would gladly be lost in her for the rest of his life.

"I had to keep you from challenging him. I had to keep you safe, my love."

All of the fear he had held in check from the moment Vale and Redding revealed her plan washed through him. He grabbed his wife and crushed her to him. He held her fiercely, knowing he would never let her go, and wished he could keep her safe forever. He held her and held her. She had wanted to keep him safe, she had put herself in harm's way to keep him safe, she had called him her love.

Her words echoed in his mind unlocking the memory of what he had overheard. His anger at the Duke had overshadowed the joy which had burst through him when he had heard her admission of love. He suddenly withdrew from her and held her at arm's length, searching silently.

"I love you," she said through a loud, happy sigh. "Even though you have yet to repeat the words you whispered on our wedding night, I have to say them, at least once. You deserve to know the extent of my feelings for you. I'm beyond grateful, beyond respectful, beyond dutiful. I'm hopelessly in love with you and I need to let you know how I feel." Tears spilled from her eyes as freely as the words tumbled out of her mouth.

"I loved you on our wedding day, but was too confused to admit it. In these past few months, I realized that I have loved you my entire life. I was too afraid to admit it to myself because you were free and I was tied to Bentwick. How could I dream to have you when I wasn't free to choose you? How could I believe you would leave your cavalier life for me? It was easier to ignore my love for you than be eternally in pain for not having you. You've been my constant, my companion, my champion and now you're my husband and I love you Matthew Edward Harrington because you're my Matthew not because you're my savior or because you're Elmvale."

Her grey eyes lit with love and relief at finally speaking the words, her rose petal lips tentatively smiled and Matthew was undone. He kissed her deeply. Salt intermingled with the sweetness she always offered him. Breath ragged with desire and emotion ran through each of them when he lifted his lips, then held her face in his hands.

"And, I love you," he said, his forehead leaning on hers. He lifted his eyes, bearing his soul to her. "I fell in love with you the day you so very blatantly informed me that you would marry to save Bentwick, but I was too afraid to admit it so I ran away to India. When I returned, I could not believe you were unmarried, so I convinced myself it was my duty to ensure a good match for you. After seeing Ellis trying to court you and our fight in the garden I knew I was desperately in love and had to make you mine. I wanted to court you, to show you we were always meant to be together... none of that matters now because I love you Charlotte and I will never let you doubt it again." He kissed her again and his hands slowly untied the cloak at her neck.

Charlotte received his kiss fully, her entire body brimming with sheer joy. After years of sacrifice and fulfilling her duty, fate had smiled upon her by turning the one man who knew her, understood her and loved her into her husband. She had married her best friend and together they had saved Bentwick. She was having his child and they were in love. The joy within bubbled out of her and she laughed as Matthew easily did away with her clothing.

"Must you always laugh when I'm trying to seduce you?" He said with his lips still firmly on hers.

"Yes," Charlotte replied kissing her husband back while helping him out of his clothes.

"I love you, Matthew," she reveled in the words now that they had finally been spoken.

"I love you, Charlotte," he replied and his body proceeded to show her just how much.

EPILOGUE

"What has you so intrigued?" Matthew asked over the rim of his tea cup. It had been a wonderful day of riding with his wife. Bentwick was fully flourishing and would soon be a formidable Earldom. Elmvale continued to thrive and Matthew knew that he was honoring Robert's memory well.

He had finally come to accept that he was Elmvale and so he had worked tirelessly to continue the legacy of his father and brother. He had become a widely respected and admired Earl. The thought made him smile for this most definitely had not been what he had envisioned for himself as a young man, yet he was so very pleased with his life.

His six-month old son, Thomas Robert Harrington, was blissfully asleep in his bassinet next to the sofa. Charlotte was slowly rocking the baby basket with one hand while intently reading correspondence in the other. Matthew took a moment to study his wife. The girl with the braid and scraped knees was now a lady of great beauty and grace. Her silken black hair was in an elegant chignon and she wore a rose-colored dress which made her ivory skin radiant. She held a private smile as she read and he was jolted by envy needing to immediately know who could produce such a smile from her.

"A letter from Isabella," Charlotte responded still smiling. "It appears she will be visiting Evangeline at the end of the season. She claims London was awful this time around," she said while continuing to read the letter.

"Isabella is quite beautiful, intelligent and as far as I know she's a lady of impeccable reputation, but she's quiet."

Her brows furrowed. "What do you mean as far as you know she has an impeccable reputation?"

"Precisely what I said. Remember, I was out of the country for five years."

"Well, I believe she's impeccable."

"That's because you're fiercely loyal," he said with a smile. "But, how can anyone know her if she's too shy to speak?" Matthew observed while popping a biscuit into his mouth.

"Most men are missing out on an incredibly loyal and worthy woman. She's beautiful, clever, extremely witty and..." Charlotte stopped when she noticed Matthew's smile widen self-righteously.

"And, I wish her nothing but the kind of happiness I've been fortunate in finding," she said with rueful smile. "I hope her journey North offers her the inspiration she needs after husband-hunting in London. I have a feeling Evangeline has some grand designs for her."

"We may visit if you wish. We didn't spend the season in London because of Thomas, but I'm positive you missed your friends. They were eerily aware of your days. The times I encountered them when I was there briefly for those few sessions, they seemed to know more than I did at times so I knew you were faithfully corresponding," he grinned when she laughed cheekily. "A visit to Hexbrook would be rather enjoyable. I could hunt with Carters, if he's in residence," Matthew suggested.

"A visit to Hexbrook? That sounds heavenly." She noticed the last two envelopes in her pile. One was from Julia and one from Westcott to Matthew.

"Odd. I didn't expect Julia to be in Hampshire so soon. She likes to remain in the city as long as she can. Not one for the country," she murmured noticing the return address. "Oh, and this is for you, from Westcott," Charlotte handed the letter to Matthew before becoming completely engrossed in Julia's news.

"It's about time. I saw him when I was in London and had been corresponding with him about an investment. Then he suddenly stopped all communication, but I've been so busy here at home I merely assumed he had moved on to another venture." Matthew was soon absorbed by Westcott's missive as well.

They finished reading their respective letters and raised their heads in simultaneous astonishment.

"Did he tell you?" Charlotte asked.

Matthew nodded.

"My goodness…I can't even begin to imagine…Julia is a stronger person than I had presumed," she looked at her husband and child ferociously willing their safety and good health. She thought of her friend with the sad green eyes and honey colored hair and hoped for her sake that her future would indeed be a bright one.

"What is it?" Matthew asked gently.

"She deserves happiness."

"Believe it or not, so does Westcott," he replied with a knowing look.

All further observations about the love lives of her friends were interrupted by Thomas' fussing in the bassinet. He yawned and settled himself back into sleep.

"Clearly our son has no intention to wake for food,"

Charlotte said staring at the cherub with great love in her eyes.

"Just as well," she sighed, "I'm trying to decrease his feedings." Despite the advice of others, Charlotte had insisted on nursing Thomas herself and she had not a single regret. It had been a magical time with her infant which was now coming to a close.

She withdrew her sketchbook and pencils. It was full of portraits of Thomas. Charlotte was obsessed with capturing her son's every expression. Sketches of her baby in his sleep were her favorite for he truly was an angel. She had not been sketching long when she felt Matthew's lips upon the back of her neck as he sat beside her.

"Matthew Harrington, are you interrupting my sketching?" Her voice playfully betrayed her desire for further interruption.

"I'm doing no such thing Charlotte Harrington," Matthew murmured in her ear while his lips teased her earlobes. "I'm saving you the trouble of sketching Thomas while he's sleeping again. You sketched him in such a state only this morning." Matthew's voice lowered as did his hand to the front of her dress, slipping into her chemise.

"You're incorrigible, but I'll have my sketching interrupted like this by you for the rest of my life," she smiled putting her book and pencils aside.

He eagerly pulled her onto his lap. With one hand cupping her face, his blue eyes darkened with emotion and his voice thickened.

"Charlotte, I'll gladly fulfill that desire for the rest of mine. I love you."

"I love you," she said with a bright smile.

He kissed her deeply. They melted into each other's arms, each thanking the heavens above for the fortune of having married their best friend.

Lady Julia Bexley, Countess of Westcott, stood with effortless elegance by her husband's side as they mingled with other patrons in The Theatre-Royal, Covent Garden. The Earl and Countess of Westcott made a striking pair. Julia perceived that behind each cordial greeting was an assessing glance as the *ton* tried to determine the type of marriage the Bexleys shared. She stole her own tiny glance in her husband's direction and chastised herself when her breath caught. Ire towards her foolish and treacherous heart filled her for daring to leap at the mere whiff of a man who treated her like a possession to be managed.

How could she help it though?

He was impeccably dressed in elegant, black evening dress. His waistcoat and cravat fit to perfection and his hands moved fluidly in pristine white gloves. But, his allure wasn't in his dress.

Lord William Bexley, Earl of Westcott, was the essence of a Byronic hero. Julia almost giggled at the intense look of consternation she would receive for daring to voice such a comparison. His dark hair was kept at a respectable length but easily went wild and showed the beginnings of peppering grey at his temples. His ice blue eyes reminded her of the Murano glass he had brought home from Venice shortly after they were married. His every move was calculated and she could not help but think of a wolf each time she studied him. A strong jaw and straight nose added to his strength. The mysterious faded scar along the left side of his face which nearly touched the outer corner of his eye completed the image of a solitary, powerful, predatory man.

"You look perfect," the precision of his words made all notions of romance evaporate immediately. He barely spared her a glance when he continued. "It will not be easy for any of the peers present this evening to deny you their support of my bills, or investments. Do try to remember the proper wording of it all this time."

Yes, the thrill of his spell was normally broken the moment words left his lips, because they were not normally of the kind variety, and even if they were, their tone most certainly was not.

Julia dared a sigh. She didn't know why she expelled her breath so loudly. She had been audience to Westcott's lectures on the fine art of seeming impenetrable, on being a cool, collected lady many times during their short marriage, yet on this particular evening she simply did not have the strength to be the lady he needed. She wanted to be herself. She had tried to be the Countess he wanted, but she never quite measured up. She suddenly realized she was tired of trying so hard. And so, on a most routine visit to the opening night of the opera for the Season, Lady Julia Bexley, Countess of Westcott, sighed audibly.

"You're not enjoying our first night at the opera?" The icy eyes turned to her with starkness, demanding to know the reason behind the very loud breath which had escaped her lips.

"The opera hasn't exactly begun." She attempted to infuse a light tone into her voice, with a brief sparkle in her eye in the hope of derailing subversive accusations.

It didn't work.

He turned his attention back to the crowd of patrons. " You didn't have to join me. Though I was under the impression you wished to help me gather support for the Spring Session. This is what we must do in order to initiate any kind of change for the better in our society."

"Yes, my lord."

"Then why the dramatics? You are aware of your duty, are you not? Honestly Julia, I expect more from you, especially after so many years of marriage."

Time almost stopped.

His tone, his words were reminiscent of all the times she had overheard her father speak to her mother with derision each time she declined an invitation to a private party.

Julia's bright green eyes mossed with tears, but they refused to look down. She drilled him with her eyes, trying to make him turn towards her and make him recall that she had never deserted her duty. Lady Westcott was the quintessential Countess, gathering support for the Earl's bills and ensuring to maintain the appearance of a happy and solid marriage. Even if she didn't exert complete poise as he always expected, the Earl of Westcott was a powerful, feared man, in part because according to the *ton*, he had the undying love and support of one of its most gentle ladies.

She stared at him hard, yet his eyes remained aloft. So many years of marriage, he said. There had been two years of marriage, and those who were syrupy romantics would still dare to call them newly married for they had yet to bear children. During those two years, she had done everything under the sun to make him happy. She had tried every tactic she found in the romance novels she kept hidden behind the tomes on household accounting he insisted she keep in her study, to stop his criticism, to make him see her, perhaps even, to fall in love.

When he barely spared her a glance, the realization of her failure crashed upon her with cold cruelty. How could she be so naïve? The heat of the crowd was suddenly drowning. Even though not a soul had heard their conversation, she felt as though every eye of the *ton* fell upon her. Her eyes remained locked on his face until he finally turned towards her with his cold blue stare. A shard ran through her exposing her very soul. The truth about her failed marriage mocked her and it was more than she could bear.

"It's stuffy in here. Perhaps I should take some air before the opera begins."

She fled. For the first time in her life, she gathered her gown in gloved hands and fled to the terrace without a care of making a scene.

Westcott watched the lovely honey blonde strands float behind the elegant neck of his most beautiful wife and buried the knife slicing at the rock-like encasement encircling his heart. Would he ever learn to speak to one whom was so beautiful and gentle? It wouldn't save his soul even if he did. He knew he was damned and being married to someone like Julia was as close to redemption as he would get. All thoughts of compassion and concern were forced aside. He evened his breath as though the most ordinary of occurrences had just taken place and placidly rejoined the throng, spotting Lord Simon Huntsbridge."

"Huntsbridge, about the bill I intend to have passed - "

"Westcott, we are at the opera. Parliament has yet to convene and you wish to discuss politics?" The shy Viscount normally nodded and assented in public because he preferred to discuss politics and business in the privacy of his study. So, when he interrupted Westcott's exacting manner, Lord William Bexley very nearly toppled onto the footman behind him. What the devil was going on? His wife had literally fled his side amidst their friends and acquaintances and now Huntsbridge, his wife's distant cousin, had shut down his intended political discussion.

"Follow her." Huntsbridge brought his tumbler to his lips.

"Pardon me?" A snarl more than a question.

"Unless you wish to lose her forever."

"Lose her? Huntsbridge, I'm married to her -"

"Marriage is the perfect place to lose one's wife," Huntsbridge retorted. "I'm not afraid of your murderous stare. I may not be a man of many words, but I'm no coward. I'll support your bills, they're normally intelligent and thoughtful. But, since you clearly refuse to move, I'll see to my cousin myself."

Once again, Westcott was left staring after a figure departing from him when he hadn't finished their conversation. There was something strange in the air tonight. He couldn't wait for the evening to be over so everything would be back to normal. He straightened his sleeves, watching with intense focus as Huntsbridge let himself out onto the terrace. He knew he should be the one ensuring his wife's well-being. After all, she was his and the *ton* knew very well that he protected what was his with vicious tenacity. Except, following her would mean falling into the artful trap of feminine control and encourage petulant behavior in future. Her cousin would ensure her safety and he would save face. He turned his attention towards a group of men, which included the Earl of Elmvale, someone he needed to speak to about a business venture in the East. With his mind firmly on the woman on the terrace, he steeled himself to continue making the most of the evening's connections.

Julia thanked the heavens above for the solitary terrace. It was too early in the year for any of the patrons to desire the sharp chill of an early spring night. The biting breeze froze her tears in place. She looked up to the starlit sky wishing the chill would move down into her heart and freeze it too. What was happening to her? She had made a career out of being the sunny Countess to the powerful Earl for the *ton*. No one, except for her three dearest friends, was wise to her internal misery. If only her friends had attended this evening, she may have been able to continue the façade.

Another sigh. Perhaps Westcott was right, she had no strength of character. She couldn't even complete an evening at the opera on her own. How had one small comment about her duty caused it all to unravel?

The stars had no response and Julia wanted to scream, but even she knew the damage that would cause and had to satisfy herself with a well intoned groan.

Was it too much to ask for a husband who loved and respected her? She laughed ruefully, remembering Westcott's proposal. If it could be called as such, for he never truly had proposed to her. The ordeal had rivalled the temperature in which she currently found herself.

The transaction had taken place in her father's study. Viscount Merriweather and the Earl of Westcott emerged, one was triumphant at his daughter's ascent in rank and the other was barely pleased that his soon-to-be Countess was from a respectable family with deep aristocratic roots and boasted an impeccable reputation. Julia's face fell into her hands when she recalled her attempt to establish some kind of connection with her future husband. Her tentative smile had been rebuked with a gruff grunt followed by a prompt exit. She saw him again six weeks later when her father delivered her to the altar on the morning of their wedding.

"Rather cold to be out tonight."

Julia whipped around and smiled when she saw Hunts-bridge approaching. "Good evening, Simon. Lovely to see you."

"We can go through the formalities and pretenses, or you can tell me why you fled so swiftly from a roomful of such refined people."

"You're very good at making a liar out of me, Simon. People never quite believe me when I tell them just how direct and eloquent you are, bordering upon insolent even," her eyes warmed at the sight of her beloved relative.

"Pretenses it is then," Huntsbridge murmured. He cleared his throat, "I prefer it that way dearest, you've always known that. Though I can't say I appreciate your attempt at discrediting my mysterious aura. It's no wonder I'm not married. Isn't that what ladies want? A man who carries mystery and secrets, someone who seems a little dangerous even? How can I accomplish that when my cousin thrice-removed is telling them I'm actually nice and just shy?"

Julia laughed melodically, throwing her head back and closing her eyes as though she hadn't laughed in a very, very long time.

"There's the Julia I know."

"And, here's the Simon I know. We are quite the pair. Everyone believes us to be something we are not." She leaned into his shoulder when he stood by her, also facing the midnight sky.

"Except, there should be at least one person who should know you better than I do."

"There is...there are actually! Evangeline, Isabella and Charlotte. My dearest friends."

"I think, dear cousin, you gathered the true meaning behind my words." His pointed look prompted a deep, mournful sigh.

"Not every marriage is meant to be a spiritual union. And,

mine, is a good, solid marriage. Any lady would be lucky to be married to Westcott. He is responsible, cares for his estates, takes his role very seriously – what's that look about? Why are you rolling your eyes?"

"Because, you, dear cousin, are a creature who delights in romance, flights of fancy, passionate devotion to your friends and family. He is cold, calculating and not at all fit to make you happy."

"Now who's being romantic? Truly Simon, I'm a mature, married woman. I can't believe in fantastical notions of love and romance. It's beneath a well-schooled mind to – can you please stop rolling your eyes at me?"

"You're being a ninny. Be honest with him about who you are. Give him the chance to know you."

"He doesn't have time for that. Besides, it won't go over well when he discovers that instead of managing the household accounts I spend my days writing poetry."

"What's the worst that could happen? You end up with a marriage of convenience in which you're expected to produce an heir? Isn't that where you are now, dearest cousin?"

"I really wish you had another dearest cousin in whose affairs you could meddle."

"Uncross your arms. That's it. Stop being petulant -"

"Petulant!"

"Oh, look everyone is moving towards their seat. Come, I'll escort you to Westcott's box."

"If you weren't a Viscount -"

"More importantly, your beloved cousin."

"Let's change that description to insufferable and overbearing. Fine. I must go and bear the punishment for my sudden exit. Oh! I didn't mean it that way Simon, truly, Westcott is a true gentleman and has never laid hand on me. But, I know he won't be happy about the theatrics."

"If it's any consolation, very few witnessed the exit. Illness can strike at any moment, you running away won't be cause for alarm. Look, see, there's Miss Burnhope nearly toppling over Lady Westmount to get closer to that group of unmarried gentlemen. You've just been forgotten."

Julia smiled in deep gratitude, ignoring the ache in her chest, and took her cousin's arm. She used their banter to elevate her spirits, so by the time she reached the Westcott box all nerves and anxiety had settled. The usual fear she felt about disappointing Westcott had vanished during her flight to the terrace. Fiery boldness crept through every limb giving her the courage to look squarely at her husband, daring him to lecture her, to make a snide remark. She grinned triumphantly when her out of character audacity left him speechless and glided by him toward her seat. Gone was the passive, dismissive wife. She denied him any chance to speak by keeping her eyes glued to the stage until she was so absorbed by the beauty and emotion of the opera, that she failed to notice Westcott's eyes hadn't once left her face.

Westcott stood the instant he sensed Julia and Huntsbridge at their box relieved to see a return to normalcy. It would not do for the *ton* to begin rumors about a weak marriage. He nodded at Huntsbridge whom left promptly. He turned with every intention of warning his wife about such theatrics in the future, but he was seared by her bold green eyes. She stared him down with such haughtiness, all reprimands stuck in his throat. He gritted his teeth when his heart beat faster upon seeing Julia's boldness.

Then her scent, lily of the valley, floated towards him and his body held the sharp intake of breath, expelling it ever so slowly as though it needed to retain her scent for as long as it could. His responses to her proximity of late had started to infuriate him. Lack of control over his reactions to his own wife was incomprehensible and unacceptable. To remedy the situation, he sat and returned to his ferocious intent of scolding her inappropriate exit, but all words were halted once again when he looked at her, truly looked at her.

Julia Bexley, Countess of Westcott, his Countess, was beautiful. Emerald green eyes outshone the diamonds at her neck. Silken honey tresses begged to be ripped out of their combs and curls. And, her creamy skin was luminous as spring's first dew. She wasn't very tall, although at his towering six foot four, most people didn't seem so. Her small, five-foot five frame made him feel bear-like around her and awkward. He didn't ever really know how to handle her delicate nature, physically or emotionally. And, it had been a lifetime since he had felt vulnerable, since he had not been in control of every detail in his life. So, he made sure to keep her as far away as he could because her beauty, intelligence and charm could prove lethal to his heart.

His wife exuded the sun's rays on the warmest of summer days. Everyone simply loved her. But, did he? He nearly scoffed aloud at the ridiculous question. He had not married with the intention of feeling anything for his wife. He tightened his jaw when the memory of the small smile she offered on the night of their betrothal suddenly surfaced. In one small movement of her lips, she had broken every barrier he had ever built to protect himself from ever feeling pain again. As a man of his word, he had not cried off, but he had ensured not to lay eyes on her again until their wedding day. A woman who could captivate so easily, was a woman who could not be trusted. At least it was what life had taught him.

Despite the hiding and all of the barriers he had placed between himself and Julia for two years, here he was being rendered mindless at the sight of her emotional response to an opera. The tears forming in the clear green eyes, the flush of her creamy cheek, the rise and fall of her most lovely bosom mesmerized him. He felt himself harden and nearly swore.

He had been with her one night to ensure the validity of their marriage. While it had been awkward, it had also been the warmest night of his life. He had disappointed her, he was sure, but he refused to touch her again until it was time for an heir. He sighed deeply for he knew the time was quickly approaching, at four and thirty years of age he needed to father his heir. Another sly glance towards his wife told him he should be happy at the prospect. But she was ten years his junior and so very gentle. How would she respond to his sudden interest in conjugal responsibilities? He certainly would never force her, but they needed a son. West-cott rubbed the back of his neck. His arousal and sudden need of his wife was beyond anything he had ever known. What had happened tonight to make him want to drag her home and have his way with her?

He tightened his jaw, forcing all desire away, because he would never allow any woman to exert such control over him again. She was the most dangerous person he had ever met; therefore, rather than trying to improve their marital relations, he had relieved his strong urges with his mistress. Tonight would be a long night indeed with Miss Lucy Taylor. He shifted on his seat to accommodate the evidence of his desire. When Julia turned to him at the end of the show in one of her usual moments of raw honesty, where she forgot to demonstrate poise and self-control, and she unabashedly smiled with exhilarating joy, he realized his desire could only be satisfied by the one woman he had vowed to keep at bay. And, he was terrified.

ABOUT THE AUTHOR

CARYN EMME loves Historical Romance. She is married with two children whom inspired her to follow her dream of publishing her work. *Capturing a Countess' Heart* is her first book and the first in *The Chronicles of the Heart* Series.

Follow her journey and receive updates about the fine ladies and gentlemen of *The Chronicles of the Heart* Series at:

https://www.carynemme.net

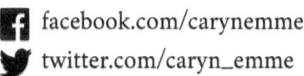

facebook.com/carynemme

twitter.com/caryn_emme

instagram.com/carynemme